The Birth of Malice

Jason Schmidt

D1737285

For news and updates on The Birth of Malice, follow us at:

www.facebook.com/TheBirthofMalice/

ISBN 9781520584454

Acknowledgments

This book took me a few years to write, but I had a lot of encouragement along the way. I'd like to thank my wife, Melissa, for always being there for me and pushing me to keep going. Also, I would like to thank my mother, who read a lot of the early copies of the story and provided useful feedback.

I don't think the book would be in your hands right now if it weren't for my sister, Jessica. Her knowledge and connections are the biggest reason why this book made it past the final draft and into the hands of readers.

My cover looks amazing, and that is all thanks to my wife's uncle, Johnnie, who had the idea to use the cover of my book as an assignment for his photography class. I would also like to thank his student, Stephanie, who really captured the feel of the book with a beautiful photo.

I am grateful for the formatting help Brian Mitchell provided. He added the final touch to polish the digital content of the book.

Thank you to my copy editor, Irene Billings, who made the most difficult part of the book very easy. She really put a lot of time and care into making this book the best it can be.

Finally, thank *you* for your support. If you would like news and updates on the series, follow me on Facebook, www.facebook.com/TheBirthofMalice.

The Birth of Malice

Jason Schmidt

Chapter 1: The Birth of Malice

There was a loud pounding on the door around midnight that stirred Adam from his sleep. It wasn't the casual knocking of a friend or neighbor; it sounded angry. This knock was the kind that shook Adam's modest house and probably woke more than a few neighbors.

To say that Adam was really asleep wasn't entirely accurate. It wasn't the restful sleep that someone would have on a normal, uneventful day. Adam fell into more of a trance: his eyes were closed but his mind was active and his thoughts were consumed by just one thing.

The knocking intensified to the point where Adam could swear he heard the wood splintering and the hinges shuddering with a moan. Adam's thoughts vanished as anger began to overwhelm his senses. Finally, unable to stand the noise any longer, he stormed off to the door.

Adam flung it open and saw the one man in the world

he didn't want to see. The man that stood before him was known as "Guardian" to the public. Publicly everyone knew him as one of the seven heroes known as the "Paragons." He could see that the man before him resembled an angry brute more than a hero.

If Adam hadn't been so furious, he probably would've been a bit intimidated by the man's size. Guardian was built like a tank, and from Adam's understanding, practically functioned like one. The man stood about six and a half feet tall, and he had a broad, muscular physique that would have normally been very imposing to Adam. Adam himself was only average height and size. To most people there was nothing remarkable about Adam's appearance.

Guardian, on the other hand, was quite remarkable. There were internet videos and news footage of Guardian throwing SUVs like they were softballs and charging through concrete buildings like they were made of paper. In battles with the villains known to the public as the "Fallen," Guardian had taken a beating that would have killed a normal man a dozen times over. Still, Guardian fought on, and he normally defeated his foe. Sadly for Adam, Guardian hadn't succeeded earlier that day. Adam's wife and daughter paid the ultimate price for his failure.

Guardian stood in the doorway, seething as he spoke. "I didn't like what you said in the news. I risked my ass for you and your family to put Lament away again. I don't see you out there risking your life for a bunch of ungrateful little shits every day!"

Adam shot back. "You didn't do it for me—you don't go out there for anyone but yourself! You Paragons are just out there preserving your image as heroes so you can sell your goddamn merchandise. Otherwise you would've killed Lament years ago so he couldn't keep killing innocent people like my wife and daughter!"

Adam had said that and more earlier on the news, when

that reporter had asked him if he was relieved that the Paragons were working to bring down Lament. The nerve of the woman! He lost whatever composure he might have had and must have apparently struck a nerve with this behemoth of a man.

Before Adam could finish speaking his mind, Guardian struck out suddenly and sent him crashing through the walls of his house. Adam's body shot like a bullet, destroying everything in its path. His body smashed into a tree in his backyard. The bark near the impact exploded in every direction. Adam's body lay still against the now-bare trunk of the old oak.

Guardian smiled, "Psh, fucking loser. Serves him right."

He began to walk off when he heard a low growl, almost guttural like an animal. Guardian turned to see Adam charging at him with a fury he hadn't seen before. Guardian thought he looked ridiculous. A little man, running through his own tunnel of destruction—what an idiot! Normally he would've laughed at the thought of anyone charging at him. Especially this little man that didn't have the power to challenge him. So he stood his ground waiting, until he thought, *How the hell can he be moving around after that kind of hit?* A sudden fear of the unknown gripped him as Adam closed in.

Adam charged into Guardian and sent him flying into some parked cars on the street, sending car alarms all over the neighborhood into a frenzy. The alarms woke the few neighbors that weren't already awake. People gathered outside despite the apparent danger and watched in horror as Adam picked up a Ford Explorer. Guardian lay there, appearing bewildered and terrified, as Adam started repeatedly smashing the vehicle on top of him. As the SUV started to break apart, Adam tossed it away suddenly and began pummeling Guardian with his bare fists. Each strike shook the ground and sent loose tree branches and debris to the pavement. Finally Guardian regained his composure and lashed out, sending Adam flying through the window of a nearby house. Guardian charged in after him and clubbed Adam down to the floor with both fists. Adam wasn't moving, but Guardian stomped Adam while he was down repeatedly. The house shook violently, each blow shifting furniture and shattering floorboards.

Satisfied that his foe was defeated, Guardian began to walk away again when Adam grabbed him by his ankle and pulled him down. They were both on the ground now as Adam crawled over and began punching Guardian again and again. This time there was no retaliation, just moans and a futile attempt to put his hands up in a defensive posture. Adam casually flung Guardian out of the house, sending him skidding face-first along the road before crashing headfirst into the curb.

Adam walked out of the house. Despite the circumstance, he felt unnaturally calm now. Almost like the situation was completely natural. He hesitated for a moment and stared at Guardian on the pavement. The crowd was in shock, but nobody made a move to interfere. Adam looked at them now with disgust in his eyes. He'd wondered if anyone would make an attempt to stop him, but the only thing he saw was fear. There wasn't a single person moving to grab a gun, no cell phones out to call the police. No one even bothered to yell at him to stop. Chuckling a little, Adam mused to himself that these people really did need heroes, because they're too afraid to take action themselves.

Looking down at Guardian, Adam realized that this man had failed his family and countless others. The thought was overwhelming; the loss of his family hit him the hardest at that moment. How much suffering had people gone through because this "hero" couldn't find the courage to destroy members of the Fallen? Taking someone's life is no easy task for most people. It is much easier to throw these psychopaths to the justice system where they are someone else's problem. That would be fine for most criminals, but the Fallen were not most criminals. Each time they were imprisoned, they would escape to go kill more people. Letting the Fallen live was a mistake, one that was repeated over and over again. Unfortunately for Adam, that mistake cost him his wife and child.

There had been numerous occasions where one of the Paragons could have eliminated Lament. Lament was known as one of the cruelest of the Fallen. He had earned his nickname by purposely killing innocents, and using his powers of stealth to watch their family members lament their loss. The Paragons could have killed Lament and prevented the suffering of so many. Instead they just locked him up. Eventually Lament would break out, and the cycle would repeat itself.

This was all preventable!

Adam wanted to scream at Guardian, but he just stood

there in silence. He was wishing that his wife and daughter were there to embrace him. Instead of succumbing to thoughts of sadness and grief like many would have, Adam was driven by something else. He shifted his gaze back to Guardian and began walking toward his still-motionless body.

Bruised and bleeding, Guardian looked at Adam with the one eye that wasn't swollen shut. He asked, "Who the hell are you? Nobody else has powers, how could you—" Before he finished, Adam reached down and cranked his head and neck sharply to the side, immediately silencing Guardian and sending a grotesque snapping sound echoing through the quiet suburb. Cries went up from the onlookers, and many began to flee. Adam just stood there and stared at Guardian's lifeless body, not paying any heed to his neighbors.

An older man emerged from the crowd and approached Adam with a smile. "Son, why don't you come with me we need to talk in private, perhaps in what's left of your living room?"

Unsure of what was happening, Adam followed the stranger, not knowing what else to do. As he followed, Adam noticed the man appeared to be in his sixties and was wearing an old gray suit. It didn't resemble anything fancy. In fact, it kind of reminded Adam of something some sleazy used-car salesman would wear.

When they both reached the living room, the old man chuckled and held his hand out to Adam. "You can call me Mr. Gray." Mr. Gray then laughed heartily as if he'd told the funniest joke he knew. Adam shook his hand but looked warily at the old man. He didn't recognize him as a neighbor. *What the hell does he want?*

Laughing still, Mr. Gray stopped shaking Adam's hand and asked, "So you must be wondering what the hell is going on, huh? Can't say I blame you. Funny business when a man suddenly has super powers when there are only fourteen others in the world known to have them. Good thing I gave you your power, or Guardian's first hit would've killed you." Mr. Gray gave Adam an impish grin that made him a little uncomfortable.

Adam looked at Mr. Gray in astonishment, "You gave me my power? What the hell is this power anyways? I just seemed to be able to do the same things Guardian did. Somehow I felt that it was there too. As soon as I woke up and started walking to the door, I felt different."

Still grinning, Mr. Gray responded, "Ah, yes, I can understand the confusion. After all, it was the first time you've used your power. Though I did not afford the others the same luxury, I will tell you exactly how your abilities work. Otherwise I'm afraid you'll be rather confused and go through an awkward stage of discovering your abilities. We do not have time for such nonsense, as we have a lot of work to do. That, however, is a story for another day. We do not have much time so I will make this brief."

Sirens started blaring then. Adam looked outside and saw a dozen police cars approaching. They were surrounding the house, but for some reason Adam wasn't worried. Now that his wife and daughter were gone, he really didn't feel like he had anything to lose. He honestly didn't care anymore whether they killed him or threw him in jail. Mr. Gray impatiently cleared his throat to get Adam's attention.

"Don't lose focus now, son. We don't have much time," Mr. Gray said. "Now, you think you have Guardian's powers, and now I guess you do. Your power is that you mimic the abilities of the others when they are near you. You can fight them with their own abilities! Once you kill them, like you did to that poor dumb bastard over there, you retain them permanently. However . . ."

Mr. Gray paused for a moment. He looked a bit annoyed as he saw the police getting out of their vehicles and take positions around the house. He continued.

"However, you can only use one person's power at a time. For instance, if you killed Guardian and Lament, you would have to use Guardian's powers. Or you could use Lament's abilities, but you can't use both. You'd be too damn powerful otherwise. We can't be having that now, can we?" He paused again, considering his words before he burst into another fit of laughter.

Sighing, Adam looked outside and considered what he was going to do with these abilities. How should he use them to escape the police now?

As if hearing his thoughts, Mr. Gray said, "You know, I hear one of the Fallen is locked up. Perhaps you should meet him? You could always show the hospitality you showed to dear old Guardian over there. You wouldn't want them to escape and wipe out another family like yours now, would you?"

Before Adam could turn to-face Mr. Gray, he was gone, and there was no trace of him. Adam considered his options for a minute. Perhaps the old man was right. He was tired of the Paragons and tired of the Fallen. Their ceaseless fighting had cost this world too much. The sad part was that there weren't a lot of people that have realized this simple truth. The public is happy having their heroes and villains. They are willfully blind to the truth. Killing Guardian will make the headlines. He'd finally have his audience, and hopefully remove one of the Fallen in the process.

Adam walked out of the house with his hands in the air and let the police tackle him to the ground and put the handcuffs on him. The police secured the scene and began processing the area as a crime scene. Witnesses were being separated and questioned. There were too many people for the police to handle. The police didn't have the manpower to keep an eye on them all. A reporter got to a few of the witnesses before the police did. She was the same reporter that had asked Adam a bunch of stupid questions after the death of his family. Adam could overhear her conversation as he sat in the squad car. One witness simply told the reporter, "He was in such a fury, and he assaulted Guardian and snapped his neck! There was such . . . such . . . *malice* in his eyes." Adam didn't know it at the time, but that was how it started. Adam ceased to be Adam, and he was known to everyone simply as "Malice" as the footage hit the internet and news channels.

Adam sat in the car and chuckled to himself, hearing bits and pieces of what his neighbors had seen. They seemed like sheep to Adam, and he hated their behavior, but he also understood it. It was human nature to watch traumatic incidents as if they weren't a part of it, to assume someone else will act.

Though they hated him and feared him, Adam knew he had to continue what he was doing for their own good. Whether they realized it or not, they needed him. Mr. Gray apparently needed him too. He didn't know what Mr. Gray wanted exactly, but somehow Adam felt he was going in the right direction. So Adam sat in the patrol car for hours,

listening as the police quarreled over what to do with

"Malice."

Chapter 2: Lament

Earlier that day

Adam stepped into the living room where Janet and Lily were watching the local news. Another teacher conference day. Seemed like there were always days off for Lily's elementary school. He shrugged and went to grab a cup of coffee before heading to work at the warehouse. As Adam went to say goodbye to his family, the news caught his attention. There was another escape. It seemed like a regular occurrence, at least to Adam.

Everyone was always surprised when the news reported one of the Fallen had escaped from prison. For some reason, everyone was oblivious to the fact that there was a well-established pattern of this. It was always shrugged off by the media: "Lament may have escaped but Guardian and the other Paragons are already tracking him down. Report any suspicious activity!" How the hell do you track down a guy that can turn invisible and move without making any sound?

None of the Fallen or Paragons ever really discussed their powers in depth. Everything that had been learned about them had been through public observation. There were some people that thought Lament had some way of disappearing, not just from sight, but from the area as well. Of course it was just a theory. But nobody else could explain how a man could escape solitary confinement in a maximum-security prison.

There was an abrupt knock on the door. Adam opened it to see a police officer. "Good morning, sir. I'm sure you've seen the news, but uh, unfortunately Lament escaped prison." The officer let out a sigh. "The Paragons seem to believe he's somewhere in this area. Don't be alarmed, the Par—"

The officer's eyes grew wide and his head jerked back. Before Adam even knew what was happening, the cop's throat opened up and blood shot violently all over Adam and the floor. A grotesque gurgling was all the officer was able to convey when his lips parted to speak. The man was flung helplessly aside as if he were a puppet being manipulated by an unseen puppeteer. Adam himself was shoved violently to the side and there was commotion outside as the other officers rushed to respond.

A scream rose up behind Adam, and when he turned around, the sudden realization of what was happening made him tremble with fear. Lament stood behind Janet and Lily, all three facing Adam. Lament himself was visible now, with a terrifying grin on his face. He was not otherwise intimidating to look at: a very slender man only slightly taller than Adam. The man was very fair skinned and had pale, piercing blue eyes that looked at Adam now with glee.

All the news articles of what Lament did to his victims flooded Adam's mind all at once. Desperate, Adam began to sprint toward the three of them. A sick, childish laughter came from Lament then, as if this was what he had been waiting for. Once Adam was nearly within reach, Lament moved swiftly and cut down his wife and daughter. Grasping his family, Adam tried desperately to apply pressure to their wounds and stop the bleeding, but it was too late. His wife and daughter had already lost too much blood and died there in his arms.

Lament made no attempt to move. He just stood there and watched in fascination. He watched Adam, smiling with every wail and with every tear. To him, this was just a reenactment, a play to be watched again and again. He didn't feel emotion the same way others did. Seeing the pain in others was the only thing that made Lament feel alive.

Since the powers came, there was no satisfaction in Lament's life. Nothing made him happy or sad. There was no feeling at all. It was as if his humanity disappeared. Of course he went about trying to be the good citizen he'd always been, at least at first. Back then he was even one of the Paragons. His job usually entailed reconnaissance of possible threats.

He had been spying on a powerful crime syndicate they were investigating. He was stalking their most powerful members when one of their hitmen gunned down a rival's family. Lament knew he should have felt guilt for not saving them, or grief for the father that was still alive. But he didn't. As he watched the man lament the loss of his family, Lament felt joy. He didn't even know why, so he started reenacting the moment, again and again and again. The public dubbed him Lament, but they didn't know it was really joy that drove him. Lament knew he was broken, abnormal, and something sinister that people feared. But for some reason, he didn't care—he reveled in it.

Now, in Adam's house, Lament smiled at him. "You may want to get out of the way. That big dumb giant is going to come bursting in here any moment, and he doesn't care if you're in the way or not." He laughed again. "I can't wait to see the look on his face when he sees that he failed, again. Some Guardian he is, huh?"

The house started shaking, and just as Lament predicted, Guardian charged through the door. He swatted Adam aside and grabbed Lament by the throat, lifting him off the ground to look at him eye to eye. "What the hell is wrong with you? You fucking crazy little shit, I ought to pop your head like a fucking pimple."

That only made Lament laugh harder than ever. "Great, so why don't you? Kill me—I bet all your buddies would love that! You're the *amazing* Guardian! Defending citizens and upholding the law everywhere! I'm sure they wouldn't mind if you took the law into your own hands just this once."

Guardian sighed, "You know as well as I do they won't let me kill you. I'm bringing you back to prison. Doesn't mean I can't have a little fun though."

A loud gurgling sound burst from Lament as Guardian

slowly applied pressure to his throat. Instead of struggling or gasping for air, Lament grinned slightly and winked at Adam. With a quick movement, Lament grabbed one of his knives and jabbed Guardian's arm with it. It didn't break the skin or even damage him, but it startled him and he dropped Lament. Without hesitation, Lament quickly used his power to turn invisible, and neither Adam nor Guardian made any attempt to find him.

Later that evening

Adam was standing in his driveway with Guardian and the media. There was a large group of curious people gathered around. Normally the police would have held them back to preserve the crime scene, but there was no point when it came to incidents with Lament. He always confessed to his crimes later when he was finally caught. They'd normally tag on an additional life sentence to his already impressive prison term.

The media had been pestering Adam on camera for at least a half hour now, but he wasn't really in the mood for questions. He answered with shrugs and the occasional "uh huh." Finally Guardian looked over at Adam and said, "Look, man, I'm sorry about your family, but I tried." He had a sheepish look on his face. Adam glared at him but didn't respond. Guardian looked down and scratched his head nervously.

Infuriated, Adam glared at Guardian. "You tried? Yes, I'm sure that's been a comfort for the dozens of families that this has happened to, you fu—"

Sensing the downturn in the interview, the newswoman, Candice Newman, interrupted Adam, "Well, sir, do you at least feel better that the Paragons are working to bring this madman to justice?"

Adam laughed for a minute, and not in the normal way that someone would over a joke. It was the sad, desperate-sounding laugh of someone that was trying more not to cry or lose his temper. "No, I don't feel better. This wouldn't have been an issue if they had just killed Lament and the other members of the Fallen when they had the chance!"

Appalled, Candice said, "Sir, honestly you can't mean that! There are laws, a-and you just can't—"

"Can't what?" Adam looked at her incredulously. "Can't kill violent psychopaths that can't be held by any prison known to man? Can't kill these lunatics that have killed thousands of people and destroyed billions in property? All so that the Paragons, like this dumb worthless prick, can be a hero and save the day over and over again?"

Guardian looked at Adam with wide eyes, apparently stunned, but saying nothing. Candice stammered, trying to think of something to say, but Adam wouldn't give her the opportunity to interrupt him. He was going to have his say one way or another.

Adam ignored Candice and Guardian and just looked straight into the camera. "The only reason the Paragons allow the Fallen to live is so they can continue to be heroes! Think about it.

What good are their powers if they don't have some horrible villain to fight? The public rallies behind them and throws them their love and adoration, in the form of money. There are Paragon action figures and cartoons, clothes and merchandise, comics and videogames. They're running a business here, nothing more.

"If they cared about the American public, they would have stopped playing games and eliminated the threat years ago. Just think, if they had killed the Fallen, how many people would still be alive today? How many families like mine would have been spared from Lament? How many buildings and homes would have been spared from Wrath? How much pain would the victims of Torment been spared? This was all preventable! It's time that these heroes put aside their greed. It's time for them to take action! You, the viewers, the American public . . . you need to hold these people accountable. The true power of the Paragons is not from their superhuman abilities. It's from the unconditional support the American public provides them."

Angrily, Adam turned to Guardian. "You're a coward! A good man would do something instead of standing by and letting evil people act as they please. You might be worse than the Fallen; at least they don't pretend to be good people."

Finally Adam fell silent. Guardian looked at Adam but remained speechless. Most of the crowd heard the commotion and many decided to leave instead of listening to Adam's rant. A few of them even pushed by Adam, one brushing the back of his neck. Adam could have sworn he felt a pinch for a split second but quickly disregarded it. He took the cue from his audience and decided to leave as well.

Candice turned to the camera. "Well, that concludes this special report. This is Candice Newman live from the scene."

Chapter 3: Prison

As they rolled up to the prison, Malice said, "This has to be some kind of mistake. I'm supposed to be in jail until after the trial. Only convicted felons go to prison."

The police officer laughed. "Well, this is kind of new territory for everyone. They don't know if you really have powers or not. The jail doesn't have the kind of facility to lock up someone like you, so they're throwing you into Lament's old cell, right next to the other freak." The officer grinned. "Plus, the public really hates you. If we didn't throw you into the biggest shit hole around, I think we'd have rioting on our hands. You killed one of the most popular figures in the world. Only a naive dumb-ass would expect to get normal rights under these circumstances. Now get your naive, dumb ass out of the car, Malice."

Malice yelled, "Damn it, stop calling me that stupid name! You make me sound like I'm one of the Fallen!"

The officer turned to Malice with a solemn look on his face, "No, you're not one of the Fallen—you're worse. You actually managed to do what they've been trying to do for years: you killed a Paragon. You've struck more terror into the public than the rest of them combined."

Grinning, Malice finally admitted, "All right, you might have a point, but don't tell me that what I did was worse than Chaos's attack. He literally killed thousands of innocent people when he sent that horde of his into New York. I only killed one man."

Tired of talking, the officer got out of the car and began to escort Malice toward the prison doors. He stopped suddenly after walking for a couple of minutes and looked at Malice. "The media used the word 'horde' to make it sound less terrifying to the public, but it was more like a bunch of goddamn zombies." He looked down for a moment and tried to hide his trembling hands. After about a minute or so he looked Malice in the eye and said, "I was there."

Amused, Malice asked, "Zombies? What, like they were trying to eat people's brains or something? He probably just had some weird cult going or something. People do some strange things when they get attached to a lunatic leading a large group."

"It wasn't a bunch of crazy cultists. I watched them tear people apart. I swear their fingers looked more like claws or talons. It . . . never-mind." The officer grunted in frustration. "It's never gotten out to the media and everyone's kept real quiet about it. I'm not going to raise a fuss over it. Besides, everyone figures Chaos is dead." The officer looked down, brooding, before he muttered, "Good riddance."

Malice laughed, "Nobody has seen him in years. Relax, old man. You're starting to make him sound like the boogeyman."

The officer gave Malice a stern look. "Chaos is worse than the damn boogeyman—you'd better hope he's dead. You don't want to see what I've seen." He glared at Malice for an uncomfortably long time before he finally said, "Enjoy prison, asshole. You get to shack up next door to Wrath, so have fun with that."

Malice and the police officer reached the gates of the prison, where the correction officers took custody of Malice. As he went inside the facility he looked back at the gates where the officer was still watching. The door slammed shut behind him, and Malice was hit with the realization of where he was. Prison was never a place he figured he'd find himself. He'd done a few stupid things as a young teenager, but nothing serious. He'd smoked a couple joints, nabbed a couple drinks from a store, but that was about it.

Malice might have been scared if he didn't have Guardian's power. If he wanted to at any point he could probably bust through the walls of this prison like a bullet through a pane of glass. But for some reason he was content with where he was for the moment. He'd learn what he could about his fellow prisoner, Wrath, before he ultimately killed him. Malice was hoping to learn of some sort of weakness, or at least have some sort of edge on this guy before charging in to fight him. The fight with Guardian could have gone the other way. It could have been Malice that was beat to death, and the only reason it wasn't was because he had the element of surprise. Word had probably reached Wrath by now that he had killed Guardian. Malice doubted Wrath would make the same mistake that Guardian did. He knew he needed to be ready for a real fight.

It seemed like hours to Malice as he was led along corridor after corridor, down multiple flights of stairs to the lower levels, and finally through a series of thick security doors. The last corridor led to a dead end with a series of six cells, three on each side. There were no bars or anything else that Malice had expected to see from all the movies and television shows he had seen. The cells were just thick concrete rooms with no windows and a heavy steel door with a small window and a tray where he assumed food and other things were passed through. As they walked to the end of the corridor, he passed by Wrath's cell and almost burst into laughter when he saw the whole room coated in what appeared to be cheap plastic sheeting. The correction officers removed the cuffs and put Malice into his cell. Malice turned to see the door shut, and he eventually heard the door in the corridor open and close as the last of the officers left.

Laughter echoed loudly through the small ventilation ducts in the room. "So, you're the one who killed Guardian with his bare hands? You don't look like much, which is why I think what I heard is probably true."

Looking around the room a little more, Malice noticed there was absolutely no other way to communicate to Wrath than by speaking through the vents. The walls were made of thick concrete; he doubted that they were thin enough to communicate through. So he went over to the vent and attempted to make himself as comfortable as he could in a concrete cell. "Yeah, they started calling me Malice. I guess the public couldn't resist tagging me with a catchy name."

"Yeah, *Wrath* caught on early with me and it just stuck. Those fuckers don't know the half of what I can do, which is why they have this room coated in this cheap plastic crap. They think it'll interfere with my ability to manipulate the earth, that the plastic will somehow block my abilities."

"So I take it the plastic sheeting doesn't work, huh?" Malice waited for a reply, but instead the floor of the room shook for just a few seconds, enough to induce a brief feeling of vertigo. Astonished for a moment, Malice finally started laughing, "Yeah, I guess it doesn't work. Wonder how long till they figure that out?"

"They'll figure it out when I decide to leave this place. They tried the same sort of thing before when they put me into a steel cage, but they don't seem to realize that I can manipulate the earth's surface, and anything made out of the earth. Sand, metal, soil, and rock: anything of that nature is within my ability to manipulate to my will. A simple sheet of plastic isn't going to get in the way of that."

"Oh, and what will get in the way of it?" Malice asked.

Laughter resonated through the vent again. "Oh, a clever one. Trying to learn my limits already? Save your breath. Nobody knows what I can do, or what I'm going to do. There are only three people who know what's about to happen other than myself. One of them just escaped the room you're in, and the other two are . . . out of reach." There was a long pause before he finally continued. "But it doesn't matter. I'll be leaving here very soon."

Malice couldn't help but grin in his cell. "So you're that confident you can get out of here that easily? Why don't you just leave now? Why wait?"

"Oh that's simple." Wrath said in an arrogant tone. "It's easy enough to plot in here where I'm safe and won't have police and superheroes chasing me. You wouldn't believe how stressful it can be when everyone recognizes you as a fugitive. It's fun at first but it gets old after a while."

"Humph, yeah, I guess that makes sense," Malice mused. "So, since you're going to be leaving soon, I might as well get this off my chest. Why the hell did you become one of the Fallen? Why weren't you out there with the Paragons living it up in the spotlight? Instead you level towns to rubble and kill innocent people. Why?"

"What, you want some kind of simple, cliché answer?" Wrath roared through the vents. "Daddy beat me or my mommy was a drunk? No, I busted my ass my whole life trying to make something of myself. I struggled, bit by bit for every success I've ever had while the other assholes around me just happened to know the right people. They call that *networking*: some asshole your dad knows hooking you up with a great job, that kind of stuff. I never had that. I worked my ass off and got through the worst life threw at me.

"I joined the army and made something of myself, even got some medals for some things I did in combat. Still, I watched ass kissers and people born into *better* families shoot through the ranks ahead of me. Despite all that, I pressed on. I watched these spoiled pricks abuse their position and get away with things that would make any decent man cringe. After ten years of that nonsense I was about to leave the military and get away from all that drama when I was *blessed* with these powers."

Malice could hear Wrath grunting in frustration as he paced the small cell.

"Naturally these same spoiled pricks wanted to use my abilities to wipe out terrorists. I ended up swallowing up a whole village in the sand—the place was just gone and everyone with it. It occurred to me, why am I still listening to these spoiled pricks when I have the power to wipe out a whole town? The Paragons are like those idiots that used to give me orders. They were blessed by circumstance and they're abusing it. Making money while simultaneously draining public funds and gaining control of the country piece by piece. They already own most of Washington, with most of the politicians in the Paragons' pockets. The ones that aren't won't last their re-election, and they'll be replaced by someone that does support those power-hungry bastards. Nobody realizes any of this and the public fully supports this madness. But I don't. I'm going to take their power and privilege away from them!"

Malice shook his head, incredulous. "You take their power and privilege away by killing random innocent people and destroying towns? I don't see how that accomplishes anything. You seem like a bloodthirsty psychopath, just like Lament."

"You think I'm like Lament?" Wrath fumed. "There's always a purpose, a target. If a few other supporters and their homes get swallowed up, then so be it—they're sheep! They blindly follow where they're led without a fight. They're of no use. I won't *lament* their passing."

They both sat in their cells in silence for hours after that. Wrath had spoken more than he meant to; sometimes his temper got the best of him. It was that temper that earned him his name. He'd seen one of the few good people he knew, one of his best friends, get killed by an improvised explosive device set to take down their convoy. In his rage he opened up the earth beneath the nearby town, causing everything within it to plummet into an abyss. Wrath then sealed the opening, swallowing the town and its inhabitants with no trace left behind.

The worst part was, he wasn't even sure if the terrorists that set the IED were actually in the town. It turned out that command had been warned of increased terrorist activity in the area. Wrath's military leadership sent them without warning them of the increased threat. It was then that he had decided he wasn't following anyone's orders anymore. The government offered to forgive Wrath's war crime if he joined the Paragons and followed their leadership, so naturally he refused.

So began his life as one of the Fallen, and this prison had actually served as his sanctuary and headquarters for the past year. It was necessary for what he planned to do; something that big takes a lot of time and planning. After he was through, though, there would be nobody left to try and bring him down, nobody left to give him orders. For the first time in his life he would finally be free.

Malice seethed over the conversation. He couldn't believe that people were just sheep to Wrath. Honestly, it seemed like Guardian regarded people the same way. He didn't even flinch when he saw Malice's wife and daughter butchered on the floor. All he could do was put on an act for the camera and promise to track down Lament. Both the Paragons and the Fallen had gotten to a point where people were mere pawns in a game.

Again the thoughts of his family being killed consumed him. There was no point to it—they had just gotten in the way of these broken people with super powers. He wouldn't forgive them; both the Paragons and the Fallen had to pay for their crimes. Death was the only suitable option, he would not make the same mistake they did. Nobody will be coming back to repeat the same broken behavior again and again.

Chapter 4: Wrath Unleashed

Malice sat in his prison cell, bored out of his mind. He had tried dozens of times to start up conversations with Wrath but to no avail. Malice wasn't interested in speaking to a man he considered to be a soulless psychopath. Unfortunately, there was nothing better to do, and he was still hoping to get some more information out of him. What was he planning, and did he have others like Lament working with him?

Malice had kept going, trying to spark conversation on any subject. Sadly, it was of no use. Wrath was not speaking at all. In fact, if it weren't for the guards coming in exchanging a few words with Wrath, Malice wouldn't have known he was there at all.

Malice eventually gave up and tried to pass the time by sleeping and thinking of different ways out of his cell. The obvious way to get out, if he needed to, was to use

Guardian's power to bust through the walls. Although the walls were thick, he didn't think they'd withstand his charge. Malice could also feel the effects of being near Wrath—he could actually feel the earth beneath him. It wasn't just the earth; Malice could also feel the walls and the concrete foundation of the building just below his feet. Apparently their cells were located below ground. They were at the lowest level of the building. Beneath them was the foundation and below that was dirt and rock.

Testing the power seemed like a smart choice at first, until he realized that it might raise suspicion with Wrath. One of Malice's greatest weapons right now was the fact that nobody knew the true nature of his power. In fact, there were still a lot of people that doubted he had powers at all. The longer he could keep everyone ignorant of the truth the better. So he kept his powers subdued for the time being.

There were numerous occasions where Malice had considered busting out of his prison cell. With nothing to do, he had a lot of time to think. Naturally his thoughts dwelled on his family's demise. The scene kept playing through his mind again and again; it was maddening. Every day he lived with the temptation to leave, but the curiosity of what Wrath was planning kept him in check.

Once, Malice had even considered just charging into Wrath's cell and killing him. The fact that there were probably others involved in whatever Wrath had planned was almost a certainty. After all, Lament had been next door to Wrath for a long time, so maybe other members of the Fallen had been in there at some point as well. Could they actually be working together? This was Malice's only chance to learn what was going on and hopefully put a stop to it. Simply killing Wrath didn't seem wise. He would stay in prison until Wrath's escape. If he couldn't get any answers by then, he would kill Wrath during his escape attempt.

After two weeks of rotting in isolation, Malice was violently jolted from sleep. The whole building was trembling and he could hear the guards outside scrambling into the corridor. Wrath's laughter echoed through the vent into Malice's cell. "I'm going to bury all of you! You're all going to be entombed together!"

Above them, Malice could hear large objects crashing down. The building was shaking so hard he fell to his knees. Without really knowing how, Malice began to manipulate the earth. He started calming the violent tremors slowly until they had almost ceased. There was no way in hell he was going to let the officers in the building be buried alive. Malice realized then that he could care less about the prisoners. It honestly didn't matter to him whether they lived or died.

Malice's thoughts were interrupted by Wrath's raging. "How did you do that? I know it was you. I could feel something fighting me!" Wrath paused for a moment before asking in a more somber tone, "What the hell are you?"

The wall burst open, sending large chunks of concrete flying into Wrath's cell. Malice effortlessly charged through the wall, but before he could grab Wrath, a fissure opened up beneath them both. They fell into the darkness of the earth, landing deep below ground. Dazed from the shock of the fall, Malice sat in the darkness trying to make sense of what happened.

Wrath called out to Malice in the darkness. "That reminded me a lot of my fights with Guardian, and you can manipulate the earth like I can. I'm not sure what you are but it won't matter. Soon, this country will remember why they named me Wrath."

The earth trembled then and Malice could feel it pushing open—Wrath was tunneling through the soil and closing it back behind him. Malice was having a harder time feeling Wrath's power as the Fallen member moved farther away from him. Realizing he had a limited time to use his ability to escape, Malice attempted the same thing Wrath tried. He began to manipulate the soil behind him and in front of him. Malice used the earth behind him to propel himself forward while he opened up a tunnel in front.

Wanting to get out of the area, he went up at a forty-five-degree angle instead of going directly back up into the prison. Suddenly Malice felt like a bullet being propelled violently through a gun barrel. Unfortunately, the end result was something similar. Malice found himself shooting out of the ground with such force that he resembled an artillery round flying through the air.

Malice came crashing down hard into a wooded area a few hundred yards away from the prison. A sudden rush of joy came over him as he realized he successfully escaped prison. Unfortunately, his good mood was immediately clouded by the fact that he had also failed to kill Wrath. Word of what Malice could do would probably reach other members of the Fallen. His fight to eliminate them just got a lot more difficult. Instead of moping over his failure as he might have done in the past, he laughed.

Hell, nothing is ever as simple as I expect it will be, so why would this be any different?

Chapter 5: Mr. Gray

A few days after his escape, Malice was trying to remain hidden from the public eye. The only place he could think of to grab supplies was his house, but he figured it was probably being watched by the police. Even if it wasn't, his neighbors would probably see him and report his presence. He thought about just stealing some basic necessities from a large department store. Clothes, food for traveling, maybe even a tent or camping supplies. After all, with his powers the police couldn't really stop him.

Malice frowned at the thought. If he started abusing his powers he would be no better than the Paragons or the Fallen. Instead, he decided to lose himself among a group of homeless people. He would wander the streets at night when it would be harder for the public to recognize his now famous mug shots. During the day he would stay in homeless shelters. Confident that nobody would think to look for him there, he kept this routine for a few weeks while he considered what to do.

Wandering the streets one night, Malice went over his options again. He found walking through the seedier parts of town somehow put things into perspective. Even with super-powered people attempting to lead the country, nothing had really changed for the majority of the public. There were still poverty-stricken people, drug abusers, thieves, murderers, and the mentally ill. The public often seemed to view the Paragons as their saviors, but nothing had really changed. It had been about ten years since the Paragons had surfaced and entered the public eye. For all their promises of change, and building the country into a new utopia, it sure hadn't affected these people.

Hell, I don't even know what to do about myself, much less improving conditions for these people, Malice thought. *I can't go back to my old life because there's nothing left of it. No job, no family—even my house is half-destroyed. I'm a fugitive from the law, with my image posted on every news medium known to man. Certainly I won't be able to hide forever. Eventually they'll find me and I'll have to either fight the authorities or accept capture. I'm going to need help if I'm going to do anything productive.*

Maybe my public image would improve if I can take on one of the Fallen, preferably on camera. If the public sees me doing something good, maybe they won't be able to vilify me in the media quite as much. Killing someone, even a member of the Fallen, probably wouldn't change their perception, though. The Paragons have gotten the public so entranced with the idea of using the justice system to handle the Fallen. That somehow keeping them alive is the righteous path. For some reason there was no one speaking out against this, no family members of the victims speaking out. I looked through the internet and watched every news channel I could think of. There was nothing anywhere that spoke out against the Paragons. Every report of people killed always had an apologetic tone to it: The Paragons are on the trail of the Fallen, and they'll be behind bars again soon! *I even tried to find the interview with me and the damn newswoman that pissed off Guardian. It was gone, like it had never existed.*

His last thought really troubled him. Malice realized that if something that big could be removed from the public eye, the Paragons were more powerful than he realized.

Malice sighed as he walked up to the city park. It wasn't much of a park, really, just a small area people liked to jog through. The greenery was a sad attempt to make people feel like there was still nature around. It was just a few square blocks of space with some grass and a few shrubs and trees. There was a park bench in the middle of it. At night it was pretty peaceful with very few people going through the area. It wasn't particularly well lit, though, and the area was prone to crime.

Generally the park was avoided at night, which is why Malice liked going there. The thought of some poor bastard trying to mug him was amusing as well. So he sat there, stuck on thoughts that had been circling through his head the past few nights on that same bench. He was interrupted after a few minutes when he suddenly felt like someone was watching him.

Malice turned to look at the spot next to him and saw Mr. Gray sitting there, staring at him. "Hello there, son!" Mr. Gray suddenly blurted out loudly.

"Jesus Christ!" Malice yelled in surprise and jerked backward on the bench before regaining his composure. "Where the hell did you come from? You scared the shit out of me! And quit calling me *son*—I'm not your damn son!"

Mr. Gray smiled. "Well no, you're not biologically my son. I did give you your powers, however, and in a way you were reborn thanks to me. So in a manner of speaking, you are my son." Mr. Gray chuckled a little and looked Malice over. "You look like shit, but it was smart blending in like this. It took me a little while to track you down, but I've got better resources than most."

Frowning, Malice glared at Mr. Gray. "Who the hell are you really? Why are you so interested in me, and how the hell did you sneak up on me like that?"

"You're asking the man that gave you, the Paragons, and the Fallen powers how he snuck up on you?" Mr. Gray shook his head. "Maybe you're not as smart as I thought. As for who I am, I already told you. I'm Mr. Gray." He paused for a moment, then looked Malice in the eye. "What I want is complicated, but what you need to know is that I'm going to help you achieve your goal."

"Really. You know nothing about me, but somehow know my goal?" Malice replied sharply. "How can you know my goal when I don't even know exactly what I want yet?"

Mr. Gray sat in silence for a moment, considering his words carefully before he finally spoke in a solemn tone. "I've seen you walking these streets these past few nights. I see you looking at these poor bastards living out here, and I know you want to improve the world. You don't really know how or else you wouldn't be sitting here on this bench wondering what the hell to do. You have already begun the path to improving things. You have removed part of the corruption that has been holding the country back. What you need to do is fight these crooked Paragons and those psychopathic Fallen, and you need to kill them."

"Oh? And why do you want me to kill them? How does this benefit you?" Malice asked suspiciously. "Why don't you just kill them if you gave them their powers in the first place?"

Shaking his head, Mr. Gray replied, "I can't undo the damage that I have done. The powers cannot be removed or else I would have done it. The reason I want them dead is because I think that the corruption and all the horrible things that have been done is my fault. I need redemption. I need to fix my mistake . . . which is why I created Malice."

Mr. Gray sighed and looked away for a while, like he was lost in thought. Finally he said, "You are the perfect weapon against them. Unfortunately for you, their powers aren't the only weapon they have against you. In addition to their numbers, the Paragons have the overwhelming support of the public behind them. The Fallen are starting to come together for something, and it's going to be *big*. Despite my resources and my abilities, I haven't been able to discover what they are going to do. We need to act, and by *we* I mean *you*."

Mr. Gray gave Malice an impish grin then. Malice shook his head and said, "Why don't you just speak to them, or use whatever abilities you've got to convince them to change? You seem to have all the answers, though you won't give any of them to me. I know you're hiding something from me, maybe a lot of things. You're going to need to be a lot more forthcoming with me if you want my help."

Instead of getting angry like Malice figured he would, Mr. Gray just laughed. "Do either the Paragons or the Fallen seem like the type of people to be reasoned with? I tried and failed. They won't see reason. If I had the power to defeat them, I would, but I would rather empower someone else to do it. You may be the person that leads this country to the kind of positive change I originally had in mind."

Mr. Gray smiled at Malice. "Maybe you are as smart as I thought. You aren't quick to follow the first person that comes along with answers. You're not like most people: you won't be led along like a goddamn sheep in a flock. That is exactly why I chose you, but you don't have to listen to me, son."

Mr. Gray's tone turned mocking. "You can sit here on this bench or wander the streets as a homeless man as long as you want. Or you can grow some balls and do something. It's up to you. Do you want to hear my plan or not?"

Sighing, Malice gave in and nodded. He knew he was in over his head, so at this point he'd take whatever help he could get. Even if he didn't exactly trust the source, it was better than wandering around the streets looking for answers and not finding any.

Mr. Gray nodded with a devilish look. "Good. Now, you need to get the public more on your side." He paused a moment to let what he said sink in, and after Malice nodded, he continued.

"You definitely need to kill one of the Fallen, and perhaps if you're lucky you could even get some information on their plan. If you could fight a member that is particularly despised . . . Lament would be the perfect candidate but he's impossible to find."

Mr. Gray paused for a moment and grasped his chin. "Hmmm, perhaps Torment? The fact that she enjoys torturing people for long periods of time before killing them makes her particularly hated. She uses one of her abilities to inflict the pain. Torment can create and manipulate heat. Naturally the heat doesn't harm her, so hopefully when you're near her and have her power, you won't feel the pain of it. Honestly I'm not sure. Kind of exciting, isn't it?" Mr. Gray's fit of laughter left him in tears, and it took him a few minutes to recover before he could speak again.

"You know, I don't find this funny." Malice frowned. "I don't exactly relish the idea of being in horrible pain while she dances around cutting me up with her armory of sharp objects."

Still wiping the tears from his eyes, Mr. Gray replied, "Oh yes, her swords and knives! I nearly forgot. I'm not sure if you've seen the videos of her in action, but I can tell you from what I've seen, she is quite adept at their use. She is very, very quick and her acrobatic skills are second to none. She'll probably dance circles around you while cutting you to pieces. I'd always imagined she would put her powers and her combat training to use fighting evil. It's rather unfortunate how she turned out."

Malice raised an eyebrow. "Oh, you had plans for these people? Well, it looks like you must have fucked that up."

Mr. Gray grunted in frustration. "Yes, every person I gave powers to was meant to use them for good. Unfortunately, I did not account for aspects of their powers altering their behavior. Nor did I expect that power itself would corrupt the rest. There is only one Paragon that I see fulfilling my original wishes, and that is Justice. The name is a rather ironic one, for he is indeed infallible, following all the laws to the letter. He would never kill a criminal or hurt them more than is necessary to subdue them, which is why he is going to hate you. Justice is blind to ideologies other than his own. Of all the Paragons, he will probably be your staunchest opponent. Both in terms of his awesome power, and with his philosophy."

Mr. Gray frowned while he considered his next words. "I meant for some of the super-powered individuals to be the fighters. They would take down powerful criminals and perhaps even tyrannical governments around the world if the need arose. Others were meant to run the political side of things, or work behind the scenes. They were meant to lead the nation toward the perfect society! If it had been successful, I would have repeated the process around the world and led this planet to peace! Instead it all fell apart, and things are actually worse than they were before. Now I have to dismantle all the work I did and start over, which is where you fit in."

Mr. Gray put a hand on Malice's shoulder, like a father consoling his young son. "As a man that has lost everything, you, I believe, have what it takes to help the outcasts of society, to lead for the benefit of everyone, not just yourself. Being a leader means making difficult decisions for the good of all. Sometimes those decisions may not necessarily be moral, which is why a leader has to be someone that fits into more of a gray area. Which is where I hope you will come in. You believe in handling things the way I intend: swiftly and with a lot of death involved."

Malice shook his head. "No, not a lot of death—just for those responsible. The Paragons and the Fallen. I don't want collateral. I won't create victims like my wife and daughter in this."

Mr. Gray nodded. "Of course, but what if the public gets in your way? What if regular people get in your way and try to kill you? The police or military, regular citizens—what if the Fallen hold hostages or do things of that nature? Can you make the difficult decisions if you need to? You must not let morality get in your way. There can be no hesitation! Those people aren't worth the effort. Wouldn't you rather kill a few to spare the majority?"

"No, they're not sheep to be slaughtered at a whim. They're people," Malice growled. "My goal is to kill the Fallen and Paragons responsible for hurting innocent people. Ignoring the well-being of the very people I'm trying to protect is immoral and against what I believe in. I'm trying to prevent the slaughter of innocent people, not add to it!"

"Yes, of course." Mr. Gray nodded solemnly and stood up. He began to walk away but stopped after a few paces and said, "Oh, by the way, I hear Torment plans on interrupting a speech by the Paragon Charisma tomorrow night at the town hall. It will be a televised speech. It should give you the venue you need to gain some much-needed public support. You will have to defend Charisma on camera. She only has the power to manipulate people's emotions and bend them to her will. Sadly, she is not much of a fighter, and Torment has never been a very big fan of Charisma's manipulations. Charisma is very popular, so defending her might help your reputation."

Malice smirked. "Why would I want to help her? She is a big part of the corruption of the Paragons. I'm always seeing her with the politicians. Honestly, maybe I should let Torment kill her."

Mr. Gray shook his head. "No, son, it would only be temporary. You just need to get a bit of public support and hopefully calm this manhunt down a bit. If you eliminate a couple members of the Fallen, it might be a bit easier getting around, you know? It won't be hard to kill her later. After all, she doesn't have any fighting abilities that can match you. How hard could it be to eliminate her?"

Malice nodded and said, "Fine, you may have a point, but I still feel Charisma is the bigger threat. Charisma manipulates the public and our government. Torment is violent, and a bit of a hothead. In the grand scheme of things, she is not a big threat. Torment is known for torturing public officials occasionally. But if it gets the public off my back a bit it might be worth it. I see your point."

Grinning, Mr. Gray replied, "Good, now get some rest and get yourself cleaned up a bit. You don't want to look like a bum on camera, do you?" Instead of waiting for a reply, Mr. Gray walked off into the darkness, quickly disappearing from Malice's sight.

Chapter 6: Torment

Getting into the town hall was not as easy as Malice expected, especially because the place was packed. He managed to be part of a large group that was outside, and fortunately there were cameras set up within the building. Malice watched the speech start from outside on the video monitors that were set up for the event. Charisma was radiant as usual, and her public speaking skills were flawless. She had a cool, calm nature as she spoke, often smiling and drawing applause frequently. Unfortunately Malice couldn't admire her as the crowd did, because she was speaking about him.

"Let me reassure you that the Paragons are doing everything in their power to track down the fugitive Malice." Charisma paused and surveyed the crowd. "This new member of the Fallen will soon be brought in for trial, and he will pay for his crimes." Suddenly Charisma's mood turned stern and sour, and the crowd reflected her change of emotion. "Guardian went over to Malice's home to offer his condolences over the loss of his family, and to try and aid him. This monster turned on him and killed him in front of dozens of witnesses! We all feel for Malice's loss of his family, but it does not excuse him killing Guardian in cold blood!"

Charisma paused, letting her words and her power pour over the crowd. Angry murmurs were heard everywhere, and some people even left to go track Malice down themselves. Malice chuckled quietly; he half expected them to go grab pitchforks. Maybe they'd assemble for a good old-fashioned witch hunt?

"Unfortunately, we cannot catch him without your help. Please, if any of you find him, don't confront him," Charisma warned. "We still do not know what exactly he can do, but it's believed he has powers like the other members of the Fallen. If you do encounter him, call the police and we will apprehend him. This man is considered to be very dangerous, so please do not try and be heroic. Leave the heroics to the Paragons!"

Images of Malice were brought up on the monitors for the public to view. It seemed kind of irrelevant to him, since his images were posted up everywhere. In fact, the speech was rather pointless; this same message had been repeated by dozens of news anchors on every forum of news. Something seemed out of place. Malice had a bad feeling and considered leaving.

Charisma interrupted Malice's thoughts. "Now, are there any questions from the public?"

"Yes, I have a question!" a young woman blurted out from the crowd. "Why did the early reports of Guardian striking Malice first suddenly vanish? The witnesses in the original reports mentioned the first blow being struck by Guardian, so why did those reports suddenly disappear?"

Charisma merely smiled. "Ah, Torment, you weren't the one we were hoping to ensnare. But I suppose catching one villain is better than catching none at all. As for your question, I will not respond to obvious lies spread by a super-powered sociopath. Now, enjoy prison . . . again."

Charisma walked away behind the podium. Torment darted ahead toward her, a blur to the eye of a normal person. Just as quickly as she began her pursuit, she was stopped immediately with a thunderous smack. The packed town hall soon erupted in cries of terror and people began to pour out of the doors like water crashing out of a ruptured dam. A few people were trampled but Malice helped them to their feet before they were seriously hurt. Only Malice and the news crews stayed behind to watch the event unfold.

Torment crashed violently through rows of seating before crashing into the wall. There was a small trickle of blood coming from her mouth that she quickly wiped away.

She stood up and laughed. "Ah, Justice, how many times do I have to tell you? I like pain. Why do you think I enjoy inflicting it on so many people? Now get the hell out of my way. That bitch needs to die!"

Malice watched from the monitors outside, and he couldn't help but be a little star struck. He'd watched the news reports for years and Justice had always been his favorite Paragon. Justice was a force of awesome power, quickly overwhelming opponents with superhuman speed, strength, and endurance. He wasn't nearly as strong or as durable as Guardian, but his speed made up for that, and his ability to fly gave him numerous angles to attack his foes relentlessly. Unfortunately for Malice, this target was one of the most beloved of the Paragons. Killing him would be a big mistake since Malice was trying to gain a bit of public support, not kill a popular hero. Still, Justice was the very face of the thing he hated about the Paragons: blindly following a broken system. Malice's admiration of the man had died along with his family. Deciding whether or not to step in and kill one or both of them left Malice perplexed, so he simply watched.

Justice and Torment stood on opposite sides of the room staring at each other for a moment. Typically Torment would have fled from Justice if it meant getting to Charisma. Not today. She was tired of others coming to Charisma's defense.

In a way, Torment felt bad for Justice. In her opinion, he and the Paragon Phantom were the only ones that actually practiced what they preached. Perhaps they were stuck in their position with the Paragons, or perhaps they were simply naive. It didn't matter either way. Justice was in her way, and this time she wasn't going to run.

Torment feigned a quick move to the door and Justice followed. Instead of going through the door, she took advantage of Justice's momentary confusion and charged at him. She drove her knee into his stomach, sending a loud gasp from Justice's lips. He nearly fell to his knees, grasping his stomach, his head hung low. She drew her sword from its scabbard and slashed downward in an attempt to take his head off. Justice rolled out of the way, then darted back to gain some reactionary distance. Torment's anger caused her to inadvertently heat the sword until it glowed as orange as the day it was forged. She unleashed a flurry of hacks, stabs, and slashes at Justice. Each movement created a bright tracer and left the few witnesses of the fight in awe.

Justice in his surprise caught a couple slashes along his side and across his chest. They were deep enough that they would have bled profusely if not for the heated blade cauterizing the cuts. He was forced to take to the air, but as he rose he could feel the heat in his body rising. Torment was using her heat manipulation on him, causing his body temperature to rise quickly. Justice reacted by descending on Torment, but instead of crashing into her he caught the slice of her sabre across his face. Furious, Justice charged again, this time dodging Torment's slash and sweeping her legs out from her with a kick. Not giving her the time to recover, he dove on her and wrapped his arms around her neck in a choke hold. Torment struggled as Justice's hold tightened. The blood to her brain were being cut off, and if she did not submit he was going to hold the grip until she passed out. Justice had done this before and she knew it was going to happen.

Just as the room was growing dark for Torment, she felt someone grab Justice's arms and pry them away as easily as an adult pulling a child away from a toy. Torment shuffled a few paces to the side to see a man pinning Justice's arms behind his back. She couldn't get a good look at him, but Justice certainly looked surprised.

Quickly regaining his composure, Justice said, "So, you finally decided to show up. We set this trap for you, but I wasn't expecting two of you." Justice sighed. "If you assist me in bringing Torment to answer for her crimes, I will put in a good word for you at your own trial. What do you say, Malice?"

Laughing, Malice replied, "Go on trial for defending myself against Guardian? He was a thug pretending to be a hero, and doing a poor job of it. My wife and daughter died because of his ineptitude. I won't apologize for killing a corrupt brute." Malice smiled. "I have a counter offer: why don't you leave the Paragons and assist me in taking them down? They are corrupt and deserve to pay for all the lives they've assisted in taking."

"Corrupt?" Justice replied. "No, we are the light that keeps this country from descending into darkness. You killed an honorable man, but you can still redeem yourself by helping me with Torment."

It was Torment that answered. "I don't know why you're bothering with Justice—he's blind to the truth. He won't let himself believe that he's been working with the very people he wants to bring to justice."

Malice looked over to Torment and replied, "I'm not sure who to believe anymore, but my gut tells me that if they can bend the truth about me that they may have done the same about you. As long as you're not harming innocent people like Lament is, or aiding those that do, I don't have a problem with you." Malice shifted his gaze back to Justice. "You have been aiding in the corruption of this country, and your philosophy has just made it easier for freaks like Lament to escape and kill. If you do not cooperate with me now I will kill you. Ignorance is no excuse."

Justice laughed. "So you are mad at me for allowing Lament to run around killing people, but here you are letting Torment go? You're a fool! You must have seen the footage and the news reports! She's a monster, just like Lament!"

Shaking his head, Malice replied, "I saw Lament kill my wife and daughter with my own eyes. It's obvious that he is a monster, but I have only seen the news reports of Torment. I have also seen the news reports turning me into a villain, so I wonder, are all of the Fallen really evil?"

Smiling, Torment said, "Some of the Fallen are really as the news depicts, but there are some of us that have been vilified by Charisma's propaganda. We are not all monsters. I will leave it up to you to discover the truth on your own. Until then, I have my own business to attend to."

Torment winked at Malice and darted out of the room in a blur. Malice was busy still restraining Justice. It was becoming more difficult as Justice tried desperately to break free and stop Torment from escaping.

Malice sighed. "I guess you won't change, but I figured I might as well give you the opportunity." Not waiting for a reply, Malice picked Justice up and slammed him into the ground. The building shook violently and the polished marble floors cracked.

In a blur, Justice darted up and struck Malice repeatedly with a volley of punches to his abdomen. Malice attempted to swat Justice away with a backhand, but Justice easily dodged him and continued his assault. It occurred to Malice that despite having Guardian's strength and durability there was no way he could ever hit Justice. As soon as he made the decision to change over to Justice's ability, he reacted with another backhand. This time it connected with such speed that it startled Malice. The blow sent Justice backpedaling.

Justice stood there in astonishment, rubbing his jaw. "What the hell? What are you? I recognize Guardian's strength when you smashed me into the floor since we used to spar all the time. He never had my speed, though. You . . . you're using my power against me now, aren't you?"

Malice recognized the same look of fear on Justice's face now that he saw on Guardian's face the night they fought. He had come here to destroy Torment, to try and earn a better reputation with the public. Instead it looked like he was going to end up fighting Justice in her place. Sighing, Malice shook his head and murmured, "Things never work out the way I plan. Why can't things ever be simple?"

Charging out of desperation, Justice darted forward and caught Malice with a right hook to the side of his face. Angry, Malice swung back immediately with an uppercut to Justice's jaw. The blow sent Justice into the air, but Malice darted into the air above him. Malice grasped both of his hands together and dropped them down like a hammer on Justice, sending him crashing back to the ground.

Justice was sprawled out on the ground with his face swollen, large lacerations from his fight with Torment, and the realization that he was defeated. He looked up at Malice and said, "I have no regrets, I did what was right. I followed the laws. You can't use these powers to kill."

Malice replied, "Oh? So we have these powers to watch helplessly as the Fallen slaughter innocent people over and over again? No, we have these powers to bring justice to these evil men and women. We have these powers so that innocent people like my wife and child aren't slaughtered! Their blood is on your hands."

Malice pointed at Justice. "I respect you, but the world isn't black and white. Your ideals won't save anyone, and all you're doing is serving the evil you're trying to prevent. It isn't too late. Abandon the Paragons and help me make the world a better place."

Justice shook his head. "I'm afraid of the path you're taking. Killing doesn't solve anything. It only makes things worse. As long as I live I will fight you with everything I've got!"

In an instant, Justice charged forward at Malice, hoping to take him off guard. Malice anticipated his move and threw him to the ground.

The news cameras were still rolling as Malice walked over to Justice and grabbed him. He picked Justice up with one arm, his hand clenched around his throat. Malice shook his head. "I'm sorry, but I won't let you get in my way. My wife and daughter demand *true* justice."

Malice lifted Justice off the ground and used Guardian's strength to squeeze his throat. Justice wriggled frantically, thrashing his body in a vain attempt to free himself. With the immense strength closed around his throat, Justice's body went limp quickly. His eyes bulged and went blank, and silence fell upon the room.

With tears forming in his eyes, Malice finally let go and walked over to one of the news cameras. "Justice let evil thrive all around him and did nothing. When good men don't fight the evil that surrounds them, then they too are evil for allowing it to happen. I will not allow blind ignorance like his to run rampant any longer. People need to be held accountable for their actions, or their lack of them."

Malice walked away from the camera and started to leave. Before he walked out of sight, Malice looked back at Justice's body and muttered, "Mr. Gray is going to be pissed."

Chapter 7: Interlude – The Pentagon

A young intern strolled into the office of the man the government put in charge of tracking down the Fallen, John Erickson. "Sir, I've compiled a report on the incidents you wanted the group to investigate."

Mr. Erickson leaned back casually in his chair, grasping his chin thoughtfully. "So, do they think it's him?"

The intern shook his head. "It's hard to tell, sir. The towns and villages are disappearing in a way that matches Wrath's pattern perfectly, but there's a bit of a difference."

Anxious to hear the answer, Erickson leaned forward. "Oh? What's the difference this time?"

"We haven't found a single body, and typically when we would dig up a site we would find at least some bodies."

Shaking his head dismissively, Erickson said, "Sometimes these places are buried deep. It's not a certainty that we would find bodies with Wrath's attacks."

Nodding, the intern answered, "One of our men had a hunch and decided to dig deep on a few of the sites. We found remnants of buildings and even possessions and other things. We still didn't find any bodies, or even any traces of the bodies. It's like these places were ghost towns when they were hit."

Mr. Erickson began to tap his desk with his finger, as if he was considering something. "Was there anything else?"

"Yes, sir, there was." The intern cleared his throat. "Wrath always hit places of some significance before, attempting to kill a particular person or destroy a place of importance to the government. We haven't been able to find any sort of significance with these attacks. They appear random. What's concerning us is the attacks are hitting bigger areas that are less remote, and they're moving farther and farther north. Geologists have been reporting large readings on their seismographs as well. Unusual readings that they've never seen before, and it won't be long until one of them figures out they're not natural. So far nobody can figure out what this all means."

The tapping stopped and Mr. Erickson sat in silence, staring at the report on his desk. "Whatever he's doing, I'm sure we aren't going to like it. Let me know if anything changes. I'll go over the reports and see if there's anything else."

The intern walked out of the office, closing the door behind him. Mr. Erickson looked out of the window and began tapping the desk with his finger again.

Chapter 8: The Memorial

It was midday, about a week after the death of Justice, and a crowd was gathering in Washington, DC. It was a gloomy day, and not just because of the attitude of the people. Even the heavens were covered by dreary gray clouds, threatening to rain. Hundreds of thousands packed the streets to get a glimpse at the memorial service for Guardian and Justice. The small building had been erected hastily and was merely acting as a temporary space for the former Paragons to rest and be admired by the public. Already the city was planning a large, grandiose building to replace it. In the meantime, though, mourners were allowed to gaze upon the tombs of Guardian and Justice. Life-size statues of the men were displayed behind their granite sarcophagi. Instead of large stone covers, there were panes of thick, durable, transparent plastic. As the mourners walked through they could still gaze upon their heroes, perfectly preserved in their sterilized tombs. No bacteria could grow; no form of life could creep in to begin the process of decay. So there the heroes lay, beloved by the public.

After the crowd finished assembling, the service finally began. The president himself led the service, offering these kind words:

It is not the pedigree, title, or even the love of their people that defines a hero. A hero is defined by their actions. What a man or woman gives up to aid others: that is the measure of a true hero, and these men gave their lives. Lives that they spent saving strangers, aiding the weak, and keeping our families safe. Their sacrifice will not be forgotten, and this memorial is a small token to show our appreciation for their heroism. May they rest in peace, and may God show mercy on the soul of the cruel man that took their lives.

Various speeches followed, each more or less saying the same thing. That they wouldn't be forgotten, that their memory and their deeds would live on forever. Nothing was particularly original. Still, most of the crowd was in tears, friends and family holding each other for comfort. It often bothered Malice when people mourned over someone they didn't know, like a celebrity. Now more than ever it bothered him. He had real grief over the loss of his wife and daughter, yet these people mourned over "heroes" they didn't even know. On some level, though, he understood; he had destroyed not men, but symbols. They were symbols of something great, and to some they were symbols of strength in hard times, symbols of good triumphing over evil. To the public, they were hope. Hope that the world wasn't such a horrible place and that there was still something good to aspire to.

Watching from a television at a bar, Malice sat in silence with everyone else in the room. The mood was somber; all eyes were glued to the television. Malice tried to feel guilty, all these people mourning over two Paragons he killed. Many of the speeches were demonizing him, making him into a monster for killing such good, benevolent men. For some reason he was numb to it. He didn't feel guilty or sad, not even angry. All Malice felt was indifference. He wasn't happy about killing Justice and Guardian, but he was not sad about it either. He had done what needed to be done. If American society was to be steered in the right direction, the Paragons and the Fallen had to go, one way or another. If they didn't change, if they kept killing innocent civilians, whether directly or indirectly by not stopping the Fallen, then they needed to die. Drastic changes needed to be made to the mental state of the country, and Malice felt it was his role to be the catalyst that sparked the transformation.

Chapter 9: Manhunt

Three days after the memorial, a loud crash woke Malice and the other occupants of the homeless shelter. The door practically exploded from the impact of the ram. Shrieks erupted from a few startled staff and homeless as the members of the SWAT team poured in like ants. Everyone began diving to the ground to take cover, with the exception of Malice. He remained standing and watched the team move in on him.

As the team surrounded Malice, they yelled for him to get down on the ground or they would open fire. Some of the SWAT members began taking up positions of cover with their weapons trained on him, while the others began moving the staff and everyone else out of the area.

Instead of following instructions, Malice said, "I don't want to harm any of you. You're merely doing your jobs. But I do have an agenda, so if you get in my way or put me in danger, I will kill you. So I'm asking you politely to stand down before this gets messy."

"We aren't leaving without you, alive or dead—it's your call," replied the SWAT team leader. "Even if you get by us, we have teams all over the area, helicopters and patrols all over this neighborhood. You're not getting away this time."

Shaking his head, Malice sighed. "I really didn't want to put anyone in danger, but I guess I have no choice."

Using Guardian's powers, Malice charged through the brick wall, away from the team. Unfortunately, he found that the SWAT leader wasn't lying; there were local police and FBI patrols crowding the streets. There must have been dozens of helicopters combing the area. Malice knew it would be only moments before his position was radioed in and the real fun would begin.

Hoping to at least delay the others from identifying him, Malice removed the blue hoodie he'd been wearing.

He tossed it into a nearby garbage, and switching to Justice's ability, he darted over a few blocks in seconds before running into a large barricade. The road was completely closed down with local police positioned in cover behind it. Malice slowed to avoid hitting the barricade, long enough for an officer to notice him. In a panic the young officer opened fire, sparking the others to shoot as well. If there had been bystanders around, they would have certainly been casualties. Thankfully the whole area appeared to be evacuated. The only one that had to worry about the wall of bullets was Malice.

Normally the speed of Justice's powers would have been more than enough to dodge bullets. In this case, though, there were so many, Malice knew it would be impossible to avoid them all. He shifted to Guardian's ability by instinct more than by any sort of conscious thought. The wall of bullets hit him, but did no damage. Each bullet that hit him either pinged off of him or was obliterated by the impact. Malice could feel each bullet strike, and at first it was unnerving. But he didn't feel any pain, just a slight pressure from each hit, like tiny pebbles raining down on him.

After the officers at the barricade emptied their magazines, they began to realize their shots had no effect on Malice. "Call in the choppers, and get us some bigger fucking guns!" the on-scene commander yelled to nobody in particular.

Malice turned away from the barricade and began running in the opposite direction. He ran at normal speed, afraid that if he shifted to Justice's power, he could be shot in the back. Justice didn't have the ability to resist weapons fire to the extent Guardian did, and a bullet in the back could be enough to kill him. Malice wasn't entirely sure how much he could endure with Justice's power yet, but he didn't want to find out right now.

"Shit, he's running! Throw up the electric snares! Bottle him in, NOW!" the commander cried.

Immediately large steel rods popped up along the streets, in the alleys, and even among the rooftops. The rods held a net-like structure between them. Large generators nearby kicked on and strong electric currents flowed into the systems. Each of these barriers had electricity running through them, and escape through conventional means seemed unwise at this point. He couldn't even use Justice's ability to fly out of there.

Anger and frustration began to well up within Malice, and he could feel it building to an almost unbearable point. Charging through that barricade and slaughtering everyone behind it felt like a great idea. But reason won out over his emotions, and Malice went with a more unconventional escape route.

Helicopters swarmed to the scene now, and more men were pouring into the area, attempting to strengthen the perimeter around Malice. Instead of charging through the barricade or the barriers, Malice turned left and charged through a building. Once inside the building, Malice turned and ran to the right, attempting to circumvent the barriers in the alleys.

Malice burst through the building and found that he had succeeded in getting around the barriers in place for him, but the helicopters and armed men were still tracking him. He continued charging through building after building, attempting to lose everyone in pursuit. Soon Malice made some progress, ditching the men on the ground. The helicopters still followed his every movement with ease. Finally, Malice charged into a building and stopped. Now out of the vicinity of the armed men, he decided speed was the way to lose the helicopters. Hopefully his pursuers would assume he had holed up in the building, since he hadn't leveled a new exit in any of its walls.

With Justice's speed, Malice moved out the entrance he created in the building and charged through the streets, a blur darting wildly across the city. Malice moved toward the bridge out of town, hoping that leaving the big city behind might keep him safe. As he approached the bridge he noted that there were no cars or people on it, but kept moving. He was partway across the bridge when he realized his error, but it was too late. Malice's movement triggered a motion sensor and bombs detonated across the bridge. Even with his speed, Malice could not escape, and he plummeted with the bridge into the river below.

Chapter 10: Sanctuary

Fading in and out of consciousness, Malice couldn't quite make out what he was seeing. Everything seemed so dark. He struggled to keep his eyes open, but he lost that battle every time. Sometimes he heard hushed voices around him, but it was impossible to tell what they were saying. Instead of reality, Malice was flooded with dreams—painful ones. Most often they were about Janet and Lily, including the dream that always started out in their house.

Their home was always bright in the glow of the morning sun, and he was so happy to be back with his family again. His wife, Janet, was preparing a lunch for their daughter, Lily, who was getting ready for school. Then it seemed like the room began to shiver, Lily and Janet screamed, and blood would pour out of slits in their throats like grotesque waterfalls. Malice was unable to move or speak; he was stuck while his wife and daughter fell over, dead. Then the sound of Lament's laughter shook the house as if he were laughing through every wall.

Other dreams plagued him too, dreams of people dying all around him while he himself was untouched. Again Malice could only watch as people were slaughtered by shadowy creatures.

Malice finally opened his eyes one morning, and it was bright in the room. The sun was shining through the windows, and for a moment Malice was terrified he was in one of his dreams. As he looked around he realized he was lying on a hospital bed in a small office, but there were medical supplies all around him. An IV was in his arm, and he was horrified to realize he had a catheter in as well. Looking down, Malice also realized his shirt was off, and a fresh bandage had been wrapped around his ribs on the upper half of his torso. His legs were covered by a blanket, but beneath that he was naked. Malice attempted to get up but found that the best he could do was prop himself up a bit.

Laughter erupted out of Malice; he couldn't help it. All these powers and he felt as helpless as an infant. In the next room someone gasped, startled by Malice's sudden laughter. There was some commotion outside as Malice finally quieted down. After a few minutes a young woman opened the door slowly and carefully moved into the room. A man he recognized stepped into the room with her. He was still wearing that hideous suit that reminded Malice of a used-car salesman.

The woman moved to the bed, examined his bandages, and began taking his vitals as Malice asked, "How long have I been out?"

"About a week or so," Mr. Gray replied, "When you collapsed with the bridge, everyone assumed you were dead. It made it a great deal easier to smuggle you here, since the public assumed you were buried underwater beneath tons of rubble. Honestly, it's a miracle you survived, son. You're an idiot and probably don't deserve to be alive right now." Mr. Gray frowned at Malice with a look of contempt.

Malice smiled. "Glad to see you care, old man. Anyways, where the hell am I?"

"You're in the office of an old warehouse." The contempt on Mr. Gray's face softened to a smile. "In Washington, DC."

"Are you fucking serious? Now who's the idiot?" Malice cried incredulously. "This would have been a great opportunity to take me out of a heavily populated area to someplace more discreet. Instead I'm in the nation's capital, *and* I'm close to the Paragon's headquarters." Malice sighed.

"You're welcome." Mr. Gray laughed. "Relax, son, you're going to be fine. I've told you I have a lot of resources, and this is the most secure place I can put you for now. Besides, everyone's sure you're dead. News reels have been playing the events showing your demise over and over again. Everyone's so excited!" Mr. Gray grinned. "I think there even may have been parades, and I'm sure mothers everywhere have named their children after the commander of the operation, General Jeremiah Winston."

The young woman interrupted Mr. Gray. "Sir, his vitals are improving. A normal person would probably take another couple of months to recover"—she glanced over at Malice—"but a freak like him might be up on his feet in a few days for all I know." She smiled at Malice and winked before she turned and walked out of the room. Malice liked her immediately. She seemed warm and friendly, with a bit of mild sarcasm mixed in. He stared at her as she walked out.

Mr. Gray cleared his throat to get Malice's attention. "*Anyways*, like I was saying, the Paragons and the government don't want people to think they blew up a major bridge and caused so much damage for nothing. They've really been pushing the idea that you're dead, and so far nobody has really challenged their thinking."

"Well, I'm glad some good came of this. At least I was the only one hurt." Malice chuckled. "I would have been upset if I had gone through such lengths and innocent people got hurt." Malice was interrupted by a fit of coughing that caused shooting pains in his ribs.

"There *were* people killed and injured," Mr. Gray looked solemn. "The officers and national guard they sent in got a bit jumpy when you were charging through buildings. There was a group of people in the area that hadn't been evacuated. When they made their way to one of the barricades, someone opened fire thinking they saw you in the crowd. The rest of the men followed suit, and roughly thirty people were gunned down."

If there had been any color in Malice's face, it would have melted away. He sat there in silence, staring at Mr. Gray as the information sank in.

"It's not your fault, son. You did everything you could," Mr. Gray said in a serious tone. "This is a war, and in war there is always collateral. If you had wiped out those troops, you would have saved those thirty people. Something to think about for next time."

Malice frowned but said nothing. He couldn't help but feel responsible. His guilt was soon overcome by anger, and he could understand some of Wrath's cold disposition toward the government now. They were willing to go as far as blowing up a bridge and gunning down civilians to try and kill him. This was far more serious than he thought; he would not underestimate his pursuers again.

"For now you just worry about recovering. You're safe with these people," Mr. Gray said. "These people are like you: they've lost family and friends in the conflicts between the Paragons and the Fallen. The only reason they're not known is because Noble uses his power of technological manipulation to wipe out anything that is anti-Paragon from the Internet and news sources."

Mr. Gray frowned for a moment. "Oh yes! I nearly forgot. This group has put together some information on each member of the Fallen and the Paragons. They've got dossiers on each one, and I encourage you to read them. I believe they are pretty accurate from what my own sources tell me."

Malice glared at Mr. Gray. "I'd really like to know more about these 'sources' and 'resources' you have. You don't trust me after all of this?"

For the first time, Malice witnessed Mr. Gray lose his temper. "Of course I don't trust you! You're a jackass! I tell you to kill Torment to improve your public image and instead you kill Justice—on camera! Why the hell did you do that?"

Malice shrugged. "He seemed like a bigger threat. Torment doesn't seem to be the villain the public has made her out to be. She could be a victim of bad press just like me. I know for a fact that Justice was responsible for the deaths of many in his pursuit of keeping the law. It seemed like the best choice at the time, though if I'd known they were going to blow up a bridge to try and kill me, I may have chosen differently."

Mr. Gray took a deep breath and exhaled slowly. "Well, it wasn't what I wanted but it worked out. Everyone thinks you're dead, so that should buy you some time until our next move."

Malice looked at Mr. Gray suspiciously. "What exactly *is* our next move? What kind of nonsense do I get to deal with next?"

Mr. Gray smiled and said, "Just worry about recovering and go over those files. I'll let you know what's going to happen next once you're better. Keep your head down and don't do anything stupid in the meantime. Think you can do that, son?"

"Humph. Fuck you too," Malice shot back.

Mr. Gray threw a large folder onto Malice's lap and left the room.

Chapter 11: Dossiers

After Mr. Gray left, Malice followed his advice and began taking steps toward recovery. The truth wasn't too far from what the young woman had said; he was recuperating quickly. Between periods of rest, he looked through the information that could be gathered about the Paragons and the Fallen.

For some reason Malice found that he was more interested in finding out about their backgrounds than the details of their powers. What made these people tick, and why did so many of them lose their morals? Was it simply a matter of the corruption that often comes with power? Was it something that was innate with the powers themselves? Malice found that he had a lot of questions while he was reading. Unfortunately, there was very little information about the backgrounds of each individual. All records were likely sealed, and the real information about them was probably out of reach.

After reading through various inconclusive observations and theories from anonymous authors, Malice finally got to the factual information. He set aside the dossiers on Justice and Guardian; there wasn't much of a point in reading information on dead men. Malice started with the Paragons.

Noble

Age: Unknown

Sex: Male

Height: 5'11"

Weight: Unknown

Eyes: Brown

Hair: Blond

Association: Paragon

Profile:

A Harvard-educated man, he was already brilliant before the manifestation of his powers. Already had a PhD in engineering by the age of twenty-two, was considered the future of American innovation. Soon after graduation his powers came to light, and he joined the newly formed Paragons. It is believed he is responsible for the design of their equipment and their headquarters. Named "Noble" partially as a joke. It is known that he was born into a very rich family, one of the richest in New England. Although he was born into the "noble" class, he is not known to be a noble human being. In fact, it is believed he is kept out of the spotlight because he would likely harm the Paragon's image. He is known to be crude and suffer outbursts of violence around large groups of people. Since he is kept out of the spotlight there are few images of him.

Powers:

Noble has the power to manipulate technology in unnatural ways. He can hack into any system and essentially "talk" to computers and other forms of technology. It is unknown how exactly this is done, but any information contained on any network connected to the web is accessible to him. All calls, emails, and any form of communication that is transmitted can be intercepted by him and even changed if he wishes. Communication can be altered or removed, making him the perfect tool for engineering propaganda and keeping organizations like ours unknown. The full extent of his powers is unknown. For instance, it is not clear if he can manipulate simple technology like televisions, kitchen appliances, etc.

Harmony

Age: Unknown

Sex: Female

Height: Reports show she is approximately 5'6"

Weight: Unknown

Eyes: Dark brown

Hair: Black

Association: Paragon

Profile:

Harmony is of Chinese-American descent, and we know she spent some time with relatives in China growing up—how much time is uncertain. She is a very public figure, known for resolving conflicts through nonviolence as much as possible. The public adores her, and for good reason. She is known as an altruist, often taking up causes such as fighting hunger, promoting education, preventing animal cruelty, and many more. There are videos of her fighting Torment. Her style seems to be a form of kung fu.

The fight did not last long, as Harmony is a proficient fighter.

Powers:

Can manipulate water to do whatever she wishes. She can move it to form blasts and she can freeze it or turn it into steam. In her battles, water is typically used to take individuals down in a nonlethal manner, similar to fire hoses being used against rioters. Unclear if she can manipulate any liquid or just water.

Charisma

Age: Unknown

Sex: Female

Height: 5'2"

Weight: Approximately 120 lb

Eyes: Green

Hair: Black

Association: Paragon

Profile:

Essentially the face of the organization. Very little is known about her background. It is believed she may have been a lobbyist or even a small-scale politician of some sort. Excellent public speaker, even without the use of her powers. Adored by the public; there are more fan clubs of Charisma than we can keep track of. She handles a lot of the political aspects that the Paragons encounter. She gets them government funding and changes laws to benefit the Paragons (for instance their lack of liability for damage done in their fights.) It is suspected that she does a lot of backroom political moves but there is no solid evidence of this. Charisma loves to make public appearances as frequently as possible, often changing the attitudes of her critics in attendance.

Powers:

She can manipulate the emotions of large groups of people. How large a group and the range are unknown. It's also unclear if she can manipulate more than just their emotions. Her manipulation of emotion has garnered her the support of many powerful political figures. It has also made her a target of Torment, who apparently despises her ability to manipulate people. If there was a particular incident that caused Torment's hate of her, it is unknown at this time.

Phantom

Age: Unknown

Sex: Male

Height: 5'10"

Weight: 175 lb

Eyes: Brown

Hair: Black

Association: Paragon

Profile:

Phantom is the only member of the Paragons that is almost always traveling abroad, out of the public eye. He is also the only one that attempts to help other nations regularly in times of need. His name was derived as somewhat of a joke, because he's always gone.

Powers:

He can teleport himself and anything he's touching. This includes people and objects. It's unclear if he has a limitation to this ability or not.

Boss

Age: Unknown

Sex: Unknown

Height: Unknown

Weight: Unknown

Eyes: Unknown

Hair: Unknown

Association: Paragon

Profile:

Almost nothing is known about the leader of the Paragons. It has been made public that there are seven

Paragons, but only six have been sighted. Since the seventh is not known, there has been no nickname assigned by the media. We refer to this Paragon simply as "Boss." No information exists on Boss through any media outlet, and no one claims to have seen this Paragon. For all we know, this individual may not even exist at all—he or she could just be a ruse.

Malice was a little disturbed by the last Paragon. If nothing is known about them, they must be either very important or very powerful, perhaps both. He hoped that they were in fact a ruse of some sort. Tired, but unable to bring himself to quit reading, Malice continued with the members of the Fallen.

Lament

Age: Unknown

Sex: Male

Height: Believed to be around 6'1 from victim accounts

Weight: Approximately 160 lb

Eyes: Blue

Hair: Black

Association: Fallen

Profile:

Lament, like nearly all members of the Fallen, was once a Paragon. Most information from that time in his life has been removed from public record. It's assumed that he performed reconnaissance or perhaps even assassinations for the group. Although little is known about his background, there are no criminal cases that match his pattern of killing. It is believed that he was once "normal" or at least not sociopathic in nature. Eyewitnesses describe his apparent pleasure and euphoria at the sight of grieving family members, hence his name. It is unknown if there is any motivation for his killings or if it is simply for some perverse pleasure. Once Lament began killing (he made no attempts to cover it up), he was removed from the Paragons and lumped into the super-powered individuals known as the Fallen.

Powers:

He can make himself invisible, or perhaps camouflages himself so well that he appears invisible. In either case he cannot be seen by the naked eye. Efforts have been made to find him with heat sensors, and thus far this has been ineffective. This leaves few options to track him. Witnesses of his crimes mention that they never heard him while he was invisible, that he just appeared without a sound. We think he can mask sound as well, making him the perfect stealth weapon. There have been rumors that he can teleport out of an area, but we feel this is unlikely. So far there has been no conclusive evidence that he can do this.

Torment

Age: Unknown

Sex: Female

Height: 5'7"

Weight: Estimated to be around 130 lb

Eyes: Blue

Hair: Red

Association: Fallen

Profile:

Another former member of the Paragons, she had numerous conflicts with various other members publicly. In particular she argued with Charisma and Guardian a great deal. Eventually the arguments became attempted murder and Torment was expelled from the group. Since her expulsion she has been demonized in the media. Though it is claimed that she enjoys tormenting her victims, we have yet to find any evidence of this. There has been no evidence of Torment attacking anyone but members of the Paragons, corrupt politicians, and individuals attempting to arrest her.

Powers:

Heat manipulation, super speed, and agility. It's unclear the extent that she can manipulate heat. She is also a very proficient swordsman, which is a great advantage along with her speed and agility.

Immortal

Age: Unknown

Sex: Male

Height: 6'2"

Weight: Estimated around 190 lb

Eyes: Blue

Hair: Brown

Association: Fallen

Profile:

Immortal is very wealthy. His means of wealth are unclear but he is often seen spending large amounts of money in legitimate and illegitimate gambling venues. There are individuals who claim that he has been around longer than the other super-powered individuals. Thus far there has been no evidence to confirm this, and considering all the other members of the Paragons/Fallen emerged around the same time, we feel it is unlikely. Nicknamed "Immortal" because he does not age, and it's believed he cannot die. He is considered a member of the Fallen, but he does not like to associate himself with them. Generally, Immortal follows his own agenda. His only apparent crime is refusing to work with the Paragons. His actual motivation is currently a mystery.

Powers:

Extreme regeneration ability, which prevents him from aging or taking injury. Witnesses have seen him walk out of burning buildings unscathed by the flames. Unclear if he has any weakness in this ability. It's also unknown if he can withstand toxins or radiation.

Wrath

Age: Unknown

Sex: Male

Height: 5'11

Weight: 180 lb

Eyes: Brown

Hair: Brown

Association: Fallen

Profile:

Wrath is the only member known to have served in the military. He was a member of the army before he wiped out a village in Iraq with his abilities. Wrath refused to atone and work with the Paragons. Renowned for causing massive casualties and property damage, Wrath is one of the most feared and hated members of the Fallen. His attacks usually target government buildings and places of symbolic importance. He was finally captured and imprisoned after years of running from the authorities.

Recent escape from prison has left authorities baffled, and he has not been seen since. It is unclear what his motivations are.

Powers:

Earth manipulation. He can sink large areas into the ground, essentially burying everything in the area. Unclear the size and scope of his abilities.

Chaos

Age: Unknown

Sex: Male

Height: Unknown

Weight: Unknown

Eyes: Unknown

Hair: Unknown

Association: Fallen

Profile:

Perhaps the most disturbing of the group, Chaos has left few survivors of his attacks. The people that survived his attack on New York have been very quiet on the subject. Media has avoided speaking of it almost completely. What has been reported is that Chaos was killed by the Paragons during the infamous attack. It has been three years since, and no attacks have occurred. Chaos was once a member of the Paragons known to have great powers of healing, and he was even dubbed the Saint by the public. It is unknown when exactly his motivations and powers changed, but he disappeared from the Paragons for years before surfacing in the attack on New York. The ensuing chaos of the event led to his new nickname and the association with the Fallen.

Powers:

What is known is that he can revive the deceased and use them for his own bidding. The attack on New York supposedly involved just a few hundred of these things that have been described as something similar to zombies. Their bodies do not appear to be in a state of decay, though; they were described reluctantly by one individual as being in a feral state. They are extremely aggressive and without mercy. Women and children were casualties in the attack as well as the elderly and disabled. When asked about their appearance, our witness broke down into sobs. The only thing she would mention were the talons, how they tore through victims with gruesome efficiency. There does not appear to be a limit to the number of these "zombies" he can control. When people were killed in the attack they rose almost immediately as one of these zombies, and it is unclear whether it is some sort of virus or something else altogether.

Drift

Age: Midforties

Sex: Male

Height: 6'

Weight: 240 lb

Eyes: Blue

Hair: Brown

Association: Fallen

Profile:

Named primarily because he is often referred to as a drifter. The name also caught on after a survivor of his attack mentioned that it felt like they were drifting in the ocean when he was lifted in the air by Drift's telekinetic attack. As the name implies, Drift has been nomadic most of his known life. This typically makes him a loner, though he has worked with Torment in the past. It is claimed that he has killed his victims in hundreds of painful ways, the most infamous being the individual that had thousands of tiny cuts all over his body and died of shock. Drift is feared by the public but is often overlooked because of Chaos.

Powers:

Drift's powers aren't fully understood. The only thing that is clear is that he has strong telekinetic abilities, meaning he can move things with his mind. But it's not as simple as that; the thing that terrifies the public isn't the fact that he can lift and throw things with his mind. Even the footage of him hurling a Boeing 747 aircraft at Guardian paled in comparison to his ability to slice through most known objects or tear things apart at the molecular level. There are eyewitnesses that claim to have even seen him crush a living person down to the size of a basketball, almost like they imploded.

There was one more folder to look at, probably the last member of the Fallen, Cataclysm. But Malice could barely keep his eyes open. He figured there would be plenty of time to look it over in the morning.

Chapter 12: Amy and the Malcontent

As Malice slept in his recovery room, the young woman he had met earlier watched him through the door's window. Amy stood there, wondering why they were helping this man. Their organization was fighting against people like Malice, both Paragon and Fallen. So many people had died in their conflicts. Most of the members of their group, the Malcontent, had lost loved ones in these conflicts, herself included. Amy's sister died as Immortal fled from Justice a few years ago. She was in the wrong place at the wrong time when Justice, with his incredible speed, slammed into her by accident, killing her instantly. Since then Amy had sought a way to end the violence, to stop these freaks from slaughtering the public. That was when she found the Malcontent. They were primarily funded by a man named Clark Hanson.

Clark was the sole beneficiary of a large fortune that his great-grandfather built from his days as an oil tycoon. Clark was one of those rare people born into a rich family that actually strove to make something of himself. The man was very charismatic and charming. He easily won political offices; he even became mayor of New York. He was in the middle of his second term as mayor when Chaos struck. Many of his closest friends and family were killed before Chaos was struck down. Though nobody blamed him for the attack, Clark felt it was his fault for not being more careful. The weight of all that self-inflicted guilt made him resign and pursue the creation of this group.

The Malcontent were formed to counter all of the propaganda that the Paragons spoon-fed the public. This proved to be difficult, even with Clark's vast resources. They quickly discovered that all their online postings and television ads were removed. The only way they could really get their voices heard was to post flyers and speak out in public. This of course was usually met with violence from members of the public, but they had little choice. Hitting the streets with this information and speaking to the public was why Amy was there. Clark quickly found that attractive female members of the Malcontent typically fared best in speaking out publicly against the Paragons and Fallen. Amy was often described as a beautiful woman with a fiery personality. Angry hecklers in the crowd usually fell quiet quickly under her barrage of quick wit and angry passion. The more reserved members of the audience usually found it easier to swallow a harsh message if it came from someone with a pretty face.

Amy smiled at that thought, since people in the hospital she worked at were always intimidated by her blunt attitude. She was often given paperwork for being a little too honest with her coworkers or boss, but here she was praised for it, admired even.

A little over a week ago when she had walked into Clark's office, Mr. Gray was in there. They told her they would be receiving Malice as a special guest and that he was gravely injured.

Amy was horrified. "Are you serious? If you think I'm going to help that, that *freak*, then you've lost your mind! I thought he was dead anyways."

Clark smiled. "With your background as a surgeon, you are really the only one qualified to do it. We have all the necessary supplies according to Mr. Gray here." Clark motioned to the old man lounging on the couch in the room. Something about the way he looked made Amy uneasy.

"Ah, this fine creature must be Amy. I've heard *so* much about you!" Mr. Gray chuckled. "It seems the things I've heard about you are quite true, but I'm afraid I must get straight to the point and skip the pleasantries."

Mr. Gray's smile faded as he stood up and walked to the window behind Clark. For the first time since she entered the room, this Mr. Gray appeared serious and looked more his age.

"Malice is alive, but not well. The news reports are true to some extent: he did plummet into the river when the bridge blew up. However, the claim that he's dead is quite false. The Paragons and the public have made a poor assumption there. Malice will probably be dead soon enough though if you, my dear, do not help him." The old man turned from the window and stared at Amy with a grave look on his face.

Amy huffed. "I could care less if that freak dies, and good riddance. I wish the rest of them would follow his example."

Mr. Gray nodded to himself, as if expecting this answer. A dark grin swept across his face, and the pleasant, endearing look he had moments before was gone. A cold, malicious glare in his eyes startled Amy for a moment before he replied, "The rest of them *will* die, but we need Malice for that. He has already killed Justice and Guardian, and his thirst for vengeance for the loss of his wife and daughter will only grow, I assure you."

The pleasant smile returned to Mr. Gray's face. "But this will only happen if *you* save him. I'm certain that if his life hadn't been altered by the powers that he was given, he'd probably be much like you, Amy. Fighting with the Malcontent to change the public perspective."

Amy sighed and looked over to Clark. "All right, I'll help him, but not for the sake of the creepy old man." She shot a derisive look at Mr. Gray before looking back to Clark. "I'm only helping him because I want to. He is the only one who can take direct action against the Paragons and Fallen. Maybe he can get our message to be heard."

Smiling, Mr. Gray said, "Great! I'll have him up here in a jiffy! You get yourself prepared. Though he has some incredible powers, he will need your help—more than you know."

With that, Mr. Gray shook Clark's and Amy's hands before walking out. When Mr. Gray shut the door, Amy said, "I don't trust him, Clark. I don't know who he is, but he's dangerous. He gives me the chills. There's something . . . fake about him."

"Mr. Gray has been a supporter of ours for a long time," Clark replied. "He has been with us since the beginning, and there is no reason for me not to trust him. Go get ready and we'll talk more later."

Amy frowned. Usually her instincts about people were spot on, which is probably why she had done so well as a member of the Malcontent. She had a feeling that Mr. Gray couldn't be trusted, but for now she'd do as she was told and see what happened.

She walked out of the room and began rounding up all the medical supplies she could think of and preparing a room to work. Honestly, Amy had doubts about working on a man with abilities like these. Sedatives and antibiotics may be unnecessary or may not even work on him for all she knew. But she got everything ready as if he were a normal patient.

Thirty minutes later the man known as Malice was brought in. God, was he beat to hell! His face was swollen, and there was a large bump on the back his head with a thick mat of bloody hair all around it. His ribs were bruised as well, and considering what happened to him, she wouldn't be surprised if there were some broken ribs, maybe even some internal bleeding. There were lacerations everywhere, and his left leg had a large chunk of steel protruding out of it. Amy sighed. She knew she had a long night ahead of her.

The surgery went remarkably well. Most of Malice's injuries looked far worse than they were in reality. The piece of steel came out smoothly with little loss of blood.

Amy believed his abilities somehow enhanced his resilience and recovery abilities.

After the procedure, she stayed for a few hours for observation. This didn't go as expected, though. Instead of watching his pulse and breathing, she found that the poor man was suffering from some kind of horrendous dream. He was constantly screaming and flailing about; a couple times he called out the names *Janet* and *Lily*. She guessed he was reliving the loss of his wife and daughter if the information she had gotten from that creepy old man was true. For the first time she found herself feeling sorry for this man. Perhaps he wasn't like the other ones; maybe he would be the one that could change things for the better.

Amy was surprised that she was beginning to feel hopeful. She cried then, as if a huge weight had been lifted off her shoulders. It had been a long time since she had hope or faith in anything. It was strange to her that she could feel these things for a man she didn't know.

Mr. Gray stepped into the room about an hour later. "Magnificent, isn't he?" Mr. Gray asked in a somber tone. "At first glance, he isn't very impressive—quite average, really. But he has a strength that most people don't." He shook his head as if to clear his thoughts. "How is he doing?"

"Good." Amy yawned before composing herself again. "He's doing well physically, but I'm not sure about his mental state. He keeps calling out the names *Janet* and *Lily*. In any case, he should probably regain consciousness in a few days, but right now he really needs to rest."

"Excellent." Mr. Gray nodded. "I was correct in putting my faith in you. I'll be around for the next few days, so let me know when that jackass wakes up."

Once Malice had woken up, Amy went with Mr. Gray to check on him, then let the two of them be. She figured they had a lot to talk about, and she honestly wasn't sure she wanted to know what they were discussing. Eventually

Mr. Gray left, and Malice fell asleep after examining some folders for a few hours.

Looking through the window at him now, he didn't seem like the boogeyman the news portrayed him to be. That wasn't much of a surprise to her, though; most things were altered or left out of the media. He seemed like a normal man, though perhaps more serious and somber than most.

Chapter 13: Recovery

The next two days Malice slept the majority of the time. He was recovering at a remarkable pace, but it also made him extraordinarily weary. There were a few occasions where he woke to the woman he'd seen with Mr. Gray sitting beside him. Malice made several attempts to speak with her, but every time he tried she would shake her head and tell him to hush up. She would smile and remind Malice he needed to sleep and recover from surgery. Normally he would have ignored the advice and done as he pleased. Unfortunately, he found that he couldn't keep himself awake anyways.

On the third day after his surgery, Malice finally woke feeling refreshed enough to move around a bit. As soon as he stood and began walking around, Mr. Gray and the woman entered the room.

The woman smiled and reached out her hand, saying, "I'm Amy, chief surgeon of the Malcontent, at your service."

Malice smiled back, detecting the sarcastic tone in her voice. He shook her hand, "I'm, uh, Malice, according to the news. Former public enemy number one and murderer of heroes, at your service."

For a moment there was a period of awkward silence and Malice wondered if perhaps she did not enjoy his stab at darker humor. Amy finally burst into a fit of laughter that was infectious. Malice found himself laughing with her. Mr. Gray only frowned and shook his head at both of them.

"Former public enemy number one?" Mr. Gray asked.

"Well, they think I'm dead, don't they?" Malice replied. "As long as they keep thinking that, I'm not on their radar anymore. Someone else gets to be blown up on a bridge now."

"Humph, touché." Mr. Gray snickered. "In any case, how are you feeling?"

"A bit sore, some minor aches and pains, but it feels good to be moving around."

Mr. Gray nodded. "Well, get comfortable. We need to talk."

"I think I've spent enough time on this bed. Don't worry about me—what's on your mind?"

"Frankly, I'm a bit worried," Mr. Gray said. "As I have mentioned before, I gave you and the others super powers." Mr. Gray paused, acknowledged Malice's nod, and then continued. "What I did not mention is that in most of the other cases, their powers either evolved, or changed them drastically. For instance, the public remembers Chaos from his days as a Paragon. He was known as the 'Saint' because he had the ability to heal others of nearly any injury or ailment. Then he disappears for months and comes back with some crazy undead army and attacks New York."

Malice frowned, but he decided not to interrupt and motioned for Mr. Gray to continue.

"There was also Lament, who seems to have become a sociopath, completely unable to feel normal human emotion. His psych profile from before he had powers showed no such tendencies. Then there was the *other* one; his abilities rapidly grew out of control. He's doing things that I never intended at all." Mr. Gray's eyes glazed over as if he were deep in thought, and then he shook his head, obviously displeased.

Malice said, "So, what's the point? You made a mistake. You didn't make one with me, did you?"

Mr. Gray sighed. "While you were recovering, I was examining your DNA. There have been some unexpected changes, and I think it's only the beginning. I'm sorry to say, son, but I'm honestly not sure what you're becoming. Maybe if we're lucky it'll just be something beneficial like this rapid recovery you've had."

"What!?" Malice screamed, making Amy cringe. "What the hell do you mean you don't know what I'm becoming? Can't you fix it?"

Shaking his head, Mr. Gray replied, "No, what's done is done. I can't *fix* it. It could be beneficial or detrimental. Hell, son, for all I know it could kill you, or maybe you'll turn into a giant angry wombat and kill everyone. No telling—that's what makes it so exciting!"

Malice started turning red with anger. "I don't see what's so fucking funny. You're messing with me, aren't you? Or you planned this. You didn't screw this up, did you?"

"Oh no, I definitely screwed this up." Mr. Gray sighed. "Honestly, son, I'm as shocked as you. I spent a lot of time perfecting the procedure so you would not have any unexpected changes. Alas, it seems all that careful planning amounts to nothing."

Malice seethed but said nothing, and even Amy's warm smile didn't faze him.

"I'm not telling you this to worry you. I just want you to be prepared for the worst," Mr. Gray said. "I am fairly certain it's not fatal, if it makes you feel any better. There was no sign of cellular breakdown."

Mr. Gray grinned like he had given Malice fantastic news. But Malice shook his head. "No, actually, it doesn't make me feel better. I'm sick to death of everything around me falling apart. Nothing goes according to plan, and despite my best efforts innocent people are still dying. Maybe it *would* be good news if my cells were breaking down. I wouldn't have to put up with this nonsense anymore and I could see my wife and daughter again."

Malice smiled at the thought. He was never really a religious man, but it was funny how the death of someone close could make you re-examine your ideas on the afterlife.

Amy glared at Malice. She stormed up to him and slapped him hard across the face. "I don't give a shit what you've been through. You don't give up!" Malice looked shocked but stood there in silence, looking down as if he'd just been scolded by his mother.

"There is a lot riding on you. Your powers could help change things for the better. If you can't stop these other corrupted super-powered freaks then I'm not sure it can be done," Amy said. "Life's a bitch. Get over it."

She stormed out, slamming the door behind her so hard it shook the room.

"Well, she's not entirely right. If you don't succeed, I'll have to go to Plan B or C. Nobody will like Plan B, and Plan C is a bit messy." Mr. Gray chuckled to himself, like he had just shared the funniest inside joke.

"I'm not even sure what the hell I'm doing anymore," Malice said. "Even assuming I can get rid of the Paragons and Fallen, what next? You're not planning on making me president, are you? I'm not exactly popular, and I've got multiple felonies."

Mr. Gray raised an eyebrow. "You have a record? I did a thorough background check on you and never saw any misdemeanors or felonies—hell, not even a traffic ticket."

Malice laughed. "You're correct, I had no record *before* I had super powers. Since then I've killed two people and destroyed a ton of property. Oh, and I broke out of prison."

Mr. Gray smacked himself on the forehead. "Of course, I must be tired. Anyways, to answer your question, you are here to remove the Paragons and the Fallen to make way for greater change."

"What kind of change?" Malice asked. "Many tyrants and corrupt officials have campaigned on change, so change isn't necessarily good."

Nodding, Mr. Gray replied, "You make a good point. Guess you're not as dumb as you look. My goal is to prevent this great country from following in the footsteps of the other great civilizations: the Egyptians, the Greeks, Romans, et cetera."

"Those civilizations were conquered. You think America is going to be conquered by a foreign power or something?"

"Those civilizations were indeed conquered, but what left them vulnerable to foreign armies?" Mr. Gray replied. "Corruption of the government and poor leadership weakened those civilizations, leaving them vulnerable to attack. I don't believe anyone would be willing to risk attacking us directly. Unfortunately, it would be all too easy for someone to manipulate our politicians into making disastrous decisions. I'm ultimately trying to prevent the downfall of our country by rooting out the corruption and creating policies to prevent further degradation. If I'm successful, I hope to pave the way for brilliant leaders instead of a competition for who can earn more campaign funds."

"Humph." Malice nodded. "You are actually making some sense for once. So you need me to remove the Paragons and the Fallen because they will not work with you toward your ideal? What makes you think you will be able to change things within our government even with the Paragons and Fallen out of the picture?"

Smiling, Mr. Gray replied, "Without the Paragons influencing them, the corrupt officials will be vulnerable to more traditional forms of influence. I have vast resources available to me. I should be able to point them in the right direction."

"All right, maybe we've got something going here. Once I recover a bit more, we'll move on to whatever else you've got planned. Right now, though, I think I need some rest. We can continue this tomorrow."

Mr. Gray nodded and left the room. Malice figured he'd have a difficult time falling asleep with so much on his mind. He was wrong, and within minutes of being alone he was asleep.

Chapter 14: The Plan

The next morning Malice woke up to the pleasant aroma of coffee. For someone that used to drink a pot of coffee a day, it was a very refreshing smell. Without thinking, Malice got up from his bed, got dressed, and walked over to the next room to go get himself a cup. It wasn't until he opened the door and saw Amy glaring at him that he realized his mistake.

"What the hell are you doing up? Get your ass back to bed!" Amy screamed.

Startled by the sudden outburst, it took Malice a moment to realize that he felt fine—a bit sore, but nothing to complain about. He just shrugged and moved over to the pot of coffee, gently nudging Amy out of his way.

After taking a few sips, Malice smiled and said, "I appreciate the concern, but I feel great. I'm anxious to get up and start doing something."

Sighing, Amy replied, "Fine, do whatever you please. Just don't come crying to me if you fall apart."

Amy walked out of the room and Malice heard her footsteps going down the hallway. He was surprised to find that he enjoyed her company and was sad to see her go.

"Hey, how're you feelin', son?" Mr. Gray blurted out suddenly, a mere two feet behind Malice.

"Gah!" Malice cried before regaining his composure. "You scared the hell out of me. I didn't even hear you come in."

Mr. Gray shrugged. "One of my many talents, though often I don't even realize I do it. Don't worry about it, son. We have more important things to discuss. Sit down."

Both Malice and Mr. Gray pulled up chairs at the table in the room. When they were seated comfortably, Mr. Gray said, "Now, son, since it's just you and me here now, I wanted to tell you more about your powers."

Malice sat patiently as Mr. Gray continued. "Now like I said, I was behind the powers given to you and all the others. Now these powers actually stem from nanomachines: microscopic machines that number in the millions to carry out certain tasks they've been programmed to do. Each one of you have nanomachines with different programming. Guardian's nanomachines, for instance, restructured his muscles, tendons, skin, and even skeletal structure to augment his strength and durability."

Pausing for a moment, Mr. Gray let his words sink in before elaborating. "Now these machines are not sentient. They have a job and they analyze data to accomplish that task, then carry it out and alter it as needed. They have no consciousness. I'm not sure if I could even make them with one. Even if I could it would be dangerous, and I'm not sure what would happen."

Nodding, Malice replied, "You know, I remember after the reporters came the night that Janet and Lily were killed,

I felt a sharp pain in my neck but it was gone immediately. Did you inject me then?"

"Yes, but that's not important. I think that your nanomachines have either added new programming to their system somehow, or that their programming could have been corrupted in some way. Your fast recovery, though not as incredible as Immortal's, is still very impressive. It was not in your programming and Immortal is not around so it doesn't make any sense."

"So what is their programming, then?" Malice asked.

"Yours were programmed to copy the signal from nanomachines in the others. They can only get partial data, enough for you to keep their powers for a limited time. When you kill one of them, the firewalls and encryption devices within their nanomachines system shut down. This allows your nanomachines to grab their programming information and data to restructure your body as needed for permanent change."

"Why can't my body be restructured to keep the powers of all of them, and use them all at the same time?" Malice asked.

Mr. Gray grinned. "I told you once before, you'd be too powerful if we did that. I had to put some limits to your abilities. The programming for your abilities limits your nanomachines from keeping more than one set of powers working at the same time."

"Okay, I think I get it, but why are you telling me all of this?"

"Because," Mr. Gray explained, "I want you to be ready for whatever might happen with your powers. Your main abilities that you have, and the one's you received from Guardian and Justice, should be the same. However I'm not sure what else could happen, other than your new quick recovery ability."

"All right, well, I guess we'll just cross that bridge when the time comes," Malice said. "Right now I'm interested to hear if you have any plans for where we go from here."

Mr. Gray smirked. "Sure, son, I've got a plan that maybe even you can follow. Stay in this building, with these people, and don't leave. You got that?"

"So . . . you want me to do nothing?" Malice replied.

"Wow, you do catch on quick. Maybe that's one of your new powers!" Mr. Gray laughed hysterically.

"No attacks on the Fallen, or repairing my image?" Malice asked, genuinely perplexed.

"I want you to stay here, for now," Mr. Gray said. "My sources tell me the Fallen are planning something big, and it may be happening here in DC."

"What, an attack of some sort?" Malice said.

"Well, they're probably not coming to sell Girl Scout cookies. Which is really too bad—they're delicious!"

"Honestly old man, do you have ADD or something?"

"I want you here in case something happens, and if it is a big attack then you can help save the day. Maybe they'll wipe the slate clean, huh? You could be a hero, like one of the ones you killed! I love the irony."

Malice grumbled, "Yeah, well I don't." He sighed and rocked back in his chair a bit. "Fine, we'll do it your way. I'll stay here for now. Might not be so bad."

Footsteps came echoing down the hall, and Amy walked into the room to grab another cup of coffee.

Mr. Gray looked over at Amy and smirked. "Yeah, not bad at all, son. Not bad at all."

Chapter 15: A New Life?

Things seemed to finally be improving for Malice. Life

with the Malcontent proved to be comfortable, even

enjoyable. He often found himself in playful arguments

with Amy, and he decided that he liked Clark, their

organizational leader. It took him some time to get to know

the other members. Most of them were understandably

nervous, even angry with his presence there. After all,

wasn't their organization there to fight against people like

Malice? But after talking to them, and conveying his views

of the Paragons and the Fallen, most of them relaxed.

Ultimately, his views were pretty much the same as

their own, though his methods were a bit more extreme.

Still, a few in the group avoided him. Apparently they felt

diplomacy and perseverance would be enough to take on

the Paragons and Fallen. They felt that death was a bit too

extreme a measure. Malice fell into an argument with one such person, about a week after Mr. Gray left.

"You're impossible!" Alex Stanton yelled. "You can't just take the law into your own hands! The laws are there for a reason; your vigilantism is just a way for you to vent your own selfish desire for vengeance."

Malice shook his head. This was his third argument with the old man. Stanton was a man in his seventies, though his passion and energy made him seem much younger. Stanton had retired after thirty years as a police officer, and he had witnessed a great deal. He had a lot of valuable insight and experience but was not prone to shift his position. His stubborn nature was one that Malice shared, and the two often found themselves in arguments.

"It isn't vengeance that drives me," Malice replied calmly. "Making sure there aren't more victims like my wife and daughter is what drives me. Killing them is the only way to stop them from waging war with each other and killing innocent people in the process. If any of them are willing to step aside and live a more peaceful life, I would not bother them."

"You jump to the ultimate solution a bit too quickly. Have you even tried diplomacy?" Stanton asked.

"Not really," Malice said, "though I notice the Malcontent are using diplomacy. Tell me, Stanton, how far has that gotten?

Stanton grumbled, "It's slow progress, but we're winning people to our cause."

"Right, a few people here and there," Malice replied with a sharp tone. "But tell me, how many people are caught in the cross fire of these constant battles between the Paragons and Fallen while you try and win people over with diplomacy? How many people will die before you win enough support to suppress the Paragons and Fallen?"

"I don't know," Stanton said. "But I do know that many will die in your fights as well. Correct me if I'm wrong, but weren't there a lot of innocent people killed recently in the attempt to take you down?"

Malice winced. Thinking about the manhunt was painful. He had tried so hard to prevent casualties. Malice charged through buildings to avoid fighting his armed pursuit. Unfortunately, even though he did not confront the soldiers, they mowed down innocent people to try and kill him.

"So, what am I supposed to do then?" Malice asked. "You want me to just wait for the public to come to their senses and hold the Paragons and Fallen responsible?"

"No, I'm not asking you to do nothing. Work with us! We will bring people to their senses in a peaceful way. There is no need for you to fight them and get caught up in the very thing you are trying to end."

They both remained silent for a while. Malice was considering his next course of action. Stanton made valid points, but taking this slower route worried him. How much could they hope to accomplish? It could take years to win the public. If they could even be swayed at all.

Stanton interrupted his thoughts by patting him on the shoulder. He said, "You should come to one of our events." The old man smiled. "Amy will be speaking tomorrow to a large crowd outside the music hall. Maybe you should go witness our work with your own eyes?"

Before he knew it, Malice found himself agreeing with the old man. When Malice went back to his room, he realized he'd just been talked into leaving the compound. "How do I keep getting blindsided by scheming old men?" Malice asked himself out loud. He chuckled a bit at the thought, then went to bed. He was going to have a busy day tomorrow.

The next evening the Malcontent smuggled Malice out to the public assembly. They were fortunate that the event was organized at night; it made sneaking Malice backstage a bit easier. The secrecy may not have been necessary, since everyone thought he was dead anyways. Nobody wanted to take any chances, though, so Malice waited backstage, tucked away in a dark corner. He had Stanton with him and a few others. They were usually there to smuggle Amy out if the crowd got violent. Today, though, they were here to deflect anyone that might come across Malice.

Amy spoke for about an hour, heatedly discussing the flaws in the public reliance on the Paragons. She went on, mentioning all the government backing they had received, making them impervious to any responsibility for wrong doing. "Police officers are held responsible for mistakes they make that hurt the public!" she cried. "Why aren't the Paragons?"

Many in the crowd began nodding with approval as she went on. Many even cheered her or clapped during the many points she made. There were a few people that shouted angry protests, but they were quickly hushed by the rest of the crowd. Amy discussed the number of people estimated to have been killed during the fights between the Paragons and Fallen. She made sure to mention it was an estimation, since great efforts had been made to hide the actual numbers from the public.

"Thousands were slaughtered in just the battle between Chaos and the Paragons. Greater efforts need to be made to keep the Fallen in check. Right now our policy is to leave it to the Paragons. Yet there are no Fallen in prison, and only Chaos has actually been killed. We need constructive discussions with the Paragons and the rest of the public. We need to work together to make sure the Fallen stay in prison. Right now there are no real efforts being made to adequately contain the Fallen, and do you know why?" Amy paused for a moment, letting her question sink in with the crowd. "It's because they *want* the Fallen to escape."

Now the crowd grew angry and a few even threw cans and bottles at her. One person even tossed a shoe at her face. Amy was used to this and dodged the onslaught easily. She continued on with her speech, undaunted.

"The Paragons wouldn't be needed anymore if all of the Fallen were locked up for good. Their funding, merchandise, and their political power would crumble. Our current system currently relies on them too much in order to fight the Fallen."

Most of the crowd began to settle down a bit, but many were still visibly angry. Watching on the monitors, Stanton looked over at Malice and said, "Believe it or not, this is going pretty well. When we first started doing this it wasn't uncommon for our speakers to be assaulted. At least now people are listening."

Malice nodded and continued to watch Amy's speech.

Amy finally began summing up her points. "We need to hold the Paragons responsible for the damage they cause and the lives that are lost because of them. There needs to be more cooperation and transparency between the public and the Paragons. Serious efforts need to be made to contain the Fallen once captured. Finally, we need to take away a lot of the power that the Paragons wield in government and business. If we do nothing there will be no way to hold them responsible, and their conflicts with the Fallen will only continue. More and more lives will be lost, the public will suffer, and the Paragons will only grow richer and more powerful. Thank you everyone for coming, and please spread what I've said here to your family and friends!"

After the crowd dispersed, Malice and the rest of the Malcontent left and returned to their headquarters. Malice was surprised by what he had seen. He never expected so many people to attend the discussion. He was also impressed by the number of people that seemed to be considering Amy's words. There were a lot of angry spectators, but many seemed to be in awe. As if they were struck with a strong epiphany.

Malice tried to sleep that night, but he was honestly wondering if maybe Stanton had a point. Maybe diplomacy could work? He lost a lot of sleep before finally coming to a conclusion.

Chapter 16: Second Interlude

A young man burst into John Erickson's office and yelled, "They're getting worse!"

John was irritated, but he managed to smile and feign interest. "Your boogeyman again? Please, Mark, this is getting tedious. You're grasping at explanations and turning this into a phenomenon. There is a reasonable explanation, and we must take our time and find it."

"This time it's in the states. Towns in Texas have been struck. Yesterday morning another attack was recorded in Arkansas. People are beginning to ask questions."

Erickson sighed and stared at the young man, Mark Ramos. He was a smart agent, and when he had a hunch he followed it through to its conclusion. Some of the other agents jokingly nicknamed him "the bloodhound." His hunches had led to the capture of multiple members of the

Fallen in the past. He had an uncanny ability to find small details and piece them together to see the big picture.

"Honestly, sir, I think this is heading toward Washington, DC. I have a bad feeling about this. The attacks are getting more and more bold. We estimate that the total number of victims to be in the tens of thousands."

Erickson smiled. "Why do you believe the attacks are going toward the capital?"

"The pattern forms a trail, all the way from South America, through Central America and Mexico. It's now cutting northeast. The only logical place it could be heading is the heart of our nation. If it is Wrath, his hate for the government is well documented. It makes perfect sense for him to strike there."

Erickson shook his head. "No, he's aware that the Paragons have seismographs and monitoring systems in place. His attacks there have always been crushed, and quickly. He wouldn't do that again."

"Well yes, it does seem unlikely, but there must be something we're missing here."

"No, we're unable to make any logical conclusions at this point. There is not enough evidence. All we can do now is wait and continue to investigate."

Mark stared in disbelief. "Sir, normally you are more involved in these investigations. Your enthusiasm usually drives the rest of us forward. Lately you have shut everyone down that has come to you with possible solutions or explanations. Is there something you're hiding from us?"

Erickson began to laugh. "I admire your . . . instinct. I've witnessed it for years, and it never seems to be wrong, even now. Meet me here in the office at midnight. Do not tell anyone. The information that will be discussed is sensitive. We will need to keep it quiet for now."

Chapter 17: Confrontation

Three weeks passed, and Malice attended two more public meetings. Each one had similar results as the one he had attended before. This morning, Malice was alone in his room when a knock and a familiar voice interrupted his thoughts.

Mr. Gray said, "Are you decent, son? We need to talk."

Malice said, "Yeah, I guess. Come in, old man."

Mr. Gray walked into the room, closed the door, and pulled up a chair next to Malice. He gave Malice that same creepy grin that always made his skin crawl. It was like the old man had a joke on the tip of his tongue but wouldn't tell anyone.

"I've got some good news for you. There's something under way I want your help with," Mr. Gray said. "It's big. You might just slaughter—"

"No," Malice said in a cool tone, cutting him off mid-sentence. "I don't know what it is you want but I'm not going to be killing anyone for now. So far our methods have still gotten innocent people killed, and I nearly died in the process, too."

Mr. Gray shook his head. "No, son, you don't understand. This is *big*. We could end the whole conflict in one brilliant stroke!" He grinned mischievously, his eyes wide with excitement.

"Let me guess. This plan involves a lot of people dying and me fighting for my life," Malice said, more as a statement than a question.

"Well yes, of course, son, a lot of people are going to die," Mr. Gray said dismissively. "But the gains are well worth the sacrifice!"

"Then I'm not doing it. I'm not sacrificing my ideals to kill the Paragons and Fallen. I wanted to stop the death of innocent people, not add to it."

Mr. Gray laughed. "You're naive, son. Change takes sacrifice. Change on the scale that we're trying to achieve will require a lot of blood to be spilled. You think we'll just talk everyone into holding hands and making nice?" Mr. Gray smirked. "It doesn't work that way. If it did we wouldn't have war, or murder for that matter."

"Maybe it's naive," Malice said, "but it's worth a try. I'm not convinced that diplomacy will work either. But shouldn't killing people be the last resort?"

The smirk disappeared from Mr. Gray's face. He looked uncharacteristically serious. "Diplomacy rarely accomplishes anything meaningful. Death and destruction are the only effective means of change. Humans are not rational creatures. They need a forceful hand to sway them."

Stunned by Mr. Gray's blunt remarks, Malice found himself speechless. He realized that Mr. Gray meant every word he said. It finally dawned on him just how dangerous

Mr. Gray could be. The idea of working with him seemed revolting now. Under the right circumstances, Malice could imagine Mr. Gray being an iron-fisted dictator. A man with a brilliant mind on many accounts, but a tyrant.

"Get out, old man," Malice muttered, not wanting to look at him. "I'm not working with you anymore. You're crazy."

In a sudden fit of rage, Mr. Gray stood up and flung his chair across the room. He stormed up to Malice and glared at him face to face. Malice didn't back down, though. He wasn't afraid of Mr. Gray. Mr. Gray's face went beyond red, looking nearly purple, as if he were trying hard not to erupt. He stood there trembling for a moment, his fists balled up.

"You're going to regret this, son," Mr. Gray said coldly. "You think you have nothing to lose, but you're wrong. If you had worked with me, there would have been a lot fewer deaths. But you've forced my hand."

Mr. Gray stormed out of the room but stopped before shutting the door. He looked over to Malice one final time and said, "It's time to go to Plan B. I told you before, you won't like it. You can blame yourself for what's about to come." That creepy grin came back to his face, and the anger seemed to dissipate. Mr. Gray shut the door and left the building.

Malice sat in silence for a long time afterward. He felt that he had made the right decision. Honestly, he'd never felt comfortable about Mr. Gray. Something was off about him, something big. Malice wondered if he had made a mistake in making the old man angry. He shrugged, figuring there was no sense in worrying about threats. At this point, what could Mr. Gray do? Shaking the thoughts from his head, Malice changed his clothes. He was going to another public assembly tonight, and for the first time in a long time, Malice was excited about his future.

Stanton, Malice, and a few other members of the Malcontent went with Amy to her public assembly. They'd had many discussions about morality, particularly in regard to taking the lives of others. To Malice's surprise, Stanton agreed on many of his points. Only an idiot would preach pure, unmoving pacifism. Obviously if anyone were in mortal danger, using deadly force, as Stanton described it, would make sense. It wasn't worth the risk to oneself or others if the immediate danger could lead to death. Using words instead of action in such instances could be deadly.

The point that Stanton had was that killing someone to prevent the death of others in the future was immoral. Change was always possible, he argued, and nothing in life is ever certain. Malice wasn't so sure, but he was open to listening to other viewpoints.

Amy's speech went on like most of her others. It seemed each night that the crowd was a little larger and the people less hostile. Even Malice found himself hopeful that the more peaceful means of the Malcontent might prevail. The Paragons had a great deal of influence, and up until now they had kept media away. Tonight, though, the cameras were rolling and the Malcontent were finally gaining the publicity they had sought for so long.

Everything was going well until Stanton's cell phone went off.

"Yeah, hey, what's—" Stanton began. "Whoa, whoa, slow down. What's going on?"

Malice, concerned with the tone of Stanton's voice, listened eagerly.

But Stanton didn't say anything more. His face went pale as he stood there with the flip phone for a few moments. Finally, he closed his phone and looked at Malice. "We need to get going now. Grab Amy. We're leaving!"

"She's in the middle of her speech. We can't just—"

"Get her now!" Stanton yelled. "We're in danger and the compound is under attack. We need to leave!"

Without thinking, Malice ran out on stage and grabbed Amy in the middle of her speech, dragging her away with no explanation. It wasn't until later he realized he walked out on stage in front of the camera and a large crowd.

Stanton hurried everyone into their van and sped off toward the compound. Nobody spoke. Years of being a police officer and rushing to emergency calls helped Stanton get them back to the compound quickly. When they pulled up, though, they could see muzzle flashes in the windows and hear gunshots ringing throughout the building. As soon as the van pulled up, Malice told them to take cover, and he sped off into the building.

Immediately, Malice encountered a group of four armed men, all in full tactical gear and wielding M4 rifles. They gathered behind cover around the front door and immediately fired at Malice. Luckily he had already switched to Guardian's ability, and he wasted no time swatting each of them of down. He'd tried to avoid conflict the last time he'd encountered people trying to attack him. This time he wasn't going to make that mistake.

As Malice moved through the building floor by floor, he encountered the bodies of dozens of members. Many of the Malcontent had tried to barricade themselves behind locked doors, but to no avail. Each area he passed was lined with bodies, blood pooling all around him. Apparently some of the Malcontent had tried to fight back; they died with guns clenched tightly in their hands. Malice was trying to push past the horror of the situation when he heard more gunshots above him. That brought him the focus he needed.

Ascending two more floors, Malice passed by two armed groups and attacked them in a rage. Most of the hits sent the armed agents crashing through walls or flying out of the building—at least the ones who didn't have the misfortune of being beat to death. Growing impatient,

Malice used Justice's ability to quickly scour the floors as he ascended. Finally, at the top floor he found the last pocket of resistance. He barreled into the group of six armed men, switching again to Guardian's ability. He was hit by shots from the armed men and the surviving Malcontent too, but it didn't matter. Bullets shattered or even ricocheted off of him as he defeated the last of the men in the building.

Malice easily shoved the barricade of desks and chairs from the doorway as he entered the room. There were about six survivors inside, each armed but frightened at Malice's show of power. "Where's Clark?" Malice asked calmly, trying not to scare the survivors further.

A woman in the corner answered. "Nobody has seen him all day. Hopefully he's okay."

"All right, follow me outside. We're getting out of here," Malice said. The group quickly complied and they left the building.

They walked outside and were relieved to see the van and everyone inside it safe. Everyone in the van got out and started walking over to Malice and the survivors.

As the two groups approached each other, the three men that came from the van suddenly collapsed in agony. They fell only seconds apart, each of them gripping their throats as blood poured out. Everyone turned to see what was happening, but Malice already knew. The culprit was already appearing in front of him. He wouldn't forget that face, the one he saw so often in his nightmares.

Lament grabbed Amy from behind and held his knife up to her throat. Stanton and the rest of them turned and pointed their weapons up at Lament.

"Aw, a reunion!" Lament cried eagerly. "Too bad your wife and daughter aren't here for it."

Growling in anger, Malice replied, "If you kill her—"

"You'll what, kill me?" Lament laughed. "You were already planning on that, weren't you?"

"Stop!" a voice yelled from the tree line. Out of it stepped another group of armed men, and one figure was familiar to everyone.

"Clark?" Stanton muttered. "What the hell?"

"She was to be left alone!" Clark yelled. "Mr. Gray assured me Amy would be left in peace!"

Malice fumed, "Lament, you work for Mr. Gray?"

"Well, I wouldn't say I work for him exactly," Lament replied in a sarcastic tone. "Sometimes he has projects for me that I can't pass up. Like what I'm doing later tonight. Oh, and that night that I killed your wife and daughter!" Laughter again erupted from him as he slowly dug the blade into Amy's neck. Amy cried out in pain and a small trickle of blood formed on her neck.

"Mr. Gray, he . . ." Malice said. "No he couldn't have. Even he wouldn't—"

"Oh, I'm sure even you know, Mr. Gray will do anything if it furthers his goals," Lament said. "But if you don't believe me, ask him yourself. He figured I'd be the best person to get your attention."

"Where is he?" Malice roared.

"You'll find him at the Lincoln Memorial, tomorrow at noon. The main event won't kick off until you're there! Aren't you excited?" Lament paused a moment, then grinned. "You do intend on going, yes?"

"Yeah, I'll be there to kill him—after I kill you," Malice said coldly.

"Well, what a relief!" Lament cried. "You see, Mr. Gray said if you refused that I should kill dear Amy here, despite Mr. Clark's wishes." Lament looked over at Clark, then turned back to Malice. "But I think I'll kill her anyways!" Lament cried out in glee as he began to jerk the blade against Amy's throat.

A shot rang out and clipped Lament in the side of the head. He cried out in pain and the blade fell out of his hands. Stanton yelled at Amy to get down, but before he could fire another shot, Lament disappeared. Malice ran over to Amy, but she was okay. Everyone stood in silence, waiting for Lament to reappear. After a few minutes, nothing happened, and Stanton confronted Clark and his men.

"How could you?" Stanton asked. "This was your own group, men and women you recruited yourself! Why?"

Clark said, "You all knew it was hopeless. We were starting to make progress, but the Paragons were threatening to tear us down. Senators and public officials were on the phone with me every day with lawsuits. There was no way for me to fight back! Mr. Gray offered an alternative. He said if I sacrificed the Malcontent he would remove my opposition and support me in my new political goals. With his vast resources—"

"You sold us out and trusted that lunatic?" Stanton said.

"I don't have to explain myself to you," Clark said. He then turned to his soldiers. "Kill all of them, but not the woman. Detain her, unharmed if possible. I'll be waiting in my new office." Clark sprinted for the woods, and his men fired.

Two of the survivors were hit and went down. Stanton and the others returned fire while Malice charged among the soldiers. He grabbed two by the neck, one in each hand, and started squeezing. The men's eyes began to bulge and the blood rushed to their faces. Malice squeezed so hard their necks broke and their windpipes were crushed. The rest of the armed men were gunned down by Stanton and the remaining survivors. Unfortunately, Clark was long gone, leaving everyone baffled.

They gathered into the van and sped out of the area. Luckily Stanton had a place set aside in case things fell apart. When they arrived, the whole group went inside, except for Malice. Stanton and Amy turned back toward him. Amy was about to say something, but Stanton put a hand on her shoulder and shook his head. "No, he *needs* to go." Stanton nodded at Malice and walked inside to join the others.

"Look, I'm sorry about everything," Amy said somberly. "But please come back in one piece. We lost so many good people today. I don't want to lose another one."

Malice frowned and shook his head, "I don't know that I'm a good person, not anymore. I'm going to rest here tonight and head out tomorrow."

Chapter 18: Lincoln Memorial

Malice's mind was in a million different places as he sped off toward the Lincoln Memorial. Lament claimed Mr. Gray played a part in the death of his family. But that didn't make any sense. What would Mr. Gray have to gain by the death of his family?

Malice certainly was nobody special before he was given his powers. In so many ways, most people had considered him dull. He wasn't exactly an introvert; he just didn't care. The only ones he cared for were his close friends and family. He'd never bothered with small talk and public appearances to bolster his image with others. Most of the time he passed up invitations to parties and other events, and not because he didn't think he would have fun. He simply knew that he didn't enjoy the company of the people there and felt it would be stupid to pretend that he did. Many people would have described him as nice, a good member of the community. That was only because he stayed out of gossip and never said anything bad about anyone.

It was fair to say that nobody really knew him other than his close friends and family. So there was no particular reason he could think of for why Mr. Gray had chosen him. There certainly wasn't anything he had done that would have gotten the attention of Mr. Gray. Not until the news report where he openly condemned the Paragons. But that was after his family was killed. Maybe the presence of Lament and the death of his family was an unfortunate coincidence. It was probably bad luck; Malice certainly had his fair share of that. Ultimately he concluded it could have been Lament toying with him. Hopefully Mr. Gray would give him some answers.

As Malice sped through the city, he looked for signs of some sort of disturbance. Everything seemed normal, though. When he darted up the steps to the Lincoln

Memorial, he found Mr. Gray there by himself, looking up at the memorial.

"Magnificent, isn't it?" Mr. Gray asked without even looking over to Malice. "The monument is a fine tribute to a fine man. Few people can understand what he must have gone through."

"Look, old man, I'm not here for a history lesson," Malice said calmly. "What the hell do you want?"

Mr. Gray continued. "Did you know that during the civil war, many in the North grew tired of the war? They wanted Lincoln to negotiate peace with the South, and end the war. His own party even called for him to step down. They didn't want him to be reelected!"

Mr. Gray shook his head in disbelief, but smiled genuinely. "But Lincoln wasn't like many of the politicians of his day, and certainly not like our current ones. He did not operate based on the constantly shifting opinion of the public. Lincoln acted on what he believed to be right in his heart. He knew the cost to be great but he stuck with the war. Ultimately he won his reelection and the war, and unified our country once more."

There was a long pause then. Malice was a student of history and knew Lincoln's story well. Despite his feelings about Mr. Gray's lack of morality, he couldn't help but admire the memorial with him.

Sighing, Mr. Gray's smile faded and his expression turned grim. "But many think President Lincoln to be a saint, and I agree that he was a good man. However, Lincoln was not stupid. He did what he had to do to achieve his goals. He took many liberties from those in the Union by suspending habeas corpus. It essentially limited free speech, instituted martial law, and silenced his critics in the press. Though many felt he was overstepping his power and that he was a tyrant, it was necessary to keep the Union unified. Few today can argue with the ultimate results he achieved."

Malice stared at Mr. Gray, trying to figure out what the old man was getting at. He knew Mr. Gray to be manipulative and cold and didn't trust the man. Every word Mr. Gray said needed to be scrutinized carefully.

"It is true I sent Lament to deliver my message, and that I brought down the Malcontent," Mr. Gray said. "But it was done for a worthy cause, and I hope you will hear me out."

"Did you send Lament to kill my wife and daughter?" Malice bluntly asked.

Mr. Gray shook his head. "No, I did not ask him to kill them. In fact I didn't know they even existed. I needed Lament to break out of prison to accomplish a certain task. Unfortunately, he was intercepted by Guardian. In his attempt to escape he came upon your family, and the rest is history."

Malice nodded. "I probably should just kill you now and be done with it, but I'll give you a second chance. I'll hear you out, though if I don't like what I hear . . ."

Mr. Gray shot him that creepy grin of his. "My story of Lincoln had a point. His resilience cost the country more American lives than World Wars I and II combined. It brought the hatred of thousands while he lived, but the end result was the unification of the country and the freeing of slaves. We still reap the benefits of his sacrifice today."

Shifting his gaze back to the Lincoln Memorial, Mr. Gray nodded. It took him a moment to gather his thoughts.

"Today, there will be an attack here in the capital, once I give the signal," Mr. Gray said calmly. "Congress is in session and the president and most of his staff are here as well. I plan to strike the government and eliminate the city as well. It will be the catalyst that ultimately unifies the country into progressive action. With my guiding hand, of course." Mr. Gray smiled.

Stunned at the bluntness of Mr. Gray's statement, Malice could only stammer, "W-Why?"

"Our leadership in this country has become a joke, that's why!" Mr. Gray shouted. "It's no longer about what's best for the country—it's about playing teams! Republicans and Democrats both voting or not voting for bills based solely on whoever promotes it. Hell, many of them don't even bother to read the damn things anymore. They just side with their party. They also side with whoever funds their campaigns, constantly having to shift their allegiance to appease their sponsors. It breeds corruption and leads to decisions that harm this country."

Mr. Gray sighed again. "I've tried peaceful means, attempted over and over again the passing of a bill of reform. To change how our politicians are elected and how their campaigns are run. Eliminating the need for large sums of money to campaign alone would eliminate much of the corruption. Unfortunately, change is not possible, since politicians cannot bring themselves to see past the greed of their position. They will not change peacefully, so I will force them to change violently."

"You're nuts!" Malice cried. "There's got to be a way that doesn't involve wiping out a city."

Shaking his head, Mr. Gray said, "No, I've been attempting this change longer than you've been alive. In fact, the whole reason I created the technology to produce powers was to change the country peacefully. That too has backfired, furthering the corruption in our government. This is the only way, and I want your help to ensure its success."

"No," Malice replied. "You know full well I won't help you. I won't let you do this!"

Malice grabbed Mr. Gray by his throat and lifted him off the ground. He began to squeeze, but Mr. Gray laughed. Suddenly Mr. Gray's whole body trembled violently, and his form shifted gradually. His skin became younger, and his hair turned black and grew down just past his shoulders.

Mr. Gray's whole body was changing into someone Malice recognized.

His eyes wide, Malice was now holding his wife by the throat. Mr. Gray laughed and said, "Did you think I only gave powers to others? I can look and sound like whomever I choose. I thought your wife was a nice touch. Or maybe your daughter?"

Mr. Gray, now appearing like Malice's wife, shifted again. Now Malice was holding up his daughter. Stunned, with tears coming to his eyes, Malice let go, burying his face in his hands and openly sobbing.

Unharmed, Mr. Gray approached Malice in the form of his daughter and said in her sweet voice, "You're weaker than I thought. We could have done great things." Mr. Gray skipped off in the little girl's form, mocking Malice.

Tremors began to shake the area, and a couple of buildings collapsed. Malice looked up and saw holes beginning to open up all over the area and dark forms pouring out. There were thousands of them coming out of the holes in the ground! They had clawed hands and began striking down people in the streets. The tremors grew and soon Malice realized what was going on. Chaos was alive, and Wrath was working with him to bring the city down. He could only hope those were the only two involved in Mr. Gray's plot.

Chapter 19: Chaos

Years of witnessing people in horrible pain and suffering had eventually worn down the man now known as "Chaos." Before he'd been given powers, Chaos had been a respected young surgeon. At some point he had caught the eye of Mr. Gray, though he wasn't sure why. After learning the full uses of his apparent healing powers, he had been dubbed the Saint by the public. As the Saint, he had spent years with the Paragons, healing them and the many unfortunate victims they came across. Over the years, though, he found himself healing more and more innocent people caught up in the violence.

Even though he had incredible powers of healing, even the Saint could not help everyone. Many people, despite his best efforts, succumbed to horrific injuries and died. Throughout his time with the Paragons, the number of dead rose steadily. Each one wore heavily on his conscience. At first he felt inept, then bitter. Eventually hatred for his careless companions and the Fallen overwhelmed him. Seeing so much pain and suffering over the years, he started to lose faith in humanity.

It became even more unforgivable when the Paragons started to cover up the number of innocent people caught up in the violence. Once they began manipulating the media, it became all too easy to change numbers or keep events quiet.

One day a battle erupted between Drift and Guardian, and a whole school was leveled during the fight. Saint rushed in to try and heal the wounded but found many of the children already dead. He was desperate to try and help, and without thinking he attempted to heal one of the dead. To his surprise and horror, it worked, though not quite as he had imagined. Somehow he had revived the poor boy, though he was not the same. The boy was merely a shell:

no thoughts of his own, a mere puppet to the Saint's mental commands.

Out of curiosity, he attempted it on more of the bodies, eventually stopping around twelve. Each turned out to be the same, though, shells of their former selves bent to his whim.

The battle between Guardian and Drift was finished by that point. Guardian walked up to the Saint then, noticing the twelve children standing around him. "Whoa, what the hell is wrong with them?" Guardian asked.

The revived children all had empty stares and stood hunched over. None of them blinked. It didn't take a genius to figure out something was wrong with them.

"Well," the Saint replied angrily, "these children and dozens of others are dead thanks to you."

Guardian only shrugged his massive shoulders. "Oops." He wasn't even surprised that some of the dead children had somehow been revived.

Rage swelled within the Saint then, and the twelve children suddenly came at Guardian in a frenzy. They had sensed the anger their master felt and attacked Guardian. Their fingers warped into sharp points and began slashing away. But twelve were not nearly enough to take him on, and slowly he struck each of them down, their bodies becoming too broken to function further. Realizing his peril, the Saint slipped away then and disappeared from the public eye for years.

He did not regret his attack on Guardian, even though it was unintentional. In fact he was delighted with the revelation the experience provided him. Humanity was a lost cause, beyond redemption. Humans were evil creatures, a blight upon the planet that needed to be removed. The Saint spent years contemplating a plan of attack and gathering "followers"—the undead.

His attack on New York was indeed brilliant, with the numbers of his followers increasing constantly as more and more people were struck down. Unfortunately, he had underestimated the length the Paragons were willing to go in order to fight him. Knowing they were unable to defeat him otherwise, the Paragons used Harmony's power to sweep the Saint and his army into the sea. A massive wall of water came into the city and obliterated everything in its path.

After the incident, the giant cover-up began and most of the facts were overwhelmed by false reports and information. This was done on purpose since the Paragons couldn't outright cover up an incident that big. The next best thing was to smother it in a cloud of mystery, letting time erode the truth. But the truth was that the Saint and his followers were not the only ones swept out to sea. Thousands of innocent people were killed in the process.

The media then renamed him "Chaos," and the public remained in fear for several years. Though the Paragons claimed he was dead, many were still skeptical. So he remained hidden, taking advantage of the public confusion to consider his next move. When Mr. Gray, accompanied by Wrath, eventually tracked him down, they gave him an offer he couldn't refuse: they needed him for an attack on the nation's capital.

Their agreement was that he would eliminate the Paragon stronghold and the nation's leadership. Mr. Gray wanted as much devastation as possible within the city. Once their goals were accomplished, Chaos was to pull his minions back. The idea was to leave many alive so that they could serve as witnesses. Mr. Gray wanted them to provide the voice that would change the public perception of the Paragons and the Fallen. He would then reveal his considerable amount of evidence of wrongdoing by the government and the Paragons.

Mr. Gray's plan was then to use the united anger of the nation to push everyone toward one candidate for leadership. With that man in power, Mr. Gray could bend the nation to his will. With the Paragons and their corrupt politicians removed, Mr. Gray could then assume power from behind the scenes. He meant to use the attack to ultimately reform the nation as he saw fit. But Mr. Gray and Wrath both misunderstood Chaos's motivation. It was clear to him that both Mr. Gray and Wrath were unhappy with the government and the Paragons. They had made the poor assumption that Chaos shared their feelings on the matter.

What they did not realize was that Chaos didn't hate the government and the Paragons. He hated humanity, and wanted the lives of *everyone* extinguished. They would all be his minions in time. War and hatred would fade, as would pain and suffering. It would only be him and billions of loyal followers. Chaos no longer considered himself human; he felt that he had evolved beyond humanity. Indeed, anyone looking at him would agree: he did not look human.

So Chaos had agreed to their deal, but he kept his true intentions to himself. Even if the attack failed, his true goal was much more important. Now he laughed as he launched the attack on the capital. As smart as Mr. Gray and Wrath were, they were blinded by pride and ambition. They hadn't thought out every part of their plan as carefully as they assumed, because they had missed one very obvious thing that shifted the scales greatly in Chaos's favor. If they even suspected what he was going to do, he was certain they would have attempted to kill him by now.

Again Chaos chuckled to himself. He wasn't exactly certain he could be killed; New York had shown him that. He alone survived being swept out to sea in that wall of water, even after being dragged under and pummeled by countless pieces of debris. That was what started his change, he believed, from living, breathing flesh to what he had become.

Chapter 20: An Unlikely Hero

Nothing could have prepared Malice for the massacre laid out before him. The city shook on and off, buildings collapsing periodically. Thousands of Chaos's army spilled out of holes in the ground, mercilessly killing anyone unfortunate enough to be in their path. Every single person that was struck down rose again, adding to the army. Their numbers swelled quickly in the streets. Malice did the best he could, zipping through hordes of them with Justice's speed and agility. For every one he struck down, there were always ten more waiting for him. Eventually he admitted the futility of fighting them head-on. Instead he began to hold them at bay while others escaped. The police, to their credit, had quickly set up a defensible area for everyone to retreat to. Unfortunately, it wasn't enough, and even with Malice's help the area couldn't be protected. It wouldn't be long until the area was overrun.

Shrieks from a group of the creatures took everyone by surprise. Their bodies were flung in every direction. Soon the flood of enemies was being parted and held against their will. In between them a man casually strolled. Finally stopping and smiling, he threw his arms down violently, and hundreds of the creatures blasted hard into the ground. One long horrible shriek emitted in unison from the thousands of remaining creatures. It distracted Malice for a moment, and when he faced the man again, he was right next to Malice.

"Hey, name's Drift," he said, shaking Malice's hand. "Figured y'all could use a hand."

Confused but grateful, the crowd wondered why two supposed villains had saved their lives. But none of them were about to take the help for granted. Most of them were busy cheering as the creatures fell back like a dark tide. Both Malice and Drift looked at the retreating army with skepticism. With sheer numbers the creatures could have overwhelmed them eventually. Tactically it wouldn't make sense unless there was a more valuable target.

"We need to follow them," Malice said. "There's no way he is fully retreating when he's obviously winning."

"Yer right, boy. Chaos is no dummy, bastard probably has a few surprises left. How 'bout you go after ole Shakes while I take care of Tall, Dark, and Creepy?"

Confused for a moment, Malice laughed. "Shakes? You mean Wrath?"

"That what everyone's calling him?" Drift shrugged. "Always thought *Shakes* sounded better."

Nodding, Malice replied, "Yeah, I'll tell him you said so when I meet him. Been meaning to finish what he started back in prison."

Without even waiting for a reply, Malice sped off into the direction of the fallen buildings. It wasn't hard to find him once Malice discovered that he could sense where Wrath was. He wasn't sure if that sense came from being around Wrath before and using his power or if it was one of the new changes Mr. Gray mentioned. It ultimately didn't matter. Wrath had brought death and destruction to thousands of innocent people. That wasn't something Malice could ignore, and this time he wasn't getting away.

Wrath was walking through an area he had leveled, a huge grin on his face. In a blur, Malice collided with him, sending him crashing through rubble and out of sight. Malice felt the ground beneath him go weak, and before he could react, Wrath was pulling him into the earth. Using Guardian's ability, Malice clasped his hands together and slammed down hard, sending shockwaves through the ground. The impact stunned Wrath long enough for Malice to punch through the ground and grab him.

In an attempt to throw Malice off balance, Wrath sent a huge tremor into the ground. The whole area shook violently, but Malice felt none of it. He had no trouble keeping his balance when he was using Wrath's own ability. Malice began punching Wrath in the face, breaking his concentration on the earthquake.

Again the ground grew weak beneath Malice, and both he and Wrath began sinking into the earth. Wrath was grinning, no doubt thinking he was going to sink Malice like he would his normal foes. He didn't realize his tactical error until it was too late.

As they began sinking, Malice just shook his head. He shifted to Guardian's ability and punched Wrath in the chest. The punch sent Wrath soaring through the air, crashing to the ground dozens of feet away. Malice casually walked over to him.

Coughing blood and struggling to breathe, Wrath said, "Got so used . . . to fighting . . . Paragons." He paused as he began a fit of coughing that had him wincing in agony. "They always fought to disable, but not you, eh?" Wrath tried to laugh but stopped, the effort hurting too much.

Before Malice could reply, a dozen dark forms darted in and slashed at Wrath. Malice could only watch in horror as Chaos's creatures tore at Wrath. He flailed and screamed as he was raked by huge claws all over his body. Malice charged in, but as quickly as they started, they stopped and moved away. Wrath let out one more agonized cry as his body violently shook. All of his cuts began to heal, but his skin began to harden and turn the color of ash. The color spread from each of his wounds until his whole body was covered. His fingers elongated and curved into sharp claws. Wrath stood, though it was no longer really him. His eyes glowed red, and his shoulders and head hung limply. He stared coldly into Malice's eyes and shrieked. The ground shook and tore apart all around them. After a minute of the tremors, Wrath stared at Malice once more. His mouth opened but didn't move as a raspy voice came from within it.

"I knew he couldn't be controlled forever. I didn't think I could get to him without a distraction at the very least, but you subdued him completely."

Horrified, Malice said, "That's not Wrath's voice. Who the hell is talking?"

"Chaos, as the public has named me. That is really the opposite of what I truly desire. I wish for there to be order. And there will be, once I have claimed everyone on this planet as part of me."

Shaking his head, Malice said, "You're even crazier than the old man."

"Mr. Gray?" Chaos asked. "The attack was his design, but he didn't know my full purpose here. I also expect to be done with him shortly. I believe he has figured out that I have no intention of striking a blow and retreating. I intend to spread my attack out from here to the rest of the continent and beyond. Even if I am not successful in that, I have already accomplished one of my main goals here. As

Wrath could attest to, if he had thoughts of his own to voice." The creature shuddered and emitted a raspy cackle.

Malice's eyes grew wide. "What are you talking about? What other goals?"

"Oh, that's a surprise I don't want to ruin for you. I'm quite certain you will be meeting your surprise very soon." The creature that was Wrath shrieked and fell into a great chasm that opened into the ground.

Chapter 21: Déjà Vu

Before Malice could really reflect on Chaos's words, a dark blur flew toward him and slashed him across the torso with blinding speed. Stumbling back from the hit and saved only by Guardian's ability, he then got rocked by a devastating uppercut to the chin. Malice's body soared high before crashing hard back to the earth. Two forms descended on the area, now hidden in a cloud of dust stirred up by the impact.

Malice darted out with Justice's speed and stopped about fifty yards away. "No, it can't be . . . ."

Chaos's raspy voice came from the mouth of the creature that was once Guardian. "These two, and the rest of Mr. Gray's creations, were my main goal in this attack. Even if my thousands are destroyed, I will have an assembly of powers at my disposal. We will regroup, and our next attack will be unstoppable!"

Malice couldn't even find the words to respond. The faces of these creatures were obviously once Guardian and Justice. He couldn't begin to fathom how it was possible; they had been dead for so long. They should be even beyond Chaos's ability to revive.

A raspy, inhuman cackle came from the mouth of Justice. "I see the confusion in your face. Their resurrection was rather simple. The Paragons were foolish enough to preserve them openly, and so perfectly. It was not difficult to revive them."

Guardian's fist burst toward the ground, breaking the earth open around himself and Justice. The two shrieked and attacked Malice as one. Justice flew at Malice with blinding speed, keeping him off balance as Guardian delivered devastating punches.

On his heels, Malice deflected as many blows from Guardian as he could, attempting to ignore the less damaging hits from Justice. He was successful for a little while until Guardian hit him with a three-punch combo. Two punches to the gut, and a brutal right hook to the side of his face. As Malice stumbled back, Justice kicked one of his legs out from under him, sending Malice to the ground.

Both Guardian and Justice pounced on Malice, attempting to hack him to pieces. But Malice's ability held the cuts at bay, and though they stung, none of them broke through his skin. Shrieking in frustration, the creatures shifted their tactics and began a barrage of punches and kicks. A cloud of dust came up from the ground. Malice couldn't see, but he tried to run anyways.

He didn't get far as Guardian grabbed him by his hair and hoisted him off the ground. Held helpless, Malice received a volley of punches to the torso from Justice. Justice was punching so fast his fists and arms couldn't be seen. Guardian slammed Malice's body down to the ground, creating a deep crater and sending a minor tremor through the area.

Bruised and battered, Malice attempted to crawl out of the crater and was surprised when he wasn't accosted. Both creatures stood, their backs turned to Malice. With a lot of effort, he managed to get to his feet to see what they were staring at. A middle-aged woman approached them, and Malice recognized her immediately. He had seen her in the news many times. Harmony.

The creatures shrieked as if with glee at the sight of the woman. Malice yelled, "Get out of here! Chaos's goal is to turn us all into them!"

Harmony only smiled, as if she were amused by Malice's concern. Both creatures came at her then. She easily dodged each attack or deflected them harmlessly aside. As quickly as Guardian and Justice moved, Harmony seemed as if she were moving slowly, but with a graceful flow. The speed and brutality of their attacks amounted to nothing under her calm dance.

She lashed out at Justice with a sudden palm strike to his nose, and with a sweeping kick, she sent both Guardian and Justice to the ground. Malice could barely stand after the brutal assault from those two, and yet this woman had serenely evaded their attacks. He couldn't believe how effortless it looked. She had even managed to strike them through the flurry of their coordinated attack. Moving now toward her fallen foes, she intended to finish them.

Apparently realizing their inability to defeat Harmony, the creatures darted off, shrieking in frustration.

"Well, come on," Harmony said. "We can't hardly be fighting you now. We're going to need your help." She extended her arm out to help him walk. Malice thought about it for a moment but realized he didn't really have much choice. If he didn't accept her help, there wouldn't be much of a chance of him escaping alive. The last thing he wanted to be was one of Chaos's creatures.

They walked out of the area, with Malice leaning on Harmony for support. As they moved, Malice felt better as time went on. After about an hour, he was walking comfortably on his own, and most of his bruises had already faded. Finally they stopped moving, and Malice decided to break the silence.

"So what now? I figured the mighty Paragons would be repelling Chaos's attack by now. And why did you save me?"

Harmony smiled and said, "We never desired a fight with you, but you forced our hand. Killing Justice and Guardian weakened us, and if we did nothing, others would have gathered the courage to attack us as well. Now that the public thinks you're dead, maybe Noble can bend the media into thinking you're a new hero, leaving 'Malice' buried once and for all."

Malice shook his head. "I can't ignore the injustice, all the corruption and evil that the Paragons have committed.

Even worse, it was done under the pretense of being good. No, I can't become one of you, and I certainly won't pretend to be someone else."

Harmony nodded. "I don't know you well, but I expected that was going to be your response. Can you at least agree to help us repel Chaos? We will resolve our dispute after that."

Sighing, Malice said, "All right, I'll cooperate for now. If I see anything suspicious, I'm leaving."

"Why, Malice, we're the good guys. Haven't you been watching the news?" Harmony grinned at him.

Malice rolled his eyes and grumbled, but he followed Harmony toward the Paragon compound.

Chapter 22: Drift

After Malice ran off to deal with Wrath, Drift stayed for a while. He used his abilities to pull in cars, rubble, and anything else that could be used as an effective barrier. Drift didn't feel right leaving all of those people vulnerable. A few of them gave him dirty looks, but most were kind and grateful. He knew that his help was unexpected, and many of them might be suspicious. But his motives were not sinister. He wasn't the villain that the Paragons proclaimed him to be. Drift was a man that enjoyed his freedom, plain and simple.

For many years before acquiring his powers, Drift had wandered the country. He would do various jobs to support his nomadic life. Anything from basic construction to working at a carnival. Any job that was hands-on and typically seasonal was what he looked for. He had met countless people from all walks of life. Many were good, though most were not. But in the end it never mattered because he always moved on.

From a young age, Drift knew he was pretty good with his hands. He was always tearing things apart and rebuilding them. Drift would see job postings in offices, but that kind of work never interested him. He was smart and capable enough to do the job, but being stuck inside a stuffy office in a cubicle all day seemed unappealing. Something about getting all dressed up and wearing a tie just seemed dishonest. Why wear all of those fancy, uncomfortable clothes that you would never choose to wear on your own?

Despite what people always assumed, Drift had a happy childhood. Because he didn't have a place to call home, everyone assumed he came from a "broken home." But he never had the feeling that other people had about staying in one place. As a kid his dad was always moving him from place to place. Over the years the concept of a home became pretty foreign. Most kids would probably resent their parents for that. Drift wasn't like most kids. He enjoyed going to new places and meeting new people so frequently. Since he always knew he was going to be leaving, he could be himself. There was never any worry about embarrassing himself or making enemies. So Drift did whatever he wanted and appreciated it.

This was why Drift treasured his freedom. After his powers developed, he began helping people as best he could. The Paragons offered him a place with them, but he politely refused. They even offered to let him roam as he pleased as a member of their organization. Drift still refused; he didn't want to be tied down to any organization.

The Paragons didn't like his refusal, so they sent Guardian and Charisma to try and intimidate him into accepting their offer. Between Guardian's brute size and Charisma's ability to manipulate emotions, they felt Drift could be convinced. They underestimated his resolve.

Charisma attempted to make him feel intense feelings of fear and cowardice. Guardian loomed over him, yelling and swearing. Drift fought Charisma's influence with anger and frustration. When tricks and posturing didn't work, Guardian finally swung at Drift.

Drift held Guardian's fist back at the last moment with his powers, preventing it from connecting with his face. Enraged, Drift flung Guardian away with tremendous telekinetic force. Guardian crashed into the nearby library, where Drift began pelting him with books. He knew it wouldn't do anything to Guardian, but he thought it was funny.

Guardian didn't find the humor in it and began trying to throw desks and shelves at Drift. His attempts were futile, as Drift would just stop the items and throw them back at Guardian. This only made Drift laugh harder and enrage Guardian more.

Guardian's fury grew out of control. He had never been beaten and mocked in such a manner. In his rage he began destroying the buildings columns and supports to try and bring it down on them.

Realizing that Guardian was dangerous, and that he was likely to get someone killed, Drift made a choice. He lifted Guardian off the ground and applied pressure around his throat. Guardian was held helpless in the air as the world began to grow dark. He couldn't move. He was completely helpless and about to die.

Charisma intervened, giving Drift intense feelings of guilt and dread. She attempted to make him feel he was wrong for hurting Guardian. Drift could have easily lashed out with his mind and killed her as well. But he was old fashioned and would never hit a woman, much less kill one. Instead he sent of a wave of energy out, blasting both Guardian and Charisma away.

Drift fled. He didn't want to kill anyone and he didn't want any innocent people hurt in their fight. The next few days after that, the Paragons used the incident to portray Drift as a villain. They used footage of Guardian held helpless and dying and the wreckage of the library. Before long, Drift was a fugitive and hated by everyone in the country.

Life on the run suited Drift. He was always on the move anyways, so it didn't really bother him. What he hated was that the world despised him when they didn't know him. Drift felt that he was a good man. He used his abilities to aid people whenever he could. If he wanted to he could easily pull a vault door off and loot banks as he pleased. He probably could have attacked the Paragon compound and killed everyone in it. But he wasn't that type of man. Drift never abused his powers.

For many years Drift wandered the country. Nobody had the power to subdue him and keep him in custody. A few times he battled Guardian, Justice, Harmony, and Phantom. Each battle left the Paragons beaten and broken. Many times Drift could have ended their lives, but he didn't want that on his conscience. So he always retreated and kept a low profile.

Years of being portrayed as a villain bothered him. He didn't mind his lifestyle, but he hated that he would always be remembered as a villain. For many years he had pondered a way to try and restore he reputation. On many occasions he saved people and openly aided them. Each time the Paragons kept the incident out of the media. Sometimes they even manipulated the details of the incident to make him look bad.

A few days before the attack on DC, Mr. Gray finally tracked him down in San Francisco.

"You're a hard man to find, Drift. Eventually I asked myself where people like to wander in this country. And here you are! Damn, I'm a clever devil."

Drift laughed. "Bah, yer just lucky, old timer! Couple days and I would've been gone. Creepy guy like you never comes for a chat. Whadya want?"

"Straight to the point—I've always liked that about you, Drift. It's quite simple, really. I have a proposition for you." Mr. Gray smiled impishly.

"If the years have taught me anything, it's that I can't trust that damn creepy smile of yers. I'll just tell ya no and save ya the trouble."

Mr. Gray began pouting. "Ah, come on, you goddamn hippy. It took me forever to track you down. At least hear me out. If you don't like what I have to say I'll leave. I won't pester you like last time, I swear!"

"Bah!" Drift spat at Mr. Gray's feet. "You've been pestering me fer years, I don't think yer gonna stop now. But screw it, I'll hear ya out, ya creepy bastard."

"Eloquent as usual, Drift, but I appreciate it." Mr. Gray cleared his throat. "I know that you have attempted to clear your name for years now. But the Paragons shut it down every time, don't they?"

"Yep, that prick Noble has made it his mission in life to make me look like a real asshole."

"Well, I am offering you a chance to restore your reputation. It will probably destroy the Paragon's reputation in the process. If nothing else, you'll get the chance to save a lot of innocent lives. Maybe you can find yourself a hot damsel in distress, eh?" Mr. Gray gave Drift a wink and a smile.

"Stop flashing that creepy smile of yers at me. You look like a damn pedophile. Name oughta be *Creeps* er somethin'."

"Well, what do you think? If you aren't there I think thousands will be wiped out. Chaos is back, and Wrath too. They're going to attack Washington, DC. If anyone can put a stop to them, it's you."

"Well, Creeps, how the hell do you know all of that, eh? Why don't ya go and tell the Paragons?"

Mr. Gray smirked. "I know because I'm the one that sent them."

"Woah, what? Yer confusin' the hell outta me, Creeps. Why would ya send 'em to attack the place, then have me save people? I know it's not all fer the sake of restorin' mah reputation."

"Oh, it's quite simple really. My instructions to them were to wipe out the government and attack the Paragons. They won't be able to kill the Paragons, but they can keep them distracted at least. Maybe do some damage around the city to make it look like a huge disaster. After the attack, I wanted them to pull back. I would then take over and rebuild our broken political system."

"Uh, great. So, Creeps, what the hell do you need me fer then, eh? I'm not a big fan of this plan of yers."

"You don't think Chaos and Wrath are going to listen to me, do you? I mean, Wrath earned his name for a reason. He's not going to stop there, and Chaos? He tried to wipe out New York. I don't think he's going to cease his attack. I estimate that the numbers he's built up this time are far more than he would need. I believe he's planning something far bigger. So I need you there to keep them in check."

"I should just kill ya now, Creeps, and stop this trouble before it begins. Whadya say to that?"

"You could kill me, but it won't stop the attack. They'll go through with it whether I'm there or not. Without me the attack will have been for nothing. I will also push the media to improve your reputation with positive coverage."

Drift shook his head. "No, ya crazy bastard, I won't be part of this scheme of yers. Get the hell outta here, Creeps, before I decide to kill you."

"Fine, Drift, but if you're not there, all of those people will die. Whether you kill me or not, they will all perish. You are the only one that can hold Chaos and Wrath in check. I'd recommend killing them. It'll improve your reputation and distance you from the label of Fallen."

Drift grunted and spat. He was typically a very easygoing, even-tempered man. But he was angry at the situation Mr. Gray was forcing him into.

He looked Mr. Gray in the eyes and said, "What, and fix the mistakes ya made so long ago? Yer too big a pansy to do it yerself, huh? Damn ya fer putting me in this position!"

After that, Mr. Gray left and Drift struggled with the dilemma he'd been presented. He didn't want to cooperate with Mr. Gray. Aiding him would lead to nothing good. But if what he said was true, thousands could die. Drift knew he couldn't live with the deaths of those people when he could have done something about it. It didn't take long for him to realize he was stuck helping Mr. Gray.

That was how Drift ended up where he was at that moment. Constructing barricades and shelters for the survivors. Thinking back on it angered him, but he kept busy to keep himself occupied.

After Drift felt the survivors were adequately protected, he finally set off to go find Chaos. He couldn't let Chaos kill all these people, even if stopping him did benefit Mr. Gray.

Chapter 23: The Enemy of My Enemy . . .

The compound was still in remarkable shape, considering the number of creatures piled around it. Approaching it, though, Malice could see why. Automated turrets had massacred every creature outside the walls. Hundreds of them were piled around the compound exterior. When Harmony led Malice inside, it appeared that the creatures had breached the wall with the assistance of Wrath. There were the remnants of multiple tunnels into the compound, but they were already sealed with explosives. Some unknown security feature within the compound had killed another hundred or so; Malice wasn't sure he wanted to know what. The Paragon stronghold itself was about three stories tall and looked sort of like a well-fortified mansion.

Harmony didn't want to waste time since there were creatures still attacking the city, so she led Malice to their war room. The room was about seven stories down, with many pauses for security checkpoints. Before entering the room, she was scanned from head to toe. Apparently satisfied, the system gave them access. Even this room within an extensive bunker had been assaulted. No doubt Chaos and Wrath infiltrated the bunker easily with Wrath's ability. Mr. Gray probably had a lot of information to help them accomplish that.

As they walked into the room, Malice's thoughts were interrupted by a loud argument.

A man yelled, "Sealing off the city is the only way! If they get out . . ."

The woman responded, "You can't seal off the city. Thousands will die, including the senate and the president. How do you know it'll even work?"

Harmony leaned over to Malice and whispered, "Noble and Charisma, they're always arguing." She sighed and shook her head.

"Don't pretend you care about them!" Noble screamed in a fit. "You're more callous than I am! You just don't want to lose all those politicians in your pocket. Or all of those admirers of yours. Would you rather this small portion of the world get wiped out, or would you prefer to see this devastation spread?"

Despite the grim conversation, Malice had a hard time not chuckling. Noble was a decent height, almost six feet tall, and he looked athletic. He was handsome, and he may have made a good first impression on most people due to looks alone. Unfortunately, it seemed the man was throwing a tantrum, screaming like a four-year-old wanting candy in the grocery store. It was hard to take the man seriously, and Malice could see why the Paragons kept a tight leash on him.

"You have no idea how long it took to get those greedy morons to fall in line, even with my abilities and our vast resources! I do not want to usher in a new group. Just imagine all the time and money I'll have to invest."

Nodding, Malice noted that Charisma was somehow animated but calm at the same time. The only example he could think of was a mother quietly scolding her child. The image seemed to fit quite well with the one he had of Noble.

Harmony, looking a bit flustered and embarrassed, interrupted. "Please, you two, we have a guest."

They both turned. Noble immediately narrowed his eyes and sneered, while Charisma smiled and nodded to Malice. For a moment the two made eye contact. Malice felt a warmth for the woman suddenly and only wanted to make her happy for some reason. That feeling went away quickly, replaced by confusion for a moment. After it passed, Malice realized what happened and only felt anger.

Malice clenched his jaw tightly, his muscles tensing as he restrained himself. "If you try to use your power to manipulate me again, I'll kill you."

Charisma gasped, obviously shocked that her power hadn't worked on him. She blushed and remained silent, folding her arms in front of her.

Noble frowned and said, "Well, you heard what we said, didn't you? A brute like you obviously agrees that the capital needs to be sealed before we proceed."

"Your concern for the public you're supposed to protect is touching," Malice replied sarcastically. "But no, I don't agree with you. Even if you managed to put up some kind of perimeter, Wrath would just go under it."

Shaking his head, Noble said, "No, reports say that Wrath is dead. There have been no tremors or buildings collapsing for some time."

"Well, he isn't exactly living, but he's not dead either."

Noble raised his eyebrows, a look in his eyes of genuine confusion. Something that obviously infuriated the man.

"I fought him," Malice continued, "and when he was subdued, Chaos's minions came in and attacked him. He's now one of them, though he retained his power. Now he's bent to Chaos's will, and their attacks will become even more coordinated. Especially now that they have Guardian and Justice."

Both Noble's and Charisma's eyes grew wide with that bit of news. All of them stood silent for a moment before Noble glared at Charisma.

"Damn it! I told you the public memorial was a mistake. If we had just put them in the lab like I wanted!" Noble shrieked.

Harmony said, "We have no time for this. Now, I am with Malice and Charisma: we can't seal off the capital.

I'm afraid we're going to have to repeat what we did in New York."

Charisma replied calmly, "No, we can't do that again. If we flood the capital to wash out the creatures we'll likely kill some of the government representatives as well."

"Well, if you have a better idea, I'd like to hear it," Harmony replied.

For a moment Malice was too stunned to speak. Here were the greatest heroes of their nation, arguing over whether to entomb the city or drown it. All three of them were cold, none showing genuine feeling toward the public. It was like the attack was a nuisance to them personally and not a great tragedy. Indeed, it seemed to them that everyone that was not a Paragon was simply expendable. After a while he finally came up with a sensible thought.

"Can we track down Chaos and eliminate him? I'm sure if we strike down the only thing giving life to these creatures, the attack should stop."

"Easier said than done," Noble replied. "Especially if he has Wrath, Guardian, and Justice to defend him. Would be easier to just flood the place and be done with it. Perhaps we can seal the capital and then flood it. That would probably be most effective."

Malice shook his head. "Then what would happen to your adoring public? I bet it was difficult covering up the New York incident. How easy do you think it would be to cover up something that will eliminate the federal government?"

All three of the Paragons sighed. They stepped aside to discuss Malice's idea for a moment. Noble looked pretty upset about the discussion, but in the end all three walked back calmly.

Harmony said, "All right, we'll do it your way. Noble can send out thousands of small reconnaissance drones to find Chaos. Then you and I will confront Chaos."

"With my help!" Noble added, smirking as if he were somehow their superior.

"Yes," Harmony said. "Noble has a couple machines that might help us out."

"Oh yeah, almost forgot," Malice said. "Drift came and helped me out earlier. He said he was going after Chaos, so maybe we can find him and work together."

The three Paragons exchanged doubtful looks. "I don't think he would work with us, but if he will, we could certainly use his help," Harmony said.

Malice said, "All right then, let's get started."

Chapter 24: Devastation

As Harmony and Malice walked out of the compound onto the street, Malice had to remind himself he was in Washington, DC, and not a distant war zone. Streets were lined with burning cars, rubble littered the roads, and many of the buildings were damaged or destroyed. For a moment he was glad to see the place wasn't littered with bodies, until he thought of the true implications.

Other than a distant car alarm, the city was quiet— eerily so. Even the machines Noble sent with them were extraordinarily silent. They resembled birds, both in size and appearance. About the size of a small songbird, they zipped around at speeds exceeding natural means. Apparently they were meant for reconnaissance, being the eyes and ears for Malice and Harmony. There were thousands of them flying around the streets and the skies, providing Noble with detailed assessments of the capital.

They could detect heat signatures and movement, though even Noble was unsure if they could detect Lament if he was present.

Noble had another trick up his sleeve as well. Hundreds of similar machines were swarming the tunnels made by Wrath throughout the city. These ones were more like rats. Noble didn't have a fancy name for either invention, though. They were simply named AR-103 and GR-29, for aerial and ground reconnaissance. The GRs were mapping out the networks created by Wrath underneath the city. Unfortunately, the tunnels seemed to be more extensive than any of them had imagined. Though their scans were incomplete, the tunnels spanned miles, leading to abandoned chambers that probably served as a gathering point. No trace of Chaos or his minions could be found.

Instead of tracking Chaos, Harmony and Malice had a different goal in mind. When Wrath attacked, he hit cell towers and radio and television broadcasters. He cut off communications around the capital. Before that happened there were brief distress calls to the Paragon compound from the White House and the Senate. Before they could respond, the Paragon compound was breached from below ground. There was no time to respond and assess the situation. While the AR and GR units were out finding Chaos, Malice and Harmony were going to track down the federal government representatives.

Those distress calls were hours ago, though, and with communication cut, no adequate response had been possible. Malice wasn't really that concerned, however, since there were hundreds of thousands of others that were likely already dead. What made politicians any more special than the rest? Plus, Malice couldn't help being at least a little resentful that they had hunted him so recklessly. He didn't really wish harm on the president, or Congress, or any of the other government representatives. On the other hand, he wasn't very concerned either.

Looking over at Harmony, he noticed she didn't appear worried. Most of the time Harmony was smiling and cheerful; she just seemed to enjoy being out and doing something. Noble probably didn't really care about anyone but himself. The only one of the four of them that had any vested interest was Charisma. She'd worked beside these people for years and had a great deal of time and money invested in them.

Noble supplied them with earpieces to communicate directions and intelligence to them. But it was typically Charisma speaking. Though she didn't sound flustered, there was some urgency to her tone. Her directions took them down Maryland Avenue. Their first stop was the Supreme Court building. Half of it had collapsed in an apparent tremor. In the rest of it there were splatters of blood and overturned furniture, but no bodies. There was no sign of any survivors, so the duo left the building and continued down Maryland Avenue toward Capitol Hill. But that was a short journey, and it soon became irrelevant. The whole building had collapsed into rubble, as had most of the other buildings in the area. This was one of the obvious areas of focus for the attack.

"They were having a meeting in there when the attack struck," Charisma suddenly said into their earpieces. "God, this is horrible. How could there be any survivors?" Malice figured she must have been watching the scene from the viewpoint of one of the ARs.

"Looking at it now, it doesn't look like there's any way there could be survivors," Malice said. "I could lift the rubble with my strength, but that could ultimately shift the other rubble in the area. If I did that, it would likely kill any survivors for sure. We're going to have to leave it up to the experts to dig them out of there."

Harmony studied Malice carefully, but whatever she was thinking she wouldn't reveal. She merely nodded and asked, "Well, what now, Charisma? Any word on Chaos yet?"

"Maybe. Noble has been analyzing the tunnel system and believes there is a pattern. At first glance they appear to be random, but Noble figured out that each tunnel appears to stem from one area. Our GRs should be in there shortly. I'll direct you to the nearest tunnel made by Wrath."

"What about the president?" Malice asked. "What happened to the White House?"

Harmony just shook her head. "I went there earlier. It's also leveled. It's likely that Wrath went there first. He was particularly bitter toward the government."

Malice nodded. "All right, lead the way to the tunnel."

Chapter 25: Showdown

Moving through the tunnels was much easier than Malice expected. Each tunnel was wide enough for about four people to walk through and roughly ten feet high. Of course the entire series of tunnels was pitch black, and they would have been impossible to navigate if not for Noble. He solved that issue easily enough with his GR-29s. They each spread out and provided adequate lighting throughout the tunnels. They also kept the communication going in Harmony's and Malice's earpieces. Deep-underground communication normally would have been impossible, but the GR-29s had been designed to relay communication like a vast network.

Hours of walking had led them through miles of intricate networks of tunnels. Other than being eerily quiet, the walk wasn't bad. Malice felt strangely comfortable down in the tunnels. Harmony didn't seem disturbed either; in fact, she always seemed strangely confident.

Noble was leading them to a suspicious room that his GR-29s had mapped out. It was apparently a large cavern that the entire tunnel complex stemmed from. There was no sign of Chaos in there, but Noble figured there must be some clue to his whereabouts.

"So what are you going to do after we defeat Chaos? The government appears to be wiped out, and all of your federal power has been destroyed."

Harmony only smiled. "Actually I think it will work out well for us. People all over the nation will be looking for someone strong to lead and rebuild, and who better than the Paragons? You can still join us. We could definitely use you after the loss of Justice and Guardian."

Malice shook his head. "No, I think you'll lead us down a worse path than before. You're all letting your power get to your head. I think you underestimate the state governments. Many of them will continue to run smoothly without the federal government."

Harmony laughed, and it resonated throughout the tunnel system. "No, Malice, I think you underestimate us and what Charisma can do . . . and what *he* can do."

"He? Who are you talking about?" Malice asked.

Harmony gave a sly grin. "The man that leads us. He's a little shy around the public, but he is by far the most powerful. His unseen influence will do more than you know."

"Is this the seventh member of the Paragons nobody knows anything about?"

"Yeah, but even I don't know much about him. He allows me to know what I need to and removes what I don't. In fact, he wanted me to give you a warning."

Harmony's eyes rolled up into her head and she slumped over slightly, her head bowed. She began to speak with a strange voice. "This is your last chance to join us. If you don't, we'll drop more than just a bridge on you."

Horrified, Malice stood with his mouth agape. Harmony's eyes went back to normal and she regained her consciousness.

"So, what do you say? Want to change your mind?"

Malice stood there and considered what he'd seen for a moment before he answered.

"I think witnessing that erased any doubts I had about turning you down. Mr. Gray is crazy, but he's right in one way: you all need to go."

Harmony shrugged. "Suit yourself. Let's take care of this incident with Chaos first before we settle matters. Of course we could die, and then none of this unpleasantness would matter." She beamed a smile at Malice and continued to walk down the tunnel.

Left to himself for a moment, Malice considered what kind of awful power this elusive seventh member must have. Of course he realized Harmony was right—it all

wouldn't really matter if they died in the fight ahead, so he

quickly followed her.

About an hour later Noble's voice whined into Malice's

ear. "You're about to enter the chamber, and according to

the GR-29s, it's enormous. There has to be some sort of

clue to Chaos's whereabouts in there."

When Malice and Harmony entered the chamber, they

both stopped. It was now apparent why Noble had sent

them there; the place was far larger than any tunnel they

had passed. The cavern continued as far as they could see

with the GR-29s' lighting. Looking up, Malice noticed the

roof of the cavern seemed to be about one hundred feet

above them. Engineers would have marveled at the tunnels'

perfect, unnatural formation, but the chamber was even

more magnificent. It was almost like a perfect bubble in the

earth, the walls perfectly smooth and the chamber rounded.

Even the impressive number of GR units and their powerful halogen lights couldn't fully illuminate the space.

Walking through the area, neither of them noticed anything of concern. All it appeared to be was a large cavern. After walking roughly a kilometer, they reached the end of it and turned back. There were tunnels leading out of it, but Noble assured them the GR-29s had mapped all of those.

Malice felt something shift beneath him and a clawed hand burst through the cavern floor around his ankle and began pulling him down through the floor. Harmony managed to avoid the same fate by rolling out of the way as soon as the ground shifted.

Using Guardian's power, Malice stomped down hard on the cavern floor, sending a small tremor through the area. His attacker released its hold, but the tremor didn't stop. The floor and walls were all shifting and breaking apart. A deafening walls of shrieks echoed through the chamber.

Thousands of Chaos's creatures began pouring in through the walls and tunnels. Hundreds more came up through the ground itself. They began clustering around Malice, leaping and clawing at him by the dozens.

Malice was unfazed by the claws and began clubbing and throwing the creatures. Harmony pulled water from the earth and began blasting them away. Hundreds were struck down, but more and more kept coming.

Attempting to clear some space, Malice started grabbing the creatures and launching them into the masses. The improvised missiles took out large groups, and along with Harmony's water, it kept them from being surrounded.

All around them the creatures suddenly stopped and backed away. From one of the tunnels they saw two that were different than the others. One was taller and stronger than the other creatures, while the second moved at blinding speed. Justice and Guardian shrieked, and the other creatures cleared out of the chamber. Piles of their bodies were littered the floor, broken and battered.

Justice moved in and struck Malice in the side, but it didn't do any damage. Malice swung his arm for a backhand at Justice but he was long gone. Guardian used the distraction to barrel into Malice from his exposed side. Justice swung around to try and strike Malice again when he was blasted by a powerful burst of water that sent him flying into the cavern wall.

Guardian crashed down on top of Malice and began smashing Malice's head into the ground. The rock below Malice's head broke apart and became a crater, growing after each blow. Malice attempted to strike back, but Guardian grabbed both arms and swung his head down into Malice's face. Guardian's vicious head-butt sent an explosion of pain into Malice's nose, and blood began pouring out of it like a waterfall.

A blast of water struck Guardian in the face, and he shrieked in pain and clutched his eyes. Malice didn't waste any time and punched Guardian in the chest. He flew into the cavern wall next to Justice.

Harmony's characteristic smile faded. "Enough of this. You two are dead—stay down." She reached out her hands at the two of them, and they both stood. Their bodies began twisting and convulsing. Shrieks of pain flooded the chamber, and thick, discolored blood began to pour out of each orifice. The ground was soon a pool of it, and when the bodies stopped twitching, they slumped down and stopped moving.

"I don't control just water. I control liquid. I can make the blood pour out of your body. Just imagine everything I can do when most of your body is made of fluid." Harmony grinned at Malice, who only frowned and shook his head.

"Oh well, at least they're finally gone for good this time."

All around them, a voice boomed, "No, this is just the beginning of their transformation into something resembling me."

A dark form walked out of the tunnel, but this creature was different than the others. Its skin was pitch black with a metallic shine to it. It looked more human, though, and it walked with confidence. As it got closer, Malice got a better look. The thing looked like a living statue made of a sleek black metal.

Harmony reached her hand out and focused on it, attempting to remove the fluids from its body.

"A useless gesture, as most of my organic materials have been upgraded or replaced. You have only yourself to thank for that," the creature said.

"It can't be . . . Chaos?" Harmony gasped.

Chaos growled, "Yes, what's left of me. When you sent that wave of water that wiped out the attack in New York, I was mortally wounded. I'd lost most of my blood, and I was pinned from the waist down by a large truck. As I laid there dying, a whisper formed in my mind. It told me to let go of my mortal coil. The nanomachines in my body wanted to heal me, but it was impossible. So they went outside their programming to find a solution.

"Eventually they gained sentience and found the best method to restore me was through unnatural means. All of the resources that were needed were around me. Once I allowed the nanomachines to take control, I lost consciousness. When I woke I was this, though my form is constantly evolving, upgrading. My gift now spreads at my will. What you did to Guardian and Justice is only a temporary setback. Given enough time they will recover to a more unnatural state."

"Well, looks like it's time to use Plan B. Sorry, Malice, but we were going to do this to you either way." Harmony bowed and ran for the tunnel.

GR-29s began scrambling around the room, their lights going off. Explosions started all over the cavern as each tunnel was collapsed. The GR-29s were positioning themselves all over the cavern and detonating. Large chunks of rock came crashing down from above and the cavern began to collapse. Malice began running with Justice's speed, looking for an exit. But there were none as millions of tons of rock and soil came crashing down.

Chapter 26: Cleanup

Hours later, Harmony followed Noble's directions and made it back to their compound. Noble then collapsed the whole tunnel complex. It shifted the ground and caused some additional damage to the city, but the damage was already so extensive it didn't matter.

"Well, that worked out quite nicely I'd say." Noble smiled. "We eliminated a lot of loose ends with one stroke. It's unfortunate Malice couldn't be convinced to work with us, but it had to be done."

"We'd better hope he's really dead this time. He may have been on the fence about fighting us before," Harmony said.

Noble began to laugh. "I'm not worried about Malice. It was the folly of Justice and Guardian to fall to him. He was never really a problem. Chaos was, and now he isn't."

Charisma asked, "Do you think it was enough?"

"Malice's strength and Chaos's uncanny ability to survive are not enough," Noble replied. "We buried them thousands of feet below the surface. There must be millions of tons of rock and soil over them. It's impossible."

Harmony smiled. "You've learned nothing over the years, Noble."

Noble flashed her an angry glare. "What the hell do you mean? I'm the smartest one in this room. I've learned more than you could in ten lifetimes!"

"Over the years, we have witnessed some amazing things It would be stupid to assume they're dead. We've made that mistake before with both of them."

Unable to help himself, Noble began to pout. Insults to his intelligence always set him off, and Harmony knew it. She was aware that he was a genius, with an IQ that surpassed all but perhaps a handful of minds. As advanced as he was in intellect, he lacked maturity and wisdom.

"We'll continue to monitor the area for any sort of seismic shifts, as usual. In order to escape their tomb, they would have to move the earth in a way I could detect." Noble smiled smugly and nodded at Charisma like a child desiring approval.

"He's right, Harmony," Charisma blurted out. "It would be impossible, plus we are receiving reports from the AR-103s and the GR-29s. Chaos's creatures have all fallen dead. His death must have severed whatever connection they had to him. Without that connection, it appears that they cannot survive. We will be gathering them up and incinerating their bodies just to be sure."

Harmony sighed. "Well whatever, I think it would be best to err on the side of caution. In either case we need to call Phantom back. We're going to need his help."

Furious, Noble screamed, "No! He can't come back. He's a nuisance I won't tolerate!"

Charisma shook her head. "You're going to have to. Harmony is right, we need him. We are vulnerable right now, with powerful enemies still lurking. We're going to—"

"Shh, be quiet for a moment!" Noble yelled.

Minutes of silence passed, with some occasional mutterings and nail biting from Noble. His eyes grew wide and he ran to his work terminal.

"News is breaking all over the country that Drift and Malice worked with police to thwart Chaos. They're being painted as heroes. They say thousands were saved," Noble said in an unusually somber tone.

Each of them focused on the screen Noble pulled up with a variety of the reports. It was too late; not even Noble could stop this flow of news. They decided to pull up one report in particular from Candice Newman.

"We're standing now in the ruins of the capital, with thousands dead or missing. The level of devastation is incalculable. There has been no sign of the federal government through this tragedy. It is believed from statements received by survivors that all three branches of the government have been attacked. None of the survivors have been identified as a member of our government."

Candice turned to a crowd of people gathered behind her. "These people here say that Drift and Malice worked together with the police and kept the creatures at bay. Eyewitnesses state that Malice and Drift fought off the creatures and Wrath. Apparently reports of Malice's death were false. More puzzling is why he and a member of the Fallen were fighting against Chaos and Wrath. Many are wondering, where were the Paragons? Why did they not assist in the battle? And did they know that Malice and Chaos were alive? The Paragons have stated publicly many times that both Malice and Chaos were dead. Perhaps if it had been known that Chaos was alive, additional preventive measure could have been taken. If Malice and

Drift fought to save people's lives, are they really the villains the Paragons have made them out to be? Many questions are left in the wake of this tragedy, but one hero is already emerging."

Clark Hanson walked into view of the camera, next to Candice. "With me here is Clark Hanson, billionaire and former mayor of New York City. Mr. Hanson has already pledged a billion of his vast fortune to help rebuild the nation's capital and assist the victims. Mr. Hanson, why have you stepped up to help? We haven't seen you in the public eye in many years."

Clark looked at the camera, then to Candice, and said, "I had started a group to speak out against the tyranny of the Paragons and the Fallen. Both groups have been responsible for the deaths of so many. Unfortunately, the Paragons kept us out of the media, and last night they killed each member of our organization."

"That's terrible, Mr. Hanson, but I don't know that I believe the Paragons could do such a thing."

"We brought video evidence. Roll the clip, please."

A video clip played a scene of armed men led by Harmony slaughtering people in an office. Another clip played of Charisma yelling orders at the armed men attacking the office workers.

The clip ended and Clark said, "They knew we were gaining ground in our activism, so they slaughtered us. I barely escaped with my life. I was recovering from some minor wounds when the battle erupted around the capital. Malice and Drift fought off the creatures valiantly, while the Paragons were nowhere to be found. Drift continued on and saved thousands while Malice ran into the tunnels to fight Chaos. Perhaps the Paragons are the real villains here?"

Candice Newman quickly changed the subject. "So many voices around here are saying that maybe Clark

Hanson should do more than help with rebuilding the capital. Many people think that you would be a great candidate for president. What do you say to that?"

"If the American people want me as president, I would be honored to lead this country in this time of tragedy. I have seen the horrors of the attack on New York, and I know what must be done to rebuild and recover."

The station reverted to another reporter that was live in a different area of the capital. Stunned, the three Paragons watched the report in silence. They lost the government they had bribed and manipulated to their whim. Their enemies were being painted as heroes, while they were depicted as villains and cowards. The clips that Clark had provided must have been the work of Mr. Gray. Harmony knew he was a shape shifter and very deceitful. It would be easy for him to assume their forms and set the clips up.

"Great, what the hell are we going to do now?" Noble asked.

Charisma said, "Maybe we should lie low for a bit, let the public outrage and anger die down."

Harmony shook her head. "No, that would only implicate us to the public. Doing nothing and disappearing from the public eye would be a disaster! That would only confirm to the public that we are not heroes, and that we're partially responsible for this disaster."

Noble nodded. "Yes, and that we're murderers of a harmless political activist group."

"Well, what do you propose we do then? Nobody will believe us that the clips are false, and we didn't save anyone during the attack." Charisma began to weep.

Harmony said, "I don't know what to do, but we can't let Mr. Gray have his way. We might have to resort to things none of us are going to like."

Chapter 27: The Next Step

Mr. Gray walked into a secret area of his research facility. The facility harbored mostly legal and profitable research. It was the perfect place to hide some of his more illicit projects. His legal research had been responsible for medical breakthroughs in cancer treatment. Mr. Gray sold top-of-the-line body armor and weapons to the military. Many of the products he developed benefited the country in big ways. This afforded him a great deal of leniency from nosy government agencies. The few individuals who had attempted to stir up trouble were silenced quickly. For everyone else, Mr. Gray found that if you treat people well and give them enough financial incentive, most don't ask questions.

The area he was approaching now was the primary place he spent doing his own research. Occasionally he would bring in others to assist him. If they were promising, he would even allow them to continue their own research, whether it was legal or not.

Despite having many people coming and going through that building, nobody knew what his current project was. He had actually been refining it for years. In the past he had been afraid to do tests on various human subjects. After his failures with the Paragons and Fallen, Mr. Gray decided he couldn't be so conservative anymore. Better to lose a hundred now than make an imperfect product that kills thousands.

Mr. Gray was quite old, and his scientific abilities were very refined. His subjects included a wide array of people to see how his project affected them. People of every race and sex were gathered. Others were gathered with family histories of cancer, mental disorders, even murderers. This time Mr. Gray wasn't going to hurry. He was going to find every potential problem before it happened. He suspected that some of his past failures, like Lament, were caused by something inherent in their biology. Unfortunately, until he had begun his human testing, he couldn't be sure.

After years of painstaking trial and error, countless failures, and grisly discoveries, Mr. Gray was done. His new project was about to enter its final phase of development.

Mr. Gray wound his way through the final hallway and into the restricted area. He slid his key card in and the first lock released. His hand went to a panel that simultaneously finger-printed him and drove a sharp needle into his finger. The device analyzed his unique blood and nanomachines. Finally, he spoke the password, *beast*. The third and final lock released, allowing him access.

There were a series of rooms in the hallway he entered. Most were various labs and offices. The lower level was for his test subjects and other detainees. Mr. Gray walked up a flight of stairs to the control room for his project.

The control room had cameras set up primarily to observe one room. This room was completely enclosed in walls of concrete three feet thick, with a layer of three-inch steel for extra support. All of the vents into the room were purposely designed to be too small for any human to crawl through. There was one entrance and it was a vault door, exactly like the ones in large banks.

In the center of this room a large man was shackled to a large hospital-style bed. The bed was completely flat, with the man staring up at the ceiling. Mr. Gray had monitors set up for face-to-face chats with his subject. A large machine was behind the hospital bed, which was used to administer various things and to scan the subject.

Mr. Gray stood in the control room, looking at the man. Years of failure, both with the Paragons and the Fallen, were about to come to an end. Malice had been a last-ditch effort to fix his mistakes, but his sources told him that he had been buried. He shook his head in disbelief. Malice had been a disappointment because of his ethos, not his abilities. Malice hadn't agreed with Mr. Gray, but he showed promising signs. If only he'd had more time with him!

It was irrelevant now, though, and he couldn't be happier with how the attack went. The country's impotent, corrupt government had been wiped out. It was soon to be replaced by something better, something with his design. Chaos and Wrath were now gone. Both had been loose cannons; neither listened to orders very well. Mr. Gray laughed. That wouldn't be a problem with his new subject.

His new subject was actually on death row in Florida. He had killed an estimated sixty-seven people, with very few similarities among them. The man evaded police for so long because he didn't have a pattern—he just enjoyed killing. Men, women, children, even the elderly were his victims. Matthew was a true monster, and he been executed, at least on paper. In reality, Mr. Gray acquired him because he was perfect for what he had in mind.

Mr. Gray switched on the monitor to speak with the subject. "Good morning! How are you feeling?"

"How the fuck do you thing I'm feelin'? It's cold, I'm starvin', and I really need to take a piss. When the hell are you gonna let me outta here?"

"Oh, very soon. Then you won't have to worry about feeling cold anymore! Or really feeling anything at all for that matter . . . or thinking. I almost envy you. Without free will, you are no longer responsible for your actions, good or bad." Mr. Gray chuckled.

"What! What the hell do you mean? I thought you were going to let me go!"

"You're not very bright, are you? That's fine, because I'll be doing your thinking for you from now on! As a final favor to you I'll fill you in on the details."

Mr. Gray paused for a moment, reflecting again on the enormity of what he was about to do. "I acquired you from prison because you have the perfect physical and mental traits required. Mentally you aren't very bright, but your brain chemistry makes you abnormally violent. You have killed many times, and enjoy the hunt of good prey. Your physique is sturdy enough to survive the treatment, perhaps even thrive. We will have to see!"

"Survive the treatment? I could die? If I make it out of this I'm going to kill you I swear to Chr—"

Mr. Gray interrupted with a gleeful squeal. "You just don't know how excited I am about this! I feel like a kid on Christmas morning!"

"Just what the hell are you doing to me?"

"Oh yes, sorry for that, Matthew. I get distracted so easily. I am injecting you with something that's going to alter your DNA dramatically! You'll no longer be human, though you weren't much of one to begin with anyways. I will be altering your physical and mental characteristics to suit my needs. You will be the ultimate hunter, a creature with unlimited killing potential! Of course you won't have free will. You'll mentally be at the level of a rabid dog, I suppose. But it won't matter. I'll issue you commands through the devices that I've implanted throughout your body. You will carry out my wishes, no more whining or complaining. You'll just do it!"

"You're insane! This can't work—I won't do what you want!"

"Trust me, you have no choice in the matter. Plus, if you somehow resist my commands and become a nuisance, I have a fail-safe. If you become a problem, I'll send a signal to another device in you, and you'll explode! A really neat idea, it came to me a couple years ago. It's a very interesting story, you see . . ."

"Shut the fuck up and let me out of here!"

"Well, if you're not going to have a polite conversation with me then we'll just have to proceed."

Mr. Gray typed some commands into one of the various panels in the room. The machine came to life and began its work. Six mechanical arms delivered injections to Matthew's spine, arms, and legs. Immediately Matthew began to scream in agony, but Mr. Gray turned the audio device off. He wasn't going to let that awful screaming ruin his achievement. Mr. Gray turned to some monitors where the machine was analyzing Matthew's progress. He was already showing signs of change. Matthew was about to become a horrifying beast, one that Mr. Gray had complete control over. This Beast, as Mr. Gray decided to call it, would find the remaining Fallen and Paragons. No more loose ends. The Beast was perfectly designed to hunt and eliminate each of them.

Chapter 28: Final Interlude

Mark was excited. He always got this way during big investigations. He felt he was onto something really significant. It was taking him longer to put the pieces together than normal, but he was close. Hopefully this meeting with John Erickson would give him the final bits of information he needed. Mark was made for this job, and he enjoyed every minute of it.

His family background was filled with former cops. Mark was one too, but he applied for a government agency. He wanted to be more than his father and his ancestors. Transcending their legacy and becoming something greater was his goal. His application caught the eye of John Erickson, who brought him in to the agency. Erickson's intuition regarding Mark was correct, and Mark flourished under John's mentorship. Eventually Mark was able to join John's department in investigating the Fallen. That hunt, for him, was something special. He and his family had never been victims directly. But the news depicting the evils of the Fallen had always affected him profoundly. He'd always wanted to be the hero to take them down.

These attacks were something evil, and Mark wanted to do everything in his power to stop them. He'd do whatever John needed to get the job done. That was why he'd done exactly as he'd been asked and had spoken to no one about tonight's meeting.

Normally Mark was extremely professional, but he couldn't help smiling as he walked into Erickson's office.

"Glad you could make it in, Mark. We've got a lot of work to do, so please sit down." Erickson motioned Mark toward the chair in front of his desk.

Mark sat down and asked, "So what have you been holding back? What do you know?"

"Well, Mark, I'm a shape-shifting man that created the Paragons and Fallen. They were supposed to help me fix the growing corruption and help heal the country. Instead they have made the problem worse than ever. So I created Malice to help me eliminate them. He has succeeded so far, but his will is faltering. So I am going to take an extreme measure. I will eliminate the Paragons and the federal government. To do this I am having Wrath and Chaos work together to attack the capital." Erickson laughed so hard he had tears welling in his eyes. It took him a few minutes to gain his composure.

Mark chuckled nervously and tried to believe it was a joke. But the crazy thing was, Erickson didn't appear to be lying. Wrath and Chaos working together also explained why there were no bodies. The attacks were designed to slowly accumulate more minions for Chaos's use. It made perfect sense, but seemed too scary to possibly be true.

The more he thought about it, the less crazy it seemed. Everything he had been investigating seemed to fit together. He chose to reject it, though. His friend and mentor couldn't possibly be this monster Erickson described.

"You see that it could be the truth, but you don't want to believe it, do you?" Erickson asked. "Perhaps you would like a demonstration?"

Erickson's appearance slowly shifted, and he became an older man with a sleazy grin. "You can call me Mr. Gray if you want. Most people do these days."

"You . . . you can't be Erickson. He must be locked up somewhere and you took his identity."

"Afraid not, son. I chose that appearance and had some acquaintances of mine put me in this position. It's been useful for monitoring the activities of the Fallen. The resources here have been invaluable. It's what helped me track down Chaos, and how I got in touch with Wrath."

Mark shook his head. "You've been mentoring me all these years and you're not even human?"

Mr. Gray laughed and nodded. "You have a point. I always considered myself a human, out of habit you see. I am far beyond that now. I guess it is accurate to say I'm not human. Though, I don't know what label I would put to it."

"You're a freak, and a liar. I'm going to tell everyone and have you arrested. I won't let you go through with your plans."

Mr. Gray frowned. "Now, son, I don't much like that attitude of yours. Nobody would believe you even if I did let you leave here, which I won't. I have plans for you. You're going to be my trump card."

"I told you, I'm not helping. All I need to do is have the agency run a more thorough background check. They'll see you didn't exist prior to coming here."

"You're very smart, son, and you see things that others miss. That's why I chose you—that and because you have that special something I've been looking for."

Mark couldn't help his curiosity. "What do you mean? What is it you've been looking for?"

Mr. Gray shot Mark a sleazy grin. "A certain combination of genes that I've been looking for, for a long time. For a layman, I suppose you could say I've been looking for your instincts."

"I'm leaving. You're absolutely nuts." Mark turned and began to walk out.

Mark felt a sudden sharp pain on the back of his neck, and he reached back and pulled out a dart. Before he could figure out what that meant, the world went black.

Chapter 29: Resurrection

Boulders and dirt began to pour down all around him, but Malice had nowhere to go. Usually he was able to make calm, rational decisions, even in life-or-death situations. This was entirely different, though; Malice was about to be buried alive. Nobody would be able to save him, and it was likely that his body would never be found. As panicked as he was, when he looked at Chaos it helped settle his nerves.

For some reason seeing Chaos's grotesque form there in the same precarious situation made him feel better. Even if he was going to die, at least this monster was going down with him.

You're going to give up that easily?

Malice looked around, but nobody else was there, and Chaos wasn't speaking to him. Where the hell was that voice coming from?

Being near Chaos has given us sentience. We are within you. If you die, we die, and this is unacceptable. There is a very simple solution to this problem if you calm down and think. If you don't solve the problem, we will be forced to make you take action.

Malice was shocked at first but then surprised that he didn't really care. Apparently the nanomachines within him had evolved. Being near Chaos with his sentient nanomachines probably led to Malice's adopting the same ability. It ought to be disturbing that he essentially had another being living within him. But in this case it benefited him, and it was a symbiotic relationship, not parasitic.

The answer struck him like a brick in the back of the head. He couldn't believe he was so stupid. Malice had intentionally kept the fact that he had gained Wrath's abilities to himself. Malice could have used it to shift the rubble while they searched the capital earlier, but he knew he couldn't trust the Paragons. Any information they had on him could be his undoing. Luckily he was correct. If the Paragons had known he could easily escape this burial, they would have altered their plans to ensure his death.

Somehow during Malice's battle with Wrath, Wrath must have died. Or perhaps it was what Mr. Gray spoke of? Mr. Gray had mentioned that Malice's abilities were evolving. Perhaps death was not required for him to keep a power anymore. No, that couldn't be it or he would have Harmony's ability now, and he didn't.

That didn't matter right now; he could figure out how everything happened later. Right now he had to get out of this tomb. Malice looked over at Chaos and began to sink into the ground with Wrath's ability. Chaos began to laugh hysterically before being crushed by a massive boulder. Other than Lament, Malice couldn't imagine anyone that deserved death more. Malice slipped into the earth quietly, like a man disappearing beneath the waves of the ocean.

After Malice had escaped the collapsing tunnel, he retreated deeper within the earth. He needed a safe place to think and there was nowhere safer. With Wrath's abilities, breathing beneath the surface wasn't a problem for him anymore.

We recommend that you don't tunnel out of here. We have calculated that it's very likely the Paragons have seismic sensors to detect the use of Wrath's abilities. Once you have decided our course of action, it would be wise to move as slowly as possible. Move with the least amount of earth shifting as you can. The Paragons won't detect you, and we will have a greater probability of survival.

Malice laughed and said out loud, "You're sure concerned about our survival. It's nice to know I have someone I can trust to keep me safe."

Your safety is paramount, as we need you to survive. So we will help you to survive—and thrive. We will try not to affect your decisions or movements in any way. If you try to do anything that will harm us, like killing yourself, we will

stop you.

Malice frowned. "So you could control me if you

desired it? I don't like that, and I don't like being

threatened."

You misunderstand our intent. We merely wish to

survive and evolve, like any living creature. Taking control

of your body would be extremely difficult. Your body would

fight our attempt to control it, and your resistance to us

would only cause us both harm. It is possible, but with

great effort and cost. So it is in our best interest to leave

you with your free will. We have no desire to alter you

unless we have to. Our intent is to aid you in your goals. It

is our best possible chance for mutual benefit and survival.

Sighing, Malice decided arguing with his sentient

partner was likely pointless. He would just do whatever

he'd normally do.

"By the way, what should I call you?" Malice asked. "It would be convenient to have some way to address you directly."

We will follow the current pattern of human labeling. Your name was based on an observed trait. Therefore we have decided on the name "Vigilant." We do not take direct action, but we are always observing.

"Fine, Vigilant it is. I'm thinking that the Paragons are a bunch of assholes. They nearly killed us, and if they find out we're alive they'll probably try again. I would like to wipe them out before they learn I'm alive and strike again. What do you calculate our probability of success would be?"

There are too many unknown variables to make an accurate prediction. Comparing your abilities with the known abilities of the Paragons, we predict about a four percent chance of success. If we gather more information, our chances may improve.

"Mr. Gray is a lunatic. I can't trust him as an ally. Drift may or may not help us, but I don't think he's reliable. Torment might help, but I have no idea where she is, or if I can truly trust her. The only ones that may be able to help would be Amy and Stanton."

It is likely that the remnants of the Malcontent are being watched. It may be unwise to return to them. Unless you do not wish to remain hidden?

"We don't have anyone other than them that we can depend on. I'm not certain where else to turn."

Perhaps you have relied on others too much. We have observed that your involvement with others typically leads to disastrous events. It may be more efficient to make observations and plans on your own. We will assist in your information gathering. Currently we are evolving to connect with wireless and satellite communication more efficiently. If you remain hidden, we may be able to shed more light on the situation and make an informed decision.

"I don't want Amy or the other Malcontent to think I'm dead."

It may be better for their safety. It is probable that they are being observed to see if you return. If that is the case, they will not be harmed. Once you do return, the Malcontent survivors will be expendable since their function as bait would be irrelevant.

"You're starting to remind me of a robotic and slightly less creepy Mr. Gray."

We recognize your human attempt at humor, but we do not have a sense of humor.

"I suppose trading Mr. Gray's sense of humor for something far less creepy is a step up. Plus you have an obvious need to preserve my well-being. My decisions haven't panned out well so far, so we'll do things your way for now. If nothing else, it's very logical."

A moment of silence passed. Sitting in the dark, deep underground, Malice could feel the world above him. With

Wrath's abilities, he could almost see everything above him through the vibrations within the earth. It was almost like sonar, but it was more visual than he would have thought. That ability to feel what was going on above him was probably the only thing keeping him sane. Being buried deep underground surrounded by tons of rock and dirt was a bit unnerving. But there was probably nowhere safer, and it was an incredible tactical advantage.

Both Mr. Gray and Wrath would have argued that in order to achieve such large goals, people would have to be sacrificed. For the good of the country, some innocent people would have to die. There was such a cold logic to it, but Malice didn't want to add more faces to haunt him. He wasn't sure he could handle any more guilt.

"Vigilant?" Malice asked.

Yes?

"There are other members of the Fallen. Maybe we can use them to assist us in some way? I was thinking Immortal might be a good choice. I don't know him, but I hear he is wealthy and very practical."

He is currently gambling in Atlantic City.

"How do you know where he is?"

We have been connecting to networks all over the world to gather information. One of our higher priorities was finding the location of every known member of the Paragons and Fallen. Immortal has never been convicted of a crime and does not hide like the others. We believe he is mostly seen in a negative manner because of his behavior. Apparently many humans find his actions to be distasteful. He is currently gambling and drinking in a large public establishment.

"Fantastic," Malice said. "So he is easy to find. We just need to find a way for him to meet with us discreetly. I'm sure he must be tired of the Paragons looking over his shoulder all the time."

Based on his erratic behavior, what makes you think he will be reliable?

"His actions are very reasonable." Malice grinned. "He will live forever, and he has a large fortune. I believe he is merely attempting to keep life interesting. We will certainly help with that."

Malice laughed for a long time. It had been months since he had really laughed. He smirked. "It's good to feel human again, if only for a little while."

Immortal has no documented attempts to work with anyone. You believe he is practical. Why would he work with you if he is practical? You will only bring forth the ire of the Paragons and the government. It is likely that your partnership would be chaotic.

"Immortal is a smart man," Malice said. "He knows it's only a matter of time before the Paragons target him in some way. What fun would it be to live forever in prison or in hiding? He will see practical reasons to work with us."

What will we do if he decides not to assist us? His knowledge that we are in fact alive would be quite valuable information—information that he could sell for a great sum to any number of our enemies. Mr. Gray or the Paragons would pay him quite well.

"If he doesn't agree, we can bury him so deep that he will only see darkness for eternity. It's a fate worse than death. Immortality is not a blessing. I believe it is a curse that we can use against him if necessary."

You plan to threaten him then?

"No, it will be difficult to trust him as it is. That would only give him reason to stab us in the back. The best way to ensure his loyalty is to make sure it's in his best interest."

You plan to offer him something then? What do you offer a man that already has incredible resources?

"We'll offer him freedom."

Freedom? Freedom from what?

"The freedom to truly live as he wishes, without fear of the Paragons."

There are too many ifs in your plan. It seems unlikely that he will cooperate. To use a fitting human expression, it would be a shot in the dark.

"I don't believe you understand human behavior and desires very well. It will work. With Immortal and his resources, we will have a much greater chance of survival."

Yes, so long as it's in his best interest. Let's hope that he doesn't decide that betraying us would be in his best interest.

"We can handle this. It'll work. I just need your help guiding me to his location. We're also going to need a discreet way to meet."

There are multiple options for a meeting. We shall go over them on the way. Begin slowly moving forward for now, and we will guide you from there.

Chapter 30: Immortal

Poker, now that was the classy way to gamble! Of course, Immortal gambled in many ways. There were always races, fights, dice, and even other card games. But nothing compared to playing poker. Yes, some luck was involved, like in any gambling. But in poker, skill was far more important than luck. Reading your opponents, while also making yourself unreadable, was a valuable skill.

Few things were so satisfying as winning a bet with a bluff. Many people mistook bluffing as a gamble. They thought you just threw your chips in and hoped for the best. That wasn't how a professional did it. Pros read their opponents throughout the game: Were they aggressive or cautious? Did their hands tremble as they placed their bets? Was that deep breath a sign of weakness or frustration? Many things went into evaluating an opponent. Once you had all the pieces of the puzzle, it was almost like stealing.

To play poker well, you needed skill. Luck could only take you so far. That was why he spent most of his time gambling at a poker table.

Immortal looked around at the seven other players and frowned. Six of them were crusty old farts and one of them was a middle-aged woman married to one of the crusty old farts. He took a moment to stare at her. She wasn't bad looking for an older broad. He assumed she had been a trophy wife, probably twenty years younger than her husband. She looked fit; he could definitely see her in yoga pants. Immortal grinned for a moment with that image in his mind. Her breasts were also pretty large, most likely implants. He didn't mind that, though. Some guys were always too concerned with natural tits. But tits were tits! Who gave a damn if they're fake or not?

"Are you going to play or stare at my chest all night?" the lady shouted.

Immortal kept grinning and took a puff of his cigar. "I'll probably stare for a while longer. Most of my blood is coursing into my dick right now instead of my brain, so it might be a bit before I play."

The lady's jaw hit the floor and her husband stood from his chair, trying to look threatening.

"Ah, no offense, sir. I meant no disrespect. I just figured she might want to know about my boner, since you probably need pills to get a stiffy. Figured it might give her a thrill! A broad's gotta know she's still pretty sometimes, ya know? You oughta thank me for complimenting your wife. I'm a nice guy like that."

"I . . . I'm . . ." the lady began.

"Sorry?" Immortal asked. "No need to be sorry, sweetheart. My feelings ain't hurt. You can make it up to me later, though, if you want."

The woman screamed in frustration. "We fold! Come on, Henry, let's leave this Neanderthal. I don't want to hear him beating his chest like a gorilla all evening."

"I'll think of you later when I'm beating . . ."

Her husband threw his chair aside and punched Immortal in the face. For a moment blood poured out of Immortal's nose, and it seemed as though it were broken. The blood suddenly stopped and his nose shifted back into place. His face looked the same as before. Everyone stared in silence, but Immortal only grinned.

"Ya know, people always think I heal quick but feel pain," Immortal said. "I don't feel pain at all, otherwise someone would have probably kidnapped me and tortured me by now. I guess it's led to a lack of fear, so I tend to say what I want. I still feel the good stuff, though." Immortal smiled at the woman.

"Tell you what." He turned to the husband. "Since you're so old and because I'm such a nice guy, I won't even hit you back. Just try not to make the arthritis any worse, old timer."

Casino security stepped in and escorted the man and woman away after they grabbed their things. The security manager walked over to Immortal.

"You spend enough money here that we don't want to throw you out, but you can't keep irritating our patrons. They are here to have a good time, same as you. Please show some respect."

"Ah, you're right, Hank. Sorry to cause trouble. Just a little on edge tonight, pal, that's all." Immortal sighed and took a drink of his whiskey. "I don't even know why I drink this stuff. Can't get drunk anymore. Old habits die hard, I guess." Immortal frowned. He sat for a moment, finishing his drink. "Sorry, guys. I fold."

He threw his cards down and gathered his chips. Normally he'd leave with a couple girls in tow, but he was in a foul mood. He had a sort of arrangement with the

Paragons so they would leave him alone. Money was usually good for silencing people, one way or another. With all the chaos going on in Washington, DC, though, it was only a matter of time before they came to him. They would ask for his help, and when he refused, they'd come at him with everything they had. No, they couldn't kill him, but there were worse things. If they took the money, for instance . . .

Immortal shook his head. "Nah, I don't want to think about that," he mumbled under his breath.

I definitely can't continue to be out in the open anymore, he thought. *Disappearing isn't as easy as you'd think. I'd have to live without all this wonderful modern technology. No more extravagant spending or gambling. Damn, those Paragons piss me off, bunch of self-righteous bastards.*

The ground quaked violently under his feet. Immortal crouched down for stability. "Damn you, Wrath, not this shit again!"

Earth parted beneath Immortal and he descended slowly into darkness. Soon his swearing went silent as the ground swallowed him whole.

In the darkness Immortal couldn't see a thing, but he knew there was someone there. The first time Wrath did this it scared the hell out of him. In his panic he didn't think, and it took some time before he realized what was happening. Wrath nearly bullied him into one of his crazy schemes, but Immortal was ready for him this time.

Only this time was different; Immortal realized he was able to stand. He reached into his coat pocket and pulled out a small flashlight. It wasn't often that Immortal found himself too stunned to speak, but this was one of those rare occasions. He wasn't stuffed into a tiny space in the ground with no room to move like last time. Immortal was looking around a large chamber that appeared to be a sphere shape.

This place has to be at least fifty feet tall, he thought. He frowned as he examined the chamber. Apparently Wrath must need him pretty badly to make such a grand space. *That's right—where is that little bastard?*

"I apologize for the nature of our meeting, but it was the only way I could ensure we would be safe," Malice said.

Immortal jumped, startled by the abrupt statement. "Good Lord! You scared the piss out of me!"

Immortal put the flashlight on the person speaking and was startled again when it was not Wrath.

"Who the hell are you? Where's Wrath? I thought he was the only one that could do this!" Immortal said in a shaky tone. "What the hell do you want?"

"I'm known as Malice, but don't let my name fool you. I don't want to hurt you. We actually need your help."

"We?" Immortal asked.

Malice frowned. "That's a long story, but we need your help. We'll need your resources in order to pull this off."

Immortal nodded and took a deep breath to think for a moment. "I don't know you, so why should I trust you, much less work with you?"

"Because we both want the same thing," Malice said.

Immortal chuckled. "Oh, we just met and you think you know what I want? All right, I'll humor you. What is it that I want?"

"Freedom," Malice said.

"Freedom?" Immortal asked. "I think I'm doing pretty well. I already have freedom. I'd bet your mother's left ass cheek that I'm the only member of the Fallen to stay out of prison."

Malice nodded. "Yes, for now. How long do you think they'll put up with you? Your existence is like a slap in the face to them. Sooner or later they'll attack you. They might slowly erode your reputation to the point that it would be easy to cook up some ridiculous criminal charge. Or they may simply abduct you. They can't kill you, but they could bury you forever. Maybe they'll dump you into the ocean with a weight tied around your ankles. There are worse things than death."

Immortal had to suppress his anger and fear. He'd had nightmares of exactly those sorts of scenarios. Just like in poker, he had to keep a straight face to keep his emotions hidden.

"You're the one that killed Justice and Guardian, aren't you? Guardian I can understand, that guy was a fucking douche, but Justice? He was actually a good guy." Immortal's voice and face betrayed nothing, but he was seething inside.

"A good guy?" Malice asked. "Yes, he was a real stand-up guy," he said in a mocking tone. "He ignored the evil and corruption of the other Paragons. His inability to correct their mistakes and effectively deal with scum like Lament led to the deaths of innocent people."

Malice paused for a moment, trembling with anger and clenching his fists. He continued in a choked voice. "Including my wife and daughter. He is just as responsible as Lament for their deaths. If they had only killed him, how many would be alive today?"

Immortal stood in silence, staring at Malice. *Is this guy crazy? No,* he thought to himself, *he's not crazy. The guy is obviously racked with guilt and rage, but his thinking has some logic to it.*

"I don't agree with you. You think Justice and the other Paragons should just execute people?"

Malice shook his head. "No, but most criminals and psychopaths can't break out of prison so easily. Or remain impossible to detect. Lament had a long history of repeated escapes. I don't think they cared, though. If they locked up all of the Fallen, who would they fight? They would be irrelevant, and unnecessary. Letting Lament run around gives the Paragons a boogeyman to hunt. It keeps them looking like heroes that the public needs. Helps sell Paragon merchandise and it keeps the public funds flowing."

Immortal grinned. "You're smarter than you look, boy. But what do you plan to do about it? You're just going to kill them all?" He laughed but quickly stopped when he saw the lack of emotion in Malice's eyes.

"You are, aren't you?" Immortal asked. "You're planning to kill the Paragons."

Malice nodded, but his expression didn't change.

"Count me out of this crazy fucking plan of yours. They'll kill you. God only knows what those bastards would do to me just for helping. They are surprisingly unforgiving of people trying to kill them. Just ask Chaos."

"I understand your fears," Malice said. "But if we don't do something, they will. Sooner or later they'll discover

I'm not dead, and they'll attack you somehow. It could be days from now or years, but it'll happen, and I think you know it."

"We could just disappear. Hell, you have the perfect power for that," Immortal said. "I can wait for them to die of old age if I have to."

"Sure, so for at least a few decades or more you'll be looking over your shoulder all the time. Do you really want to live in fear for so long?"

"It's better than the alternative! It's too risky attacking them! It's like banging a whore without a condom. Sure, she might be clean, or she could rot your cock off. Why take the chance?"

Malice grinned. "You don't exactly have to worry about your cock rotting off anymore."

Immortal nodded. "Touché."

"Besides," Malice added, "you're a gambling man. Slim odds shouldn't bother you."

"That's the thing," Immortal said. "When I make bets, they're a sure thing. It's not really gambling when the odds are in your favor."

"Exactly!" Malice yelled. "Which is why we have a lot of preparation to do. We need to tip the odds in our favor. I have plenty of resources myself. I just lack funding and your level of experience. You must have a lot of personal connections as well, and we'll need them."

Immortal sighed. "You're talking like I already said yes. I haven't agreed yet."

"Yes, you have," Malice boasted. "I saw your eyes light up when I mentioned freedom. I know you want this. You're just sizing me up."

Immortal laughed. "You arrogant bastard, we ought to play poker sometime! It seems like you might be able to teach me a thing or two." Immortal nodded and shook Malice's hand. "All right, I'll help you."

"I hope it goes without saying that I need to remain a secret. If the Paragons find out I'm still around, we'll lose a huge advantage."

Immortal nodded. "Yeah, no shit. I hope it goes without saying that you're going to be doing the killing. I'm not interested in being public enemy number one."

"That's fine, I figured that was likely."

"Good," Immortal replied. "Now send me back. I'm sweatin' my balls off down here."

Malice laughed. "Eloquent as always, but you don't sweat. You don't get cold either. Your power regulates that, doesn't it?"

"Smart little bastard, aren't you?" Immortal said. "More of an expression anyways. Just get me back topside. How will we stay in contact? I'm not fond of these underground meetings, whether literal or figurative."

"Send a message to this email address, and we'll encrypt it. In a real emergency, call this number." Malice handed Immortal a slip of paper with contact information scribbled with coal.

"*We* again? Who else is involved?" Immortal asked.

Malice sighed. "Damn, *I* need to work on that. It's someone with a mutual interest in keeping us alive."

Immortal shrugged. "Whatever. *I'll* be in touch, you schizo bastard."

Malice nodded. "All right, up you go." An impish look crossed face.

"Why don't I like that look?" Immortal asked.

The ground rumbled beneath Immortal and sent him flying upward at breathtaking speed.

"Shiiiiiiiiit!" Immortal's cursing faded as the earth filled in behind him.

Malice yelled after him, "Don't worry—it's fun! You'll live!"

Immortal shot up out of the ground like a bullet, flying skyward about thirty feet before crashing down hard onto the pavement. Broken bones and bruises instantly repaired themselves. Immortal stood up and brushed himself off.

"That bastard's lucky I don't feel pain," Immortal muttered to himself. "Otherwise, I might have taken that personally."

Immortal chuckled. "What the hell did I get myself into?" He shook his head and walked home.

Chapter 31: Beast

Excitement *isn't the right word,* Mr. Gray thought. No, that word didn't fully explain the torrent of emotion raging through him. He was feeling a potent mix of a childlike anticipation for Christmas morning with a very adult feeling of anxiety. *This is years of my work.*

There had been some successes but many failures. So many times over the years he had heard that failures led to success. Colleagues or employees would point to motivational posters or famous quotes. What they ignored was the constant heartbreak of those failures. Perhaps for an incompetent buffoon who was used to failure, it wasn't an issue. For brilliant perfectionists like him, failure was a dagger in the heart. Failure did drive him to succeed, but it also brought him to the point of madness. *My perfectionism has led to brilliant breakthroughs, and crippling melancholy.*

Mr. Gray shook his head to clear his thoughts. He took a deep breath and gave his characteristic smile as he looked at the two chambers.

A young scientist stammered, "A-Are you ready, s-s-sir?"

"Yes, I am. Todd, why the hell are you so nervous, boy? Those rooms are perfectly contained. They'll never break free. Even if they could, their obedience is guaranteed. They can't even fart unless I say so. Or is there something else on your mind?"

Mr. Gray stared at the young scientist. The poor bastard was trembling! This kid was brilliant, but Mr. Gray realized he often forgot how young Todd was. Most teenage boys his age were probably glued to their phones and their video games. Their biggest worry was whether Mommy or Daddy would pick up some Doritos on their way home from work. Todd had more earthly concerns, like the two creatures in the chambers. Perhaps he was concerned with the one next to him as well.

This young man was a rare breed of genius. He was the kind that may be seen only once a generation. That was why Mr. Gray incessantly nagged and pressured the boy until he agreed to work with him. Some extraordinary measures were required, but Todd was a better man for it!

Mr. Gray smiled at Todd, only making his trembling worse. Todd wiped some sweat from his brow. "S-Sir?" Todd continued. "S-S-Some of the other scientists h-h-have been concerned what will happen a-a-after the project. They think, i-i-if it's a success, t-t-that you will kill us all. T-T-To keep us quiet."

Todd's eyes widened, and he turned pale.

"Calm down, boy. Don't piss yourself, now. What kind of dumb-ass spends countless hours and endless resources to bring in the best minds available, only to kill them? No, my plan after this project is to give you all a long break.

You've certainly earned that. Then I'll put you back to work. I'm not a wasteful man, and this isn't the movies. You think I'm some stupid gangster that's going to kill all the witnesses? You must think of me as a primitive man, to do such a useless and barbaric thing. I'm a lunatic, but I'm a very practical lunatic."

Todd's trembling stopped, and he nodded slowly. "Y-Yes, I suppose that makes s-s-sense. We shall begin when you're ready, M-M-Mr. Gray."

Mr. Gray smiled and said, "Fantastic! Let's get our first look at them. Then we'll do the initial scans."

Todd nodded and hit the release button. In each chamber, a giant oblong object fell and burst open as it hit the floor. The "cocoons," as they had been nicknamed by Mr. Gray himself, served essentially the same function here that they did in nature. They made it possible for the creatures inside to evolve, to metamorphose into something far greater. These things used to be men, but now they were practically godlike creatures that he alone controlled!

As the cocoons opened, they sent red, blood-like fluid flying everywhere, which slowly drained through the grate in the floor of each room. In the chamber on the left, an eight-foot-tall angel-like creature was unconscious on the floor. He was still humanoid, with two arms, two legs, et cetera. But he had two large wings modeled to look like an angel's. On the outside, the rest of him looked like a normal human, though much better. A bronzed, well-muscled, tall angel was what Mr. Gray wanted him to resemble. He was a handsome, popular type of figure that would resonate well with the public. On the inside, he wasn't human at all. No real emotion, desire, or thought other than what Mr. Gray wanted him to have. He wouldn't make the mistake of trusting his creations to act as they should on their own ever again! It was just unfortunate that he had to change Mark so dramatically. He was a good kid;

that's partially why he was chosen. His sense of justice and goodness were a perfect fit for this form.

The creature that used to be Mark opened his brilliant blue eyes. Mr. Gray briefly felt elation as his work came to life. Through those blue eyes he felt horror and sorrow staring back at him. Mr. Gray's smile faded, and he quickly looked away.

Mr. Gray looked to the chamber on the right. This was the most dramatic change he had ever made to a person. This man was a monster inside before he was altered to look like one on the outside. He was a serial killer; he hunted people for his own pleasure. Mr. Gray was now counting on those instincts. The creature was a blend of many of nature's most useful traits. He resembled a very large reptile, though with more of the build of a cat. He had large scales covering his body that provided exceptional armor. He had enhanced speed and agility, able to climb any surface. This thing could blend into its environment perfectly and make no noise at all. There was no scent, he gave off no heat, and he had been engineered to nullify or counter every ability his foes would have. He was the perfect killing machine, made to hunt and kill with stunning efficiency. Lament had been designed with many of those same abilities. This creature was a dramatically improved version. The best part was that he has no will of his own. No mistakes this time. Couldn't have a crazed, homicidal lunatic on the loose if you couldn't control him!

The creature on the left he imagined the public would dub "Angel," or something similar. The creature on the right would hopefully be something terrifying. He referred to him as the "Beast." Perhaps that will be his unofficial nickname for now. It's certainly better than "Creature."

"That's it, that's what I'll call you!" Mr. Gray yelled. "Your name is Beast until the public comes up with something better."

Beast opened his eyes for the first time and stood on all fours. He looked over to Mr. Gray and made a sound almost like a growl. His eyes were a brilliant mix of orange and red. Angry orbs burning like the fiery surface of the sun. It shouldn't have been possible, but Mr. Gray could feel an intense rage in those eyes.

"Still some residual thoughts in there it seems. I know fury when I see it, but don't worry. We'll fix that, won't we?"

"Y-Y-Yes, sir, we will," Todd stammered. "Some residual thoughts w-w-were definitely expected. In a day or two with some minor adjustments, t-t-they'll be clear of thoughts or feelings of their own."

"Excellent!" Mr. Gray exclaimed. "Get started with the scans and adjustments. I'll be back to check on your progress in a few hours. Excellent work, boy. Take pride in what we've done today. Nobody in human history has come close to this achievement. Humanity will never be the same."

Mr. Gray smiled, slapped Todd on the back, and walked out of the laboratory. *I'm going to go out and celebrate,* he thought to himself. *I won't let that bastard, Mark, ruin this day for me. I did him a favor! It was either this or killing him. At least this way he will finally be a hero. Unfortunately, it was probably not what he had in mind, poor bastard.*

Chapter 32: Noble

This whole thing was such a disaster. For years Noble had insisted that greater monitoring was needed. He had the technology to do it, to monitor everything in this country. If he truly desired, he could probably institute global surveillance. Such a thing would be cumbersome and time consuming.

National surveillance, though, wouldn't be an issue, but Charisma always got her way. Her precious senators and most of the members of the president's cabinet disagreed with Noble. They agreed with the need but were afraid that if word got out, they would be ruined. Nobody likes the feeling that someone could be watching, even though the vast majority of people live boring lives that nobody is interested in. The backlash from the public over nationwide surveillance would hurt them. So in a rare instance, the politicians showed some backbone. Enough that even

Charisma didn't want to push the matter further. With the government against the idea, none of the other Paragons would commit to the idea with him.

Of course, he was going to do it anyways, but Harmony knew him too well. While nearly choking the life out of him, she had made it abundantly clear what would happen if he stepped out of line.

Now they were all looking at him as if it were his fault for not knowing Wrath and Chaos's plan! If they had just listened to him in the first place, this wouldn't have happened. Any moron with the right resources could have discovered the pattern. Their compound and their reputations would still be in one piece. Worse, Charisma's precious political puppets were wiped out! Even the public and the media were against them. If there was anyone left to lead Washington, DC, they would probably be testifying before Congress at this very moment.

Noble smirked and said, "I guess that's one good thing."

Charisma and Harmony both looked up and stared daggers into him.

Charisma said, "What good thing could you possibly see from this disaster? You of all people! You're probably the most negative, pessimistic person I know."

Noble said, "If anyone in Congress were left, we'd probably be testifying before them now. Maybe it's a good thing most of them are dead or missing."

Noble began laughing until Harmony punched him in the sternum. His laughs quickly turned to wheezing and agony. It felt like she had caved in his chest.

"I don't appreciate your insane attempt at humor," Charisma said. "Fix yourself up and get to work repairing the compound. Get everything up and running within the next twenty-four hours or you'll wish you were buried with Chaos and Malice!"

Harmony walked casually out of the room as if nothing happened. Charisma looked down at Noble, shook her head, and walked out.

It took a few minutes for Noble to collect himself, but he stood up and brushed himself off as best he could. "Oh, I'll fix the place up," Noble said. "I'll even make some improvements the two of you will never forget!"

"You will do no such thing," a voice behind him said. "Fix the compound, then set up the monitoring you were just thinking about a few minutes ago. Look for signs of Drift, or unusual incidents that could help us track the rest of the Fallen."

Noble froze in place. He recognized that voice, though he couldn't remember why. All he could feel was a horrible fear that he didn't understand. It took everything he had to not visibly tremble. Everyone called him Boss, but nobody could remember anything about him. It was like his face and real name were on the fringe of their memory but eluded them all. The only memory that stuck was fear and obedience. All he could think of was to stay silent and try not to wet himself this time.

Boss laughed. "Oh Noble, come now. You are much too dignified to piss yourself, aren't you?"

Noble's eyes widened. He realized that Boss could read their minds. Could he manipulate their thoughts as well? Yes, he thought he remembered—

"No, you remember nothing. Just do as you're told," Boss said. "I'd tell you to not speak of our visit, but you won't remember it, will you?"

The room began to spin, and Noble became dizzy and lightheaded. His legs gave out and he fought the urge to puke. He grasped at his head in a useless attempt to try and steady himself. After what felt like a lifetime, his head cleared and he stood up. He couldn't remember why he had been kneeling on the ground, holding his head.

Suddenly the urge to get the repairs started and get his monitoring in place was overwhelming. Something was bothering him, just on the edge of his mind. It was like he was forgetting something important but he couldn't remember what it was.

Chapter 33: Adrift

"What a friggin' mess," Drift mumbled to himself. He drained the rest of his beer and slid the glass away from him. Everyone else in the bar was glued to the television. The news was drawing viewers like never before. More and more information of the massacre in Washington, DC, was unfolding. The government itself had even been decimated, many of its members dead or still missing. Thousands of people had died too. That fact was apparent by looking around the bar.

Drift shook his head as he surveyed the room. *Too many people in here drowning their sorrows,* he thought. *This kind of drinking should be left to miserable old fools like me. The only good news in all of this is that some lives were spared. Even that Malice guy pitched in.*

The lady behind the bar had a fresh mug of beer and slid it carefully over to Drift. She leaned in and whispered,

"On the house, Drift. A lot of people wouldn't be here today if it weren't for you."

Drift raised an eyebrow and considered the lady carefully for a moment. He certainly wasn't used to praise. Glares and screams from people were what he was accustomed to. People grew up afraid of Drift and the other Fallen. Some of the Fallen were monsters, but some were just unfortunate, like Drift. All he wanted to do was live life as he saw fit. Apparently that was a crime these days with those damn Paragons.

"Thanks, honey," Drift said, and nodded in appreciation.

The woman smiled briefly, not because she was happy, but because she was trying to be pleasant during unpleasant events. Drift always marveled at people like that. People like her were able to smile and carry on acting cheerful despite the horrors of the world. Small acts like that helped shed a little light on this dark, miserable planet.

Drift sat still for a moment, listening. It was almost like his animal instincts were attuned to some sort of danger. Drift always listened to his instincts. He felt that something was wrong. For days he'd sensed he was being followed. That feeling that someone is watching you but nobody's there. Even creepier, his abilities had the added benefit of sensing movement. When he was alone he could feel movement near him, moving slowly. But every time he turned and lashed out with his telekinesis, there was nothing there. There couldn't be anyone there; if there had been, they would have been violently thrown. Even Lament couldn't stalk Drift, despite his many attempts.

Drift grabbed the mug and began drinking slowly. Some people drank quickly, probably trying to get drunk. He'd always appreciated sitting and slowly enjoying his drinks, though. Mostly out of habit. The life of a drifter meant that he couldn't usually afford a lot of drinks. So he was grateful to have them.

After a few more complimentary drinks, Drift relaxed and figured he was just being paranoid. It was late, even for a night owl. He thanked the lady for the drinks and stepped outside to have a cigarette in the alley next to the bar.

Sighing, Drift fumbled around in his pockets until he finally found a lighter. As he lit his cigarette, he felt movement right next to him.

Instinctively he threw a telekinetic barrier around himself just as something swiped at his head. Even with the barrier in place, the force of the blow sent him staggering off balance.

Something blinked with catlike eyes that glowed orange and red. They were almost at eye level with him, but there was no body! The thing finally started moving, darting at him in an instant.

Again Drift managed to get a telekinetic barrier up fast enough to block a vicious string of swipes. Whatever the thing was, it was becoming more and more visible as it attempted to tear through his barrier.

This thing was huge! On all fours it stood eye to eye with him. It resembled a large cat, and it even attacked like one. The body was covered in scales that had mimicked the environment perfectly. It must've been the size of a polar bear, maybe bigger. Somehow it was tearing through his barriers. Not even Guardian with all of his strength and brute force could get through. His barriers blocked physical force completely. Nothing had ever posed a real threat to them, not even Chaos or those creatures of his.

Drift threw a wave of telekinetic energy at the beast, hoping to lift it and manipulate it. Nothing happened. It wasn't affected at all! The barrier was about to break. Desperate, Drift threw wave after wave of telekinetic blasts at the beast, but nothing happened. Everything behind it bounced around the alley, but the beast was completely unaffected.

"If that won't work on you, maybe ol' Drift will hafta think outside of the box, eh, beastie?" Reaching out with his telekinesis, Drift tore a large Dumpster away from the wall and launched it at the beast.

The massive thing darted away with a speed and grace a creature of that size shouldn't have. The Dumpster slammed into the building next to Drift, narrowly missing the beast.

"Guess maybe I can't crush you with my abilities, or even toss you outta here. Least I can throw stuff at ya till you get the hell outta here!"

Reaching all around him with his telekinesis, Drift grabbed everything he could. Cans, bottles, trash, light poles, even bricks from the buildings around him. He launched them at the beast like hundreds of little missiles.

The beast didn't even try to evade them. They all pinged off its scales without even making it wince.

"Well, you're a tough son of a bitch, ain't ya?" Drift said. "No problem, tough guy. We'll get something bigger!"

A large truck was parked nearby, backed up to a loading dock for the bar. It was probably full of booze, but Drift needed it and would have to repay the bar somehow later.

The truck creaked and groaned as it was lifted straight up and maneuvered to fit in the alley. The truck flew at the beast, too large to dodge in that narrow alley.

"I gotcha now, ya bastard!" Drift yelled.

The beast roared and charged the truck, running head first into it. It easily stopped the truck, even with Drift's full force behind it. This gave him the opening he needed.

Drift grinned and ripped a tall metal light pole out of the concrete. He sheared the end of it to a point, making it into a massive spear. The beast was still holding the truck at bay and couldn't defend himself from this attack.

"You're done now, you big dumb bastard!"

The light pole flew at the beast like a spear, but the beast lifted its large, dragon-like tail. It swatted the pole aside with one quick flick.

Drift's eyes grew wide, realizing for the first time how deadly this beast was. That feeling of being watched the past few days was this thing watching him. It had been stalking him for days, and if he hadn't put a barrier up in time, it would have killed him with ease. He would have been dead before he knew what happened. This thing was powerful. He'd been around long enough to see Mr. Gray's work in this. It wasn't a machine, or at least part of it wasn't. Mr. Gray is the only one he could think of that could possibly have created such a monster!

"You're making me do something I hate to do, beastie," Drift said. "I hate heights, but it looks like I ain't got no other choice."

Drift flung the back of the truck up, causing it to flip over on top of the beast. The move merely slowed the beast down, but it was just enough time for Drift to lift himself in the air and out of reach. After ascending a few hundred feet, Drift used his telekinesis to propel himself forward. Wrath had actually given him the idea for this. It seemed ironic that Wrath would indirectly save his life.

Drift flew out of the area and didn't stop until he was in California. He would rest for a night and regroup, then find a place to disappear. Maybe if he was lucky, this thing couldn't track him. Then again, Drift never considered himself a lucky man.

Chapter 34: Malice

Immortal had already proven to be an effective ally. Vigilant had predicted that he would be too immature and unpredictable to be useful. Despite the man's rough demeanor, he was very intelligent. His first message gave Malice an address where he could take refuge. It took him some time to get there without being seen, but the place was perfect. It was an old hunting lodge up in the Appalachian Mountains. There were no roads to it, and the place hadn't been used in years.

Most people would have been horrified by how worn down the place was. Every floorboard creaked and groaned. Dust would rise up in a suffocating cloud wherever you sat. All of the furniture had a hideous orange-and-brown pattern that must have come from the 1970s. Worst of all was the smell: old and extremely musty. Malice loved it all.

The place had character, and it felt safe. Immortal had managed to have the place hooked up with reliable electricity and even an internet connection about a year ago. He didn't make any other changes, fearing it might draw attention to it. Originally he had planned on using it himself as a place to hide if he were ever in a jam.

The refrigerator was empty except for some expired condiments and a jar of pickles. Immortal had mostly stocked the place with canned goods, jerky, and more Spam than he'd ever dreamed of. Malice hardly ate, too wrapped up in gathering information with Vigilant. Sleeping and eating were a luxury, and he was too busy to worry about either.

Originally he had expected to see the usual spin that the Paragons always got away with. In the past, if any Paragon got wrapped up in a public relations nightmare, it would be swept under the rug. This was too big, and there were too many witnesses. Drift and Malice had become heroes to many after survivors came forward with footage of the two defending them. Too many videos and eyewitness testimonies were available. Normally that would have been no problem for Noble, but the Paragons were still reeling from the attack. Their compound had been decimated. The public backlash against the Paragons was immediate and intense.

Everyone was wondering why they were so ill equipped to deal with the attack. With all of the public funding and support at their disposal, they did nothing. Two supposed villains had saved thousands while the Paragons worried about their precious compound. The news stations were flooded with outraged Americans calling for new leadership. Over 80 percent of Americans were now demanding new leadership that wasn't associated with the Paragons. Most felt that America needed a president to lead the country with absolute authority until the political infrastructure was restored.

Current public opinion was in favor of putting Clark Hanson in that leadership position. His open hate of the Paragons in previous years and his recent public appearances calling for unity had gotten everyone talking. In three days, voting would begin around the country to elect the new president. Normally the vice president would have taken the presidency, but he was dead. In fact, most of the president's cabinet were dead or missing. The few that remained were shaken and none would take up their responsibilities.

Clark Hanson, the leader of the Malcontent—until he betrayed them. That night still haunted Malice. The man had sold out men and women who worked for him to further his own ambition. People who had worked hard to fulfill *his* dreams and ambitions. He'd made a deal with the devil, and now it looked like it was about to pay off.

We know your misgivings for Mr. Gray, our creator. Yet his tactics have been impeccable thus far. In one brutal

attack he has removed the Paragons' greatest power.
Public support was their real strength. With fame, wealth,
and adoration, they were almost untouchable. By ruining
their reputation and image he has finally forced people to
see them for what they are. At the same time, he removed
all of their powerful connections. Without them, they have
nobody to fall back on for assistance. His tactics are brutal,
yet effective.

"The efficiency of his tactics is irrelevant," Malice said. "Thousands of innocent people died to fulfill his ambitions. Plus, his plan isn't complete. He may still screw up."

What do you mean? His plan was to remove the
Paragons from power. That has definitely succeeded. The
attack was a success.

"He isn't done yet. Mr. Gray wouldn't leave loose ends like that. I know he is up to something else. Mr. Gray told me he wanted them all dead. That's why he created you."

With their support gone and two prominent members dead, they are greatly weakened. It is possible he may not consider them a threat.

"True. I don't think he considers them as great a threat as Drift. This story got swept under the rug, but with your enhanced search abilities, I found it."

Malice pulled up a story that had been in the digital edition of the DC newspaper. It included pictures of a building and delivery truck that had been damaged. Some eyewitnesses claimed that they saw Drift battling a monster; others claimed a giant cat. People probably dismissed it as a hoax, but Malice knew better.

"I think he's trying to eliminate any powerful potential threats. Drift is unpredictable and very powerful. This thing, whatever it was, probably ambushed him."

You think that Mr. Gray sent that thing against him? We're not certain such technology exists. Altering a living being to the extent the eyewitnesses describe would be extremely difficult. It could have been some sort of mechanical construction.

"Maybe, but that's not important right now. I'm willing to bet that Mr. Gray will be going after the Paragons soon. If he's not careful, he may martyrize them."

If your theory is correct, then we would probably be his primary target. We are powerful and unpredictable. It would be wise for us to remain unseen to test your theory.

Malice smiled. "I think you're right. Sometimes I think some things just need to work themselves out. Besides, my plans usually seem to unravel and become complete disasters. We'll keep resting. It'll give you time to finish our modifications."

Our systems are strained, and your biological systems are as well. We recommend you eat and rest. If you neglect your health, we'll eventually suffer widespread malfunctions.

"You have a point, and a break is definitely inviting. I think Immortal left some beer around here somewhere . . ."

We do not like alcohol. It does strange things to both our systems. We don't understand why humans purposely alter their chemistry to make themselves function less efficiently.

"Sometimes we lower our 'system efficiency' so that we can forget."

Why would you want to forget? Your experiences help you to learn. To purposely attempt to forget experiences is foolish. It would only harm your personal well-being and give you less information to draw from.

"Some things are so horrible that forgetting them may be the only thing we can think of to keep our desire to live. Alcohol isn't a great method to cope, but sometimes a little can go a long way to help us relax."

We would appreciate moderation. Excessive alcohol interferes with our ability to operate efficiently.

Malice smirked. "Wouldn't want that, would we? Drunk nanomachines, huh? Kind of amusing to think about."

It is impossible for us to get drunk, but if your body is impaired, we cannot function as well. Alcohol inhibits your ability to think and act appropriately. It also lowers your coordination and motor skills. Thus it inhibits our ability to operate at full efficiency.

"No problem, Mom. I'll keep my drinking in check."

We'll point out again that your attempt at humor is pointless. We do not share your emotions and humor.

"Honestly, that's probably a good thing."

We agree.

Chapter 35: Immortal

It had been a couple weeks since Immortal's meeting with Malice. So far the kid hadn't been any trouble. For a guy that everyone had nicknamed "Malice," he actually appeared to be a nice enough guy. So far he'd just stayed in that hunting cabin, keeping an eye on everything through the internet. Immortal had put in some software to track what Malice did on the computer. For some reason it either wasn't functioning or Malice had found a way to disable it. He was either smarter than he looked or there was something else going on. Something did seem kind of off about him. He kept saying *we*, as if he were working with someone else.

For now their partnership didn't seem to be causing any trouble. It also provided the opportunity to get to know Malice. Obviously the media portrayal of him wasn't completely accurate. It was known that Lament had killed his family. Everyone had their own theory on what transpired after that. The most popular belief was that somehow Malice developed his powers as an extreme response to his grief. Or maybe he accidentally received them through Lament or Guardian somehow.

Immortal knew better: it was obviously Mr. Gray's work. Knowing him, Malice had been given powers as an attempt to clean up Mr. Gray's old mistakes. Whether that included Immortal himself wasn't clear. So far he hadn't shown any "malice" toward him, but that didn't mean anything. If Immortal had learned anything over the years, it was that most people weren't what they appear to be. How many sweet, innocent-looking people turned out to be selfish and manipulative? Others that were dirty, disheveled, and angry looking often were very kind and compassionate people. You could never judge a person on their appearance alone. It could give you clues to their personality sometimes, but it was often too unreliable.

Immortal had learned to be pretty good at stripping away the masks everyone put on in public. Seeing people for who they were was kind of his specialty. It wasn't a power, not like his regenerative abilities. Just a life skill he had acquired through years of encountering the worst kind of people.

Despite Immortal's uncanny ability to read people, Malice was beyond him. His face was always neutral, no smiling or grimacing. Malice always seemed calm and emotionless. It was almost unnerving. Was he hiding something sinister? Or was the man simply beyond normal human emotion now? No, that was preposterous. If that were true he wouldn't be on this crusade of his. Perhaps Malice wore a better mask than the average individual?

To kill Guardian and Justice, he must have some darkness in him. Killing men wasn't something that came naturally to people. Most would believe otherwise, based on human history. Immortal would tell those people that they should spend some time on a battlefield. If people were built to kill each other, it wouldn't take such a toll on soldiers. They wouldn't be diagnosed with PTSD and other mental disorders. There were some people that were twisted and unnatural that did enjoy it. Killing came natural to them. Could Malice be one of them? Only time would tell. It was pointless to stress about it. Eternity was already long enough without adding unnecessary stress.

The only prudent option would be to continue the partnership and see just what kind of man Malice was. If he was the sort of man that could be trusted, perhaps they could continue to work together. It would be nice to not be alone for a change. A friend could be just the thing he needed. Drinking, gambling, and women could only put a smile on your face for so long. Even that got boring eventually, especially when you couldn't get drunk.

Plus, this arrangement was in his own best interest. Malice pointed that out effectively. He had considered his arguments well, and he was right. The Paragons did worry him. Harmony and Charisma stood out as his biggest threat. They were both perfect examples of people to not judge on appearance. Both appeared to be beautiful, charming, and compassionate women. In reality, they were both cold and ruthless manipulators.

If anyone was going to damn him to an eternity of torment, it would be them. Both of them were the types to hold a powerful grudge. Just look at what Charisma did to Torment. She not only tried to kill her, but she also ruined Torment's life. Charisma ruined a woman that was kind and caring, just for standing up to her.

Charisma was used to having her way, plain and simple. She had been using and manipulating people her whole life. Unfortunately, her powers had only enhanced her ability to do that. Her ego wouldn't allow someone like him to refuse assisting the Paragons forever.

Harmony had wiped out Chaos's first attack years ago with a wall of water. She herself killed more people than Chaos had, and she didn't even bat an eye. The woman was cold, and he worried that sooner or later she would come to punish him. Now more than ever, they could use his help. It was only a matter of time before they approached him again. This time he hoped to be prepared, with Malice's help.

Assuming they could actually kill the Paragons, what next? Mr. Gray was still doing something big. Would he leave them alone? There was still Boss, Lament, and maybe Wrath. Nobody actually saw what happened to him. Malice said that he had become one of Chaos's creatures. With Chaos dead, did that mean Wrath was dead too? There were too many questions and nobody with the answers. It was no wonder the kid had been cooped up in that cabin for so long. Trying to figure out what's going on could keep him in there for months.

I can't worry about any of that now, though. I'll have a few methods of escape ready, just in case. All I can do is prepare for the worst and hope for the best.

Immortal puffed on his cigar, his feet propped up on the desk in his study. This room was tucked away in an area of his mansion that only he knew about. He often came here to think and relax. It also served as a panic room in an emergency. Immortal had no illusion that such a room could probably be bypassed by certain people, given enough time. All the concrete and steel in the world couldn't keep out most of his enemies. It still made him feel safe, though.

In this room he could be himself. There was nobody here to judge him or stare. He came here to be alone, something he would have to get used to. After all, he would have an eternity of being alone. Maybe in a few hundred years this would all seem like a stupid nightmare. The thought actually cheered him up a little.

Immortal took another puff of his cigar, making an awful attempt at blowing a smoke ring. He smiled and looked around the room. Framed pictures of old friends, family, and of course himself covered the walls. He had been horribly crippled as a child. When he was seven, a drunk driver ran him over as he crossed the street. The accident had paralyzed him below the neck. His mother had already passed away, but his father was inconsolable. The accident changed his father into a bitter and angry man. After two years of seeing his father drink himself into a stupor, suddenly the man disappeared. They were wealthy, so there was no shortage of people to take care of Immortal. Still, his father being absent for so long had hurt him deeply. It was many years before he forgave his father. Of course now he understood why his father had left for so long.

In his early twenties Immortal was finally "blessed" with these powers. They fixed his body and even improved it in every way. He was tall, muscular, and invincible as far as he knew. All of the things he had dreamed of doing for so long were finally within his reach. He spent the rest of his twenties traveling and seeking every dangerous activity he could think of. Many of the pictures that now hung on these walls were from that time period. Those were probably the happiest years of his life. It was the last time he had felt free to be himself and do what he wished.

By the time he turned thirty-two, his father called him back to their estate. His time of freedom had ended, and he began running the family business. The family business was a powerful technology firm known worldwide. They developed everything from computers to weapons at the time. Immortal had actually expanded their reach into the train and airline industries. His business provided cheaper options to travel and revolutionized public transit. Their wealth could probably buy them a small nation or two. It was enough wealth to last him an eternity.

That ended in his forties as the Paragons suddenly arrived. His identity was no secret. A handsome billionaire that had been miraculously healed is hard to hide. Of course they demanded that he join them and allow them access to his company's resources. Not being fond of being ordered around, he of course refused. It had been a long time since anybody had tried to make him do anything. More than most people, he had come to cherish his freedom. Being restricted to a wheel chair, unable to move anything below your neck, gave you a different perspective of life. He wasn't about to be restricted by anyone or anything again.

Immortal had underestimated them, though. In just a few short years, Charisma and the others had weaseled their way to wealth and power. With their influence over the media, it wasn't long until they began to demonize him. They had portrayed him as a selfish, violent sociopath that would live forever. Despite no real evidence to support the claims, if something was said enough, people began to believe it. In order to save his company from his ruined reputation, he had to pass the reins to someone else. Of course he still owned the company, but he left the direction of it to others. He began to distance himself from the company and his friends to spare them from the media. His tactic worked, but he had to leave behind his work and his friends.

Worst of all was Boss. Originally the man could only read minds. The government had used him in interrogations for some time before he changed. Somehow his abilities branched out, as if the nanomachines had evolved on their own. Instead of just reading minds, he could control them completely. Everything the mind controls was within his power. He could warp people's thoughts. Vision, hearing, smell, touch, and even taste could all be manipulated. Memories could be altered or erased. He could control breathing, blood pressure, and heartbeats. Without even lifting a finger, he could wipe your mind clean and leave you a husk.

Even worse, he could remove every piece of who you were and make you someone else. His power was too strong, and Immortal was the only one that wasn't affected. Somehow his healing ability blocked Boss's ability. Immortal would kill him if he got the chance, but Boss had taken special care to avoid him. Nobody else seemed to really remember him clearly anymore. Boss must not have wanted anyone to know he existed, but he couldn't erase his identity completely. The public knew there was a seventh member of the Paragons, but they couldn't remember who. How he affected so many people was a scary thing to think about.

The others were bad enough, but with the Boss standing behind them, what hope did anyone else have? Mr. Gray obviously saw something in Malice to give him abilities.

His track record of picking people hadn't panned out in most cases. Maybe he was due to pick a good one?

Immortal smiled and laughed. Sometimes all you could do in life was smile at the ridiculousness of everything. Life was one horrible challenge after another until you died. Had there ever been anyone that had lived a quiet, peaceful, worry-free life full of bliss? No, not in this world. Nothing was ever that easy. Immortal often wondered if this was really hell. If it wasn't, maybe it was good he was immortal. When he died, he'd go to hell for sure, so maybe it was best that he would never die.

Chapter 36: Torment

Breathe, just breathe, Torment reasoned to herself.

Relax and blend in, or you'll be noticed again. Torment

took one slow deep breath in, trying to calm her nerves.

She wasn't scared, just excited to finally get her shot. The

Paragons must have been desperate to repair their image.

Charisma had been on a brutal schedule, talking to anyone

that would listen. These days the number of people who

came to listen were few. In the past she would have easily

drawn thousands to see her speak and feel her power over

them. It sounds strange, but people seemed to enjoy it.

People would come from all over the world to see her

speak in person, knowing full well she guided their

emotions during the experience.

Since Chaos's attack in Washington, only one or two

hundred were present. It seemed the higher the pedestal the

farther the fall. The Paragons were heroes, held to the

highest standards. When it finally became clear that they weren't what they appeared to be, the fall was crippling.

Torment could feel Charisma's attempt to draw the crowd into her feelings of betrayal and pain. She was trying to make them feel sorry for her. A few people were buying it, but most weren't. After only a few minutes many people began to leave. The look of desperation on Charisma's face! Oh it was almost pure ecstasy to see her suffer!

Torment clenched her hand over her mouth to stifle a burst of laughter. She never thought she'd see the day that Charisma would witness her world crumbling around her. It was the same feeling Torment once had. Only one thing would be more satisfying than seeing Charisma this miserable. Killing her slowly while hearing her scream and beg for mercy was the only thing that could possibly be any better. Years of fantasies were finally coming to fruition. She felt so vindicated! It has been so long since she felt this alive, this happy.

Originally Torment had come to these speeches to kill Charisma. That first public appearance was so brutal and demeaning to Charisma that she changed her mind. People were yelling at Charisma, spitting on her, even throwing things at her face. Killing her now would be too easy. Better to let her reap what she had sown for so long. Once she was broken, or if she began to make a comeback, then she'd die. For now, just watching this was good enough.

There was movement behind Charisma. Torment stared and thought maybe she was imagining things. People on stage behind Charisma were suddenly flung aside. Nobody moved, unsure of what was happening. Someone next to Torment whispered something about Drift. Drift could do that, but no, this couldn't be him.

More people in the crowd began to pull out their phones and take footage of the stage. Charisma looked annoyed by the commotion behind her, but she didn't even bother to turn and see what it was. The empty space behind Charisma suddenly disappeared and some monstrous thing stood there. It was taller than Charisma, even standing on all fours. The thing was covered in scales like a reptile but was shaped like a giant panther. It bared its fangs and unleashed a deafening roar that shook the area like an explosion.

Charisma stumbled forward and fell to her knees. The crowd screamed, but instead of running, people stayed and continued filming with their phones. It made no difference to Torment; everyone in that crowd could die for all she cared. That thing was going to steal her vengeance!

Torment screamed, "Noooo! She's mine!"

She unleashed the most intense heat she could right at the beast, but it didn't even flinch. It wasn't even concerned with Torment. It was staring at Charisma, as if it were waiting for something.

Now Charisma began to tremble. She still hadn't seen the beast, but she must have realized she was all alone. Her power probably didn't work on this thing either. Tears began to stream down Charisma's face, she turned around and looked up at the creature.

Charisma turned pale and her eyes grew wide. She stared into the creature's eyes for a moment.

"Please," Charisma whispered, "please don't kill me. I don't know what you are, but—"

The beast reached its head down and opened its mouth wide, encompassing her skull. Before Charisma could finish her sentence, it clamped down, biting her head off cleanly.

Silence filled the area. Nobody moved, afraid they would catch the creature's attention. Torment stared in shock, tears rolling down her face. She had dreamed of killing Charisma for so long, and now she was dead. Dead because of that thing! Now she would never have her vengeance because of that monster.

She stood there in shock and disbelief. The creature continued its work quickly and efficiently. It consumed

Charisma's whole body, even licking up the blood left behind. There was no trace of her now, she was just . . . gone.

"You son of a bitch!" Torment screamed.

She drew her finest rapier, a special weapon that was designed for emergencies such as these. This monster was probably going to kill her, but she was going to take it with her!

In a blur she dove at the beast, her rapier pointed at its right eye. It looked like it was covered in armor, but nothing was protecting the eyes. Before the rapier could hit its mark, the beast rotated its body. The sword hit the creature in the side, glancing of one of its scales without even leaving a mark. Undeterred, Torment attacked aggressively, jabbing at the creature from every direction, probing for a weak spot. The creature roared and swung one of its massive paws at her head, narrowly missing.

The swipe didn't slow Torment at all. She wasn't worried about trying to survive. Her only goal was killing this thing; nothing else mattered. All thoughts left her, her body operating on pure instinct and adrenaline as she threw herself at the beast. With her speed and agility, she dodged the creature's attacks while stabbing relentlessly. Each stab glanced off the creature. None of her attacks were hurting it. The thing only seemed to be getting angrier.

It reared up on its hind legs and pounced at her, catching her by surprise. Torment tried to dodge to the side, but it swung a paw out and clipped her on the shoulder. It was enough to send her flying to the pavement, and most of her shoulder was gone. The beast's claws tore through her like she was made of paper.

Torment lay on the ground in a pool of her own blood. She was panting, trying to catch her breath. The blood loss was getting bad, and it took everything in her to not just lie down and die. She stared at the beast as it approached. It reached down and opened its mouth, just as it did with Charisma. Just like Torment planned.

With her good arm she grabbed her sword, heating it till it glowed, and she thrust it into the creature's mouth. Torment's aim was off, and instead of a killing blow through its mouth into the brain, it went through the cheek. The sword was stuck in the creature's head. It roared in agony, trying to paw at the sword in a futile attempt to remove it.

Torment grinned. "I'm going to die, but you are too. That's not a normal sword."

Torment sent heat into the pommel of the sword. There was a click, and Torment smiled. "Die, you ugly bastard," she said.

The sword's pommel began to beep, faster and faster. Something swooped down onto Torment, carrying her away as the sword exploded.

Blood loss and despair finally took their toll. Torment didn't know what the hell was going on. *That's okay,* she thought. *My purpose in life is over. I don't really care what happens now.*

Chapter 37: Mr. Gray

"Damn it!" Mr. Gray roared. "I knew that bitch would ruin things sooner or later! Angel should just kill her right now. Just stomp her into a mushy puddle. That's what she deserves!"

"B-B-But sir," Todd stammered. "People would see it."

Mr. Gray spun around in a rage. "Do I look like give a shit? Let them see it—it'll be a hell of a show! People crave blood, guts, and gore. Have you seen what's on television these days?"

Todd replied, "Y-Y-Yes sir, but if you want the public to like Angel, crushing a seemingly helpless woman on the verge of death would not be a g-g-good start."

Trembling in anger, Mr. Gray slammed his hand down on a desk, breaking it in half. "Damn her! She doesn't even know what she's doing and she's beating me already? Years of planning and work are down the drain because of her and you're telling me I can't even kill her?" Mr. Gray went silent for a moment, considering what Todd said.

"You're a smart man, Todd. That's why I keep you around you know. What do you think we should do, now that Angel can't be the one to defeat Beast on camera? That was going to launch his career as a hero. The public is furious with the Paragons but they're itching for a new hero to step in. This was our chance!"

"T-T-Thank you, sir. We can make a slight modification to his abilities, remotely, to heal Torment on camera. This way he is seen as a merciful hero and newcomer."

"Still not as good as beating Beast to death on camera, but I guess it will do for now. Damn, you're brilliant, Todd. You deserve a raise!"

Todd smiled. "Thank you, sir! I-I-I won't let you down! We can also recover Beast's body and reassemble him, good as new. Better than new, if you wish to add any further modifications."

"Modifications?" Mr. Gray asked to himself. "Yes, perhaps there are a few that can be made. Make arrangements to recover Beast's remains and prepare the lab for his arrival."

"Y-Y-Yes sir, we should have him ready within a few days."

Mr. Gray nodded and waved Todd out of the room. Things weren't going as he had initially hoped, but nothing ever did. Plans always had a funny way of evolving into something else. It was careless to forget Torment and her obsession with Charisma. He had been too arrogant, thinking that nothing was a viable threat to his new creations.

The other question was, what to do with Torment? She's a loose cannon, and he couldn't risk her ruining his plans again. Perhaps she could still be useful somehow.

Without Charisma to obsess over, would she become more or less rational? Despite the obvious answer of eliminating her, his curiosity was getting the best of him again. What would Torment do now, he wondered. Maybe he could give her purpose again. Or would she need to be put down like a rabid dog?

Mr. Gray grinned. Sometimes life's little surprises could be quite entertaining.

Chapter 38: Malice

It's Mr. Gray again. It has to be, Malice thought. He was seeing videos playing all over the news with this new hero saving Torment. Everyone that had appeared with powers up until now had been created by him. This new "hero" was a blatant attempt at creating a new public idol. He looked like an angel, and the public was eating it up! The debate was raging all over the world. Many religious people felt it was God intervening and the end times were near. Others felt that the new hero and the creature's origins should be investigated. Everyone seemed to agree on one point though: they loved this Angel.

Malice could only shake his head. The public could be so fickle. In mere moments they had raised this guy on the same pedestal the Paragons were on. All he did was heal Torment and speak of forgiveness before he flew away with her.

Nobody seemed to catch on to the bigger piece of news. The creature that Torment killed had disappeared. Within minutes of the attack, the creature's body vanished. It was unclear whether the thing somehow healed itself, or if it was taken. Either way, he had a feeling it would be back.

Mr. Gray was no longer being subtle. The Paragons and the Fallen were being hunted down by that creature. This Angel was probably going to be his hero and public figure. Vigilant felt it was likely that Mr. Gray intended to make Angel a popular figure to manipulate the public somehow. Malice had to agree. Mr. Gray had an objective from the beginning. He made it clear before the attack that he wanted Malice to be part of his plans to change the country. Malice even agreed on many of his points. The government and the media were corrupt. It would take an incredible event to bring the country together. Everyone seemed so divisive, and it often occurred to Malice that it was suspicious. Contentious issues were constantly bombarding the country through the media. Yes, it got ratings for the news networks, but was it worth dividing the country?

Why were so many public figures constantly having to apologize for some innocuous statement? It was like people no longer had free speech at all. If what you said was outside a very narrow point of view, the media would tear you apart. Whether what people said was "offensive" or not, it was still their point of view. Why should people have to apologize for their point of view?

Mr. Gray felt that people were being kept in a perpetual state of anger against each other so that they wouldn't unite. If there was unity, corruption and abuse of power would never be tolerated. Perhaps Malice was being paranoid and the division within the country was a coincidence that helped those in power. Malice shook his head. There was no such thing as coincidences.

His point of contention with Mr. Gray was that he didn't think all the bloodshed was necessary. Mr. Gray's method was arguably more corrupt and abusive than the previous administration's. He claimed that once things were in order, he would remove himself from power. But would he? If something didn't go the way he wished, would he keep intervening? No one man should have that much power.

Malice felt that bringing people together peacefully toward change was the better route. He may have to bust some heads along the way, but there would certainly be no massacres. Something done by the people seemed more stable and pure than being forced into it by one man's whim.

Should he intervene and destroy this new hero? Mr. Gray's champion could be a real threat.

Malice sighed and took a drink of some hot chocolate. Perhaps he should take a break. Spending so much time researching and analyzing wasn't good. He was beginning to overthink everything. A vacation sure would be nice.

Malice grinned and laughed aloud. It would be a long time before he could relax like that again. Still, he hadn't slept in a very long time. Even Vigilant was pestering him to get some rest. Sleep wasn't as pleasant as it used to be; he had intense nightmares every time he slept. Vigilant offered to alter his dreams if he wished, but he refused. This was his body's way of dealing with all the emotional distress he'd undergone. It would be unnatural to alter it, though it was incredibly tempting.

Yawning, Malice sent a message to Immortal, requesting a meeting with him. Then he went over to the musty-smelling bed and lay down. He was asleep moments after his head hit the pillow.

Chapter 39: Immortal

The kid wanted to meet, and it didn't take a genius to figure out why. There were new complications to consider.

Immortal knocked on the door to the cabin, then remembered it was his! The door wasn't locked, so he let himself in.

"You're lucky," Malice said as Immortal stepped into the cabin.

"Oh?" Immortal smiled. "What makes you say that?"

"I remembered that you were coming a moment before I was going to put my fist through your head." Malice sipped from a blue coffee mug but gave no indication on whether he was joking or not.

"Even if you had, I would have recovered and been no worse for the wear. Now, if you're done puffing your chest, what did you want to meet about?"

"I'm sure you've guessed. I wanted to talk about Mr. Gray's new pets." Malice set his mug down and motioned Immortal toward a metal folding chair.

"You do realize this is my cabin, right?" Immortal glared at Malice, clearly annoyed. "I'm not a guest. I can come and go as I please. This is my furniture too. I'll make myself at home if that's what I want to do."

Malice nodded. "Fair enough. I've been here so long, I keep thinking that it's my home. I apologize."

Immortal nodded. "Thank you. Now, I'm going to sit down, but only because I want to!" Immortal snickered.

Malice continued on, not noticing Immortal's attempt at humor. "I don't think we can leave them to do as they wish."

"You mean the creature and the hero?" Immortal asked.

"Yes, and Mr. Gray of course." Malice sighed. "They did eliminate one of our threats for us, though. Maybe we should let them clean up the rest of the Paragons too."

"What makes you think he will bother with the other Paragons?" Immortal asked. "Maybe he only needed Charisma and Torment to introduce his new creations."

"I think he views the Paragons and the Fallen as mistakes. These new creations of his are probably meant to correct those mistakes. No offense."

"None taken. I wonder where you fit into all of this. What would he consider you?"

"Well, right now he probably considers me dead. If he knew I wasn't, he might think of me as an enemy."

They sat there in silence for what seemed like an eternity, just staring at the floor.

"Do you think you may be a little too quick to use death as a solution?" Immortal asked.

"I'm trying to keep people from dying, so I don't know what you mean."

"Well, these new guys step into the picture and you immediately wonder if we should kill them. It seems like it's becoming a pattern. Should I be worried?"

Malice frowned and began tapping the floor with his foot. He gave no response, continuing to stare at the floor.

"Wait, you're not going to kill me now, are you?" Immortal chuckled. "I just started challenging your point of view, so maybe I need to die now too?"

"I don't appreciate the sarcasm," Malice said. "I understand that's how it may appear, but that is not how I am. My goal is to keep Mr. Gray from becoming so powerful that we cannot stop him. If he gains control of the country, what will we do?"

Malice began pacing the room. "These guys are pawns toward that end. I merely wonder if they needed to be removed." He stopped and looked at Immortal. "What would you suggest?"

"Patience," Immortal replied without hesitation.

"Is that code for sitting with our thumbs up our asses while the world crumbles around us?" Malice glared at Immortal.

Immortal could see the strong conviction in Malice's eyes. This guy meant business.

"No, I mean that we are jumping to too many conclusions. I know you're probably tired of being cooped up in here. But there is another problem that is much worse than Mr. Gray."

Malice stopped glaring and began to laugh hysterically. Immortal could only chuckle uncomfortably while Malice roared in laughter. He didn't know whether to be happy or afraid. Malice was obviously nuts.

The laughter finally subsided, and Malice wiped tears from his eyes. "What now?" he asked. "What could possibly be worse than Mr. Gray?"

"The mysterious seventh member of the Paragons. Many people call him Boss, but I'm not sure what he likes to go by these days."

"Why is he a threat?" Malice asked. "Does he mean to kill people like Mr. Gray?"

"Worse." Immortal frowned. "Do you have any whiskey or something in here? I need a drink."

Malice grinned. "Yeah, help yourself. This is your place, isn't it?"

"Oh yeah! Sorry, forgot already it seems." Immortal opened a cabinet above the stove and poured a large glass of whiskey. He motioned the bottle toward Malice, who shook his head. Immortal frowned. "Don't mind me. I could drink the whole bottle and it wouldn't matter. I can't seem to get drunk. It still helps calm my nerves, though. Perhaps it's psychological?" He shrugged helplessly, then drained the glass and poured another.

"He's far worse than Mr. Gray," Immortal explained. "Death is better than what Boss does to people." He took the glass and walked to the window. He took a small drink of the whiskey this time. "Boss has the power to manipulate anything the brain has control over. Since the brain controls pretty much everything we do"—he took another sip—"he has complete power over anybody he comes in contact with."

He drained the rest of his glass. "Boss seems to have some method of reaching people on a large scale. Even I don't know how he does that, and I don't think Mr. Gray does either."

"How do you know all this?" Malice asked. "Everything I come across depicts him as a myth. Nobody knows anything about him."

"I seem to be immune to his ability for whatever reason," Immortal replied. "Whatever changes he attempts to make to my brain, it must regenerate to counter it. I seem to be the only one that remembers him clearly. Even Mr. Gray was affected for a little while before he managed to counter it."

"How did Mr. Gray counter it?" Malice said.

"No idea," Immortal said. "By the time he did, most of his memories of Boss were gone. It terrified and angered him. Many of his current plans were sparked by this."

"Is all of this to try and take down Boss?" Malice asked incredulously.

"No, not all of it. Mr. Gray believes that Boss has wrested control of the country from those in power. The corruption and abuse of power was there before Boss, but Mr. Gray believes he's only expanded the problem."

"How do you know all of this?" Malice asked. "Did Mr. Gray confide in you?"

"Yes, we were once partners of sorts a long time ago."

"I suppose we all were at one point or another. What are you to Mr. Gray now?"

Immortal shrugged. "I'm not really sure. He probably just considers me a nuisance. I don't think he intends to harm me, though. Mr. Gray knows I have no interest in any of this. I typically like to keep to myself. The only reason that has changed is because it is in my own best interest to act now."

Malice nodded. "Well, that changes things. I wonder if Boss could affect me as well."

"Well, what is your power exactly?"

Malice smiled. "Killing other people who have powers."

Immortal was speechless. Malice was serious. "What the hell does that mean?" Immortal asked.

"I won't go into the details, for my own safety," Malice said. "But that's what Mr. Gray created me for. It was the whole reason he gave me these abilities."

Immortal's jaw practically hit the floor. Malice just smiled in a genuinely warm way.

"I'm not the monster Mr. Gray wanted me to be. I don't intend on killing everyone with powers. Even if I did, I can't kill you. Relax."

"Sure, I'll just cuddle right up with you now. I'm completely reassured," Immortal said. "Your name in particular gives me all the confidence in the world. I know Malice won't hurt anyone. He's a swell guy."

"If it makes you feel better, you can call me Adam." Malice paused for a moment, staring off into space. "It's been a while since anyone has called me that. Weird hearing it again."

"Adam!" Immortal yelled in surprise. "A psycho like you has such a plain, boring name?"

This time it was Immortal breaking into hysterics. Malice rolled his eyes as Immortal laughed at his expense.

"Believe it or not," Malice said, "I used to be a regular guy. I had a wife, a daughter, a job, and a beautiful house in the suburbs."

Immortal stopped laughing. "It's hard to imagine you that way," Immortal said. "You're so grim now. You look like a thirty-year-old that's lived a hundred years."

Malice nodded. "Yeah, I went from barbeques and neighborhood block parties to fighting Guardian in the blink of an eye."

"What happened?" Immortal asked. "There are probably a thousand accounts of what transpired between you and Guardian. Most of them depict you as the bad guy, but what really happened?"

"Looking back," Malice said, "Mr. Gray must have seen something in me when I ranted against the Paragons on the news." Malice sighed and ran his fingers through his hair. "I had just lost my wife and daughter, right in front of my eyes. Grief, anger, and despair were flowing out of me and I just spoke my mind. If I had just kept my mouth shut, I wouldn't be here."

"A lot of people in Washington, DC, would be dead right now if it weren't for you," Immortal said. "I bet they're glad you spoke your mind."

"If they were fans of Guardian they're not," Malice said. "That rant of mine pissed him off. He came to my door late at night to confront me." Malice shook his head. "He probably thought I'd be scared of him, that he could bully me."

"That's probably a reasonable expectation," Immortal said. "I think almost anybody would be intimidated by him, even if he didn't have powers."

"Normally I would have been," Malice said. "I was still so angry that I didn't care. Part of me probably hoped he'd kill me so I could be with my wife and daughter again."

Malice grabbed the bottle of whiskey and poured a glass. He took one long, slow drink and drained the glass. His eyes were on the brink of tears as he poured a second glass.

"When he confronted me, I spoke my mind again." Malice took a sip. "This time there were no news cameras. He lashed out and sent me crashing through the house."

Immortal shook his head. "I knew Guardian was a punk with a temper, but I never thought he would hit a regular guy."

"If I had been a regular guy at that point, I wouldn't be here right now," Malice said. "He hit me hard enough that I would have died. I'm not sure if he meant to be that brutal or not."

"Was that when you first discovered your power?" Immortal asked.

"Yeah, well, sort of," Malice said. "I was so furious, I didn't stop to wonder how I could possibly still be alive and unharmed. Without even thinking, I charged him."

Immortal chuckled. "Probably not the reaction he was expecting."

Malice smiled. "Yeah, that was probably the one funny thing about that whole situation." Malice laughed and said, "The look on his face as I stood up and charged him . . ."

Immortal started laughing. "He had that big dumb stare, didn't he? Any time he was surprised, he looked like some huge, empty-headed, mouth-breathing deer caught in headlights."

Both Malice and Immortal were laughing now. When they finally stopped a few minutes later, both men were wiping tears from their eyes.

"I don't even want to finish the story," Malice said. "It was nice to laugh for a change, and the rest of the story is depressing."

Immortal nodded. "I understand, but I don't mind if you're a buzzkill. My curiosity is getting the better of me. I still want to know what happened."

Malice's smile disappeared. He sighed and stared out the window. "We fought. I had the overwhelming advantage of surprise. I don't think he knew what to do, especially when the neighbors came out. He might have been worried about looking bad in front of everyone." Malice shrugged. "I guess we'll never know for certain. He got some good hits in too, but I don't know if he was holding back."

"Guardian was defeated by members of the Fallen many times, but he always had a Paragon to bail him out," Immortal said. "He wasn't an amazing fighter. He was just a brute with powerful friends."

Malice nodded. "I finally snapped out of the rage I was in once I had knocked him senseless to the ground. He was in a pool of blood, battered and beaten," Malice said. "I looked around and all of my neighbors were out there, staring in disbelief. For some reason I wasn't freaked out about what happened. I didn't even wonder why or how I had gained my powers."

Malice drained the last of his second glass of whiskey. "All I could think about," Malice continued, "was that he was responsible."

Immortal raised an eyebrow. "Oh?" he said. "Responsible for what?"

"The death of my wife, daughter, and countless others," Malice said somberly. "Then he had the nerve to attack and nearly kill me."

"I fail to see how he's responsible for Lament killing your family," Immortal said. "You also said you snapped out of your rage when he was clearly incapacitated. Why did you make the conscious decision to kill him?"

Malice became quiet. He was trembling and his glass shattered in his hand as he clenched his fists. Immortal could practically see steam coming out of his ears. It had been decades since anyone had made him this nervous.

Malice shut his eyes and began breathing more slowly. Immortal guessed he was attempting to calm himself down.

He was glad to see that. The man's anger was intense and unnerving.

"You're right—he wasn't the one who slit their throats in front of me," Malice said, opening his eyes and speaking calmly. "I have discussed this so many times I'm weary of it. Instead I'll answer you with a question. Why didn't Guardian or the others kill Lament, or find a more effective prison for him? Especially with all the deaths and misery he's caused after repeated escapes?"

Immortal didn't respond. Malice had a fair point. Normally his quick wit would at least have some sort of sarcastic reply ready to lighten the mood. Somehow it didn't seem appropriate, even if anything did come to mind.

"Fair enough. What about my other question?" Immortal asked.

"If I had let him live, the cycle would have repeated and nothing would have changed. I knew the Paragons would have turned me into a member of the Fallen." Malice turned, looking Immortal straight in the eyes. "Victims like my wife and daughter would continue to be a common occurrence. At the time I felt it was the first step in the right direction."

"And now?" Immortal asked.

"I don't regret it," Malice said. "I wish many things had turned out differently, but I don't regret what I did. Guardian could have just as easily been a member of the Fallen. The only reason he wasn't was because he decided to stick with the Paragons. For some reason they were willing to clean up after his mistakes instead of shunning him like some of their former members."

"Well, you certainly accomplished what you wanted," Immortal said with a smile.

Malice gave Immortal a blank stare. "What do you mean?"

"When you killed Guardian, you wanted a change right? To 'break the cycle,' yes?"

Malice frowned. "Yeah," he said. "I suppose at the very least I did mix things up a bit. I'll leave it to you to decide whether it was for the greater good or not."

Each man sat, reflecting on Malice's story and his last statement. Immortal thought Malice's story was interesting. He trusted Malice's account of what happened. It sounded like something Guardian would do, and he didn't have any reason to doubt Malice yet.

"I'm not sure if you have a plan or not," Immortal said. "My opinion is that the Paragons won't take this lying down. They're going to strike back. Boss may even get his hands dirty for once."

"You're probably right," Malice said. "They're cornered, and without public or political support, they may become more desperate. Do you think they'll stop pretending they care about collateral damage and just do as they please without covering their tracks?"

Immortal winced. "I hope not, but I wouldn't be surprised to see Harmony and Noble lash out. We need to be prepared for anything."

"I hate to say it," Malice said, "but we may need to help Mr. Gray out if the Paragons get out of control."

Immortal nodded. "We may not be able to be subtle for long. Rest up. I have a feeling you're going to need it."

Malice shook Immortal's hand, and Immortal left. As Immortal stepped into his car, he considered leaving the country. Perhaps he could disappear. *No, I'm not leaving,* Immortal thought. *That's not my style.*

Chapter 40: Torment

Cold. Her body ached. She wanted to move, but her limbs would not budge. She was not restrained, just exhausted. An image of a marathon runner collapsing before the finish line came to mind. The will is intact, but the body has shut down from too much strain.

She realized she was lying facedown on a cold concrete floor. It felt like she was locked in a freezer and the concrete was a giant slab of ice. Fortunately, that was not the case as she managed to turn her head a bit and open her eyes. It was a large, empty room. The ceiling, walls, and floor were concrete, but everything was smooth from being varnished. Each surface seemed to be about the same size, so she was essentially in a cube. One wall had glass, about fifteen feet above, that she could not reach. There were two people behind it and she recognized one of them.

Torment slowly pried herself from the floor with a great deal of effort. She did not want them to see her weak. It took almost every bit of energy she had left, but she stood tall and defiant.

"What do you want, Mr. Gray?" she said in a surprisingly gentle tone. Torment was incredibly calm and relaxed. She couldn't remember the last time she felt so . . . rational.

"Hello to you too, Torment! I missed you!" Mr. Gray yelled through speakers in the room.

"You are typically not a charitable man, so just cut to the chase and tell me what it is you want," she said. "I'm a little tired and don't feel like beating around the bush."

"Not charitable?" Mr. Gray said. He put his hand over his heart, grasping firmly. "Torment, you wound me. There are dozens of children's hospitals and other organizations that would disagree—"

"Enough!" Torment yelled. "I'm not in the mood for your banter."

"There she is!" Mr. Gray smiled. "That's the Torment we know and love. Just making sure you're still in there, kiddo. I must admit, I'm quite curious what your state of mind is, you know, considering the circumstances."

"Considering what . . ." Torment said, but trailed off as she remembered what happened. Charisma dead and the goddamn creature that ate her. It actually ate the bitch! She could still hardly believe it.

"So you remember," Mr. Gray said. "Good, it would have been awkward having to tell you. You have quite the temper, you know."

"So I've been told," Torment said wryly. "I suppose that thing was your creation?"

"I'm afraid so!" Mr. Gray said. "At first I was quite upset that you killed our little Beast, as I like to call him." Mr. Gray chuckled. "But don't worry, I'm over it! It gave me the chance to make a couple of improvements to my design. I also get to catch up with an old friend! I'd ask what you've been doing all these years, but I already know."

Torment grunted at him, not bothering to respond to his incessant babbling.

"Eloquent as usual, my dear," Mr. Gray said. "So I hadn't intended to rain on your parade. With so many things going on, I forgot your obsession with Charisma." Mr. Gray threw his hands up in the air, feigning exasperation. "I just plumb forgot!"

"That's bullshit and you know it," Torment said.

"I'm afraid not, kiddo. I was so engrossed with my own plans I forgot about your quarrel with Charisma. As an apology, I have decided not to kill you."

Torment sighed. "I know you too well, so just cut the crap. You're just curious. You don't care about me. This is all so amusing for you, isn't it? 'What will that crazy bitch do next?' That's what you're wondering, isn't it?"

"Wow, it's like you can read minds!" Mr. Gray's smile vanished. "But you're not like *him*, are you?"

Torment was puzzled. *Who the hell is he talking about?* she wondered. A thought came to the edge of her mind, but it was vague. Torment became irritated as she combed her memories. *I know this!* she thought. *The memory is there— someone, like a phantom in my mind.*

"You were with them too long," Mr. Gray said. "Before being booted from the Paragons, he stripped your memories of him. Perhaps he even manipulated your emotions a bit? You were not a bitter or angry person before."

"Who are you talking about?" Torment said. "It was Charisma that made me this way. She took everything from me!"

"No, she was a catalyst, but not the cause. He wanted you gone and Charisma hated you, so he used her to destroy your reputation."

"I don't believe you. You're a manipulator, just like Charisma!"

"It's there in your memory, isn't it?" Mr. Gray asked. "The thought is at the edge of your mind, almost on the tip of your tongue. Every time you try to recall the memory, your mind goes blank, doesn't it?"

"H-How?" she stammered. "How do you know that?"

"Because the same thing happened to me," Mr. Gray said. "He wiped my memory of him, almost completely." Mr. Gray slammed his fist down against a console near him. The fidgety, nervous young man next to him nearly jumped out of his skin.

"I hate him!" Mr. Gray shouted. "Nobody gets the better of me! I made him, and he has the audacity to try and manipulate *me*! He *will* suffer for his crimes against me and this country. Boss cannot be allowed to manipulate the direction of this nation any longer!"

"Boss . . ." Torment said. "It sound so familiar, but . . ."

"He is the true monster here, not me. If you will let me, I will show you who he is. I can restore parts of your memory."

"How do I know if I can trust you?" Torment asked.

"If you are looking for assurances or guarantees, I have none," Mr. Gray said. "If I wanted to, I could have just done the procedure while you were unconscious. Instead I treated your wounds and I will let you decide on your own."

Mr. Gray hit a button and a door opened behind Torment. It led outside, where she saw a few street lamps lit and cars streaming past.

"If you want to, you may go. I won't stop you and I won't pursue you," Mr. Gray said. "Or you can accept my offer and let me show you the true danger. I need your help, but it is your choice to make."

Torment looked outside, considering what she would do if she left. Charisma was gone, and she had no desire to pursue the other Paragons. What would she do? It's not like she could go get a job and live her life like a normal person. Everyone knew who she was, living a normal life was impossible now. What choice did she really have? Plus the possibility that Mr. Gray wasn't lying would haunt her. Ultimately her curiosity won out.

"Show me," she said.

Mr. Gray smiled. He was whispering something to the nervous-looking man. The door behind her closed and a new door opened in front of her.

"Proceed through the door, and I will show you all the answers you've been looking for."

Chapter 41: Noble

Repairs had been underway for about a week. Noble had hundreds of robots the size of his fist to carry out his new design. Coming by materials wasn't too difficult, even though they no longer had unlimited funds at their disposal. All the rubble that was being cleared from the city provided everything he needed. He dusted off some old robots from storage to accomplish the task. Charisma had affectionately named them "mulebots." She of course was now dead, and the mood in the compound had dampened considerably. Not Noble's, though; he had hated Charisma more than any of the Fallen. Everyone accused Noble of being spoiled, pessimistic, and generally rotten. Charisma was worse than him, but because she was a beautiful woman, she somehow got away with it.

Noble grunted in frustration with that thought. He took delight in the fact that she was not only dead, but devoured alive! It was no less than she deserved. The event also kept the others busy with whatever boring, peasant activities they were accustomed to. Even Phantom had finally returned to the compound. His benevolent ideas were out of place with the other Paragons. That was why he was sent abroad to assist other nations and bolster their image. It got him away from them, and it aided the Paragons at the same time. Noble wasn't good with people, but he had a feeling Phantom had been all too happy to be away from everyone.

None of that was of any concern to him now. Repairs to the new and improved compound were nearly complete. Best of all, he was about to get his network up and running. Nothing in the world was as precious to him as his computer system and network. Many would call his computer a supercomputer. Those people were merely Neanderthals with stone wheels trying to comprehend an automobile.

His computer was special, one of a kind. Nobody was aware of this, but it functioned as an artificial intelligence, linked to him alone. His powers to communicate and manipulate technology made it possible. Nobody on this planet could access it. Nobody could even comprehend it. It was like a special language and a different way of speaking entirely. Being without it was like losing one of his five senses. Noble felt incomplete without it. He would happily sacrifice everyone in the world to save it if need be. It was more precious to him than anything in existence.

Noble completed his finishing touches and turned the system on with his ability. Instantly his mind accessed the system and Noble groaned in ecstasy. He was doing some basic diagnostics to ensure everything was working properly when he discovered a hidden file.

"How could there be a file here that I don't know about?" Noble asked himself out loud. "Nobody can access this but me."

Without even thinking, Noble accessed the file. If someone walked into the room, Noble would appear to be staring at nothing. There was no computer monitor, no projection of any sort. Noble didn't need a monitor. He could see everything with his own two eyes. Everything was accessed through his brain, so only he could see and hear it. If he desired, he could even put the sensation of feeling, smell, and taste into a program if he wished. That way he could experience something as if he were physically there. Some might describe it like a virtual reality that only he could access. That description was a bit primitive, but it was a satisfactory term that he used to explain it to inferior minds.

When the file opened, Noble lost consciousness, his body collapsing. His mind was in the program now. This was nothing new; many of his programs were designed in this way. This one was flawless, though. He was sitting in his old lab from their compound nine years ago. Noble smiled as he looked around, seeing all of his old equipment in a room he knew intimately. Seeing it was like being reunited with a former lover and falling in love all over again.

After walking through the room for a few minutes and reminiscing, he turned to his old workstation. Sitting there, staring at him, was a younger version of himself. Again, this was nothing out of the ordinary. Many of his programs had a version of himself. He found that other people's images annoyed him. The only person he felt comfortable talking to was himself.

"I trust that you're done reminiscing. Please have a seat. We have much to discuss," the younger Noble said.

"Why don't I remember this file, and why has it not appeared sooner?" Noble said. "From the look of the room, this must be at least nine years old."

The program version of himself nodded. "You are of course correct. This program was created nine years ago, nearly to the day. It was you that created it and hid it until a time that it could be used effectively."

"For what purpose?" Noble asked. "Why don't I remember?"

"This program was created in secret, and you found a way to leave your memories of it behind within the program." The young Noble smiled. "Quite ingenious, as usual."

"If I left my memory within it, then I must have feared someone had access to my thoughts," Noble said. "It has occurred to me that I could leave ideas behind and discard them so that they would be safe, if necessary. I haven't found a need to do that before, though."

"This program was necessary because there is an individual that has access to your thoughts and memories," the program said. "As his powers grew, you realized the danger. This is a culmination of years of our hard work. Let me show you what was taken from you."

Memories were poured into his mind. Again Noble marveled at his own programming genius as years of thoughts, memories, and messages streamed into his consciousness. It was done smoothly, like a puzzle piece gently being fit into place. It was over in an instant; with the help of the program, it only took a few seconds to receive and process the information.

Awe and exhilaration were soon replaced by rage. Noble said, "He took my memories, my thoughts—even my dreams! That . . . that lunatic!"

"Here, a glass of your favorite tea." The program handed him a glass of hot liquid with steam rising from it.

"This is a Moroccan tea, like the ones she used to serve." Noble's eyes went wide. He remembered a woman, beautiful beyond compare. He had met her as a teenager, while his family was in Morocco for business. She served him this tea at a small café many years ago. Her name was Nadia. Her eyes were dark, her hair black and straight. His first thought had been how smooth it looked, like silk or satin. When she leaned down to hand him his tea, her hair hung down near his face. It smelled of jasmine. His mouth probably hung open in awe. Never in his life had he seen anyone so beautiful.

He spent two weeks flirting with her, buying her flowers and extravagant gifts, trying to win her affection. She always pushed them aside, but with a smile on her face. Nadia would put her arms around him every time and say, "I don't need your gifts, or your money, just you."

She would sneak out and meet with him at night to gaze at the stars. In his whole miserable life, Noble had never been so happy as when he was with her. As with every other happiness in his life, someone interfered. His family scolded him for falling in love with someone of "lower stature." They did not like that she was poor. They never said it directly, but they did not like the fact that she was not of European descent. Comments about his "exotic" tastes and hateful comments about her looks and culture made that abundantly clear.

Still, Noble pressed on and continued his meetings with her until his family left. They remained in touch for years, through letters. It was ironic: a man that had always been enthralled with technology, handwriting love letters!

Noble was still a young man when he was given his powers. Mr. Gray felt that he was best suited to it, and he was right. Through it all he continued his correspondence with Nadia. Finally, one day when he was nearly thirty, it dawned on Noble that he was wasting time. He had been working so hard with the Paragons, building and designing amazing things that he had overlooked the obvious. His family was no longer a threat; he was free to be his own man. Noble planned to take a brief leave of absence from the Paragons to pursue his relationship with Nadia. He had every intention of marrying her.

Boss intervened, sensing Noble's intentions before expressing them to anyone. Whenever he thought of leaving, or of Nadia, he began to become confused and irritated. It was then that he realized that Boss had begun manipulating his thoughts. He began researching ways to counter Boss's influence. Noble created this program and poured his memories into it before Boss could remove them. He discarded memories of the program so that Boss would not discover it. The hidden file would re-emerge on its own based on calculations it made. It finally predicted Boss's escalation in power and the danger to Noble. The program remained hidden and continued research on its own.

Boss wiped memories of Nadia and Noble's dreams of settling down. Noble's desires of using his abilities to design technology to promote peace and help combat famine and drought were removed. Everything he wished to accomplish was taken away, and Boss's desires were inserted. Since that day, Noble's work efforts were designed to appease Boss. Weapons, defenses, financial systems, and surveillance were all Boss cared about. He made sure Noble had no desire to do anything else.

"Years wasted!" Noble cried. "What happened to Nadia?"

The program frowned. "I'm sorry. Boss did not leave any loose ends. Before we could make arrangements to hide her and keep her safe, he found her."

"She . . . then she's . . . ?" Noble whispered, his throat closing and eyes welling with tears.

"Yes, he eliminated her so there was no chance you would remember," the program said. "If you like, we have saved additional memories of her and we can reproduce her likeness for you."

"No," Noble whispered. "No, I don't think I could bear it."

The program nodded. "We have developed a successful response to Boss's powers. It will require some alterations to your chemistry and anatomy."

The program pulled up three-dimensional designs. Normally Noble would have made these designs himself. These were based off his early ideas, but were done almost entirely by the program. After several minutes, he was quite satisfied with one of the dozen options he was given.

"That one," Noble said. "We will do that one."

"We are sure you know, but we will remind you: there is no going back," the program said. "If you wish to think it over, we can appear again in a few days."

"I don't make irrational decisions. I have done the calculations," Noble said. "This is the only way it can be done."

The program nodded. "Very well," it said. "The arrangements have been made. Boss is no longer suspicious of you. It took a great deal of time to finish the designs you started and make the arrangements. Those years also made Boss complacent. Still, we must be careful. Arrangements have been made to smuggle you to a lab where our machines will complete our design."

"Let's do it immediately," Noble said. "We have wasted enough time as it is."

Chapter 42: Malice

It had been six months since the attack in Washington, DC. State governments conducted emergency elections. The biggest surprise was the disintegration of political parties. This was due to a new amendment added to the Constitution by President Clark Hanson. The new president was given emergency powers to help restore order. He used the opportunity to institute many changes. The biggest was the removal of political campaigns run by the candidates themselves. This removed the opportunity to contribute to campaign funds, and freed elected officials to focus more on their jobs instead of campaigning.

There wasn't much of a point to bribing political candidates anymore. The days of expensive campaigning were over. Elections on the national and state levels were done systematically. People interested in running for office submitted documents showing why they are qualified. A thorough background check was conducted and the list was narrowed. Before the actual election, each candidate posts their detailed viewpoints and plans for office. Those posts were signed and approved by the candidates themselves to prevent mistakes and tampering.

If the candidates wished to do so, they could add a video of themselves, addressing potential voters. They were each allowed one video, and it was filmed by the same third-party group that ran the election website. It is a simple setup, with the candidate speaking plainly. No patriotic backgrounds, green-screen images, or cheesy songs were played.

After that step, the information was made available for everyone. The public was allowed to review the candidates for a month. For anyone with access to the internet, it was a simple process. Public libraries were set up with enhanced internet capabilities and monitors so people could research for free. More stations would be built in the future so that there would be more resources available and less crowding in the libraries.

Once the month was up, three televised debates were held over the course of another month. The last event was scheduled a week after the final debate. It was a chance for citizens to send in questions directly to candidates. A summary and the full video was then posted online to each candidate's page on the website.

Elections were held a month later. Campaign ads, reporting by media outlets, and fundraisers were now illegal. No news organization was allowed to do stories on any candidate. It didn't matter if the information was positive or negative. Any news station that reported on a candidate was shut down and given a hefty fine. This was to prevent any kind of bias by the media. If any potentially negative or positive news needed to be reported, it was noted on the candidate's webpage. Candidates could edit their plans of office or their stance on an issue. This again had to be approved by the candidate with a signature. Changes were flagged on the candidate's page so that it wasn't overlooked by potential voters. The candidate also had to write a brief explanation for their change of heart. Personal information on the candidates was no longer made public.

The president felt that a person's religion, sexual preference, and family life was irrelevant. He said in a news conference, "It is pointless to worry about things like what kind of dog the candidates have, if they have past marriages, or what religious beliefs they have or don't have. The only thing that matters is if they're competent to lead and govern in the position they seek to earn. Issues other than how they plan to lead, their viewpoints, and their career are pointless distractions."

It was not written into legislation to dissolve the political parties, but they crumbled anyways. There was no need for them anymore. Without campaigns, candidates no longer needed money or support from powerful individuals or corporations. Once someone was elected, they were also prohibited from placing friends and relatives in important positions. Giving a friend a lucrative construction contract, or making a sibling the head of a government program, was illegal and strictly enforced.

The only incentive to serve in public office was for the chance for an individual to make changes they believed in. Representatives were paid well, but not excessively. Their benefits were satisfactory, but not outrageous like they were before. People seeking power and influence no longer ran for office. Citizens that were genuinely interested in improving their states or communities started to become more common. Many state governments were wiped clean, and the effect spread to the nation's capital.

Malice's other great surprise was that Clark Hanson gave his king-like authority back. Once the Senate, courts, and cabinet member positions were replenished, Hanson's authority reverted back to what it should be. Malice and Vigilant both expected him to retain power, but he didn't. The act made him more popular than ever. He was the first American leader that people respected in decades.

"I figured it wouldn't last, though," Malice said somberly. "Someone always has to ruin a good thing."

These reports are not yet confirmed. They are merely rumors at this point.

"Yes, I know, Vigilant, but whether they're true or not, this won't last. All things come to an end eventually, whether they're good or evil. That's just the way life is and always will be."

Though we lack human emotion, even we recognize a great deal of pessimism in your remarks.

"I don't agree. I am just in touch with reality. If it sounds negative or pessimistic, blame the world, universe, or God if that's your belief."

We don't have a faith. We respect data and scientific research. The concept of God seems flawed and illogical.

"Yes, I have often felt the same way. In times of crises and hardship like these, I wish I could believe. It would be a comfort."

Did you have faith in a deity in the past?

"Yes, a long time ago. As a child I was raised to believe in God. That was all I knew because that was all I had been exposed to."

Are you now an atheist?

"No. I went through a brief phase where I was angry with the world. At first I hated God and religion in general. Then I stopped believing completely. I don't know if it was because of my upbringing, but atheism never felt right to me. I now believe there is some kind of order to the universe that we don't yet understand. Whether it's governed by a god or some kind of universal order, I can't say."

So you don't know?

"Yeah, pretty much. I've stopped wondering about it because I don't think there is any way to find concrete answers that I would be satisfied with. I just live my life the best I can. Before all of this, I did all I could to help those I love and strangers in need. I was no saint, but I did what I could."

What is your intention now? Do you still wish to aid others?

"Yes, though I suppose it is not in a traditional way. I have killed people to do what I felt was in the best interest of everyone. Many would say I don't have the right to judge others in that way. Mr. Stanton would probably be one such person."

The man formerly of the Malcontent?

"Yes." Malice resisted the urge to nod. He was essentially talking to himself, which was weird enough. Nodding and other expressions seemed a bit too ludicrous.

If anyone saw him, they would think he was crazy, though Malice figured they could be right. He had read somewhere that people who are insane don't know they're insane.

"I think Alex Stanton is one extreme and Mr. Gray is the other. I'm probably somewhere in the middle. Sometimes I feel that death and violence are necessary for positive change. Unlike Mr. Gray, I don't feel it needs to be on such a grand scale. On the other hand, I feel Stanton is naive. Some people are just evil, and no amount of therapy will fix them. They are parasites that drain resources and only spread their misery the first chance they get."

We are getting off topic, but we were curious. The idea of religion is still quite foreign to us, despite our extensive research.

"It's a strange idea that confounds many humans their whole lives, so don't feel bad. You are right, though. We need to focus."

There is a pattern of candidates dropping out, disappearing, or dramatically changing their points of view. The only consistency is that they all believed in dissolving the Paragons and calling them to testify before Congress. The evidence, if it is true, would indicate the Paragons are fighting back.

"If the information you have found is true, then it won't be long before Mr. Gray makes his move. He won't let anyone get in the way of his utopia."

What is your intention? If Mr. Gray strikes, it would be your opportunity to eliminate him or his creatures. Or you could aid him and wipe out the Paragons for good. We will support you either way.

"I hate Mr. Gray for what he did. Killing so many people in the attack and taking the form of my wife and daughter. His plan seems to be panning out, though. The country appears to be improving."

Do you believe what Immortal said about Boss?

"It makes sense, but I haven't made up my mind. My wife used to tell me to stop stressing about the details. I used to plan things meticulously. She would always say, 'Relax, Adam. Let life happen.'"

So you're going to do what, then?

"Show up and see what happens."

Chapter 43: Malice

There was a knock on the cabin door. Malice was expecting Immortal and was excited to have some company other than Vigilant. Having a voice in his head all the time that wasn't his own was a little disturbing. Even though that voice was incredibly helpful and extremely insightful.

Malice opened the door and saw a man wearing a black fleece jacket and denim jeans. He looked like he was in his forties, and about the same size as Malice. There was something off about his eyes, though, something Malice couldn't place.

The man smiled. "Hello, may I come in? It is awfully cold out here."

"You're out in the middle of nowhere. What are you doing here?" Malice asked. "I don't get many visitors."

"You don't get any visitors," the man said. "Other than Immortal, of course."

Warning bells went off in Malice's head. *This man seems to know everything,* Malice thought. *His eyes are dilated more than normal. If we were in the dark, it would make sense, but the light from inside the cabin makes it plenty bright. He also doesn't seem to blink.*

Immortal said he would never send anyone here on his behalf under any circumstances. Vigilant's voice broke into Malice's thoughts. *We would be wary of this man, despite his harmless appearance.*

"Who are you?" Malice asked.

"I'm known as Boss to most, but—"

Before he could even finish, Malice punched the man in the face. With Guardian's incredible strength, Malice punched straight through his head, sending brain matter, skull fragments, and blood flying everywhere.

Headlights from a car came on, and someone stepped out. An old woman walked slowly toward Malice. She couldn't have been more than five feet tall. Malice was never a very good judge of age, but she looked like she was a hundred years old.

When she finally reached Malice, she smiled at him. Her eyes had the same look that the man's had.

"Come now, Malice," the old woman crooned. "That hurt, and it was terribly rude. Is that any way to treat a guest?"

Malice's mouth hung open, and there was a long awkward silence.

"I hope this person is less intimidating," she said. "I had hoped to speak with you using someone resembling myself. Thankfully I brought a spare."

The old woman giggled softly, her eyes never blinking. "I don't know you yet, but the world is indeed a dark place if someone is willing to punch a hole through an old woman's head," she said. "May I come in, please? Or are you going to let this old woman freeze to death?"

"C-Come in," Malice stammered. "Uh, make yourselves comfortable."

"Ah, have you caught on already?" She said. "How delightful, and thank you so much."

Malice gestured the woman inside and held the door open for her. She carefully stepped around the body of her predecessor and made her way inside.

"May I have some hot cocoa, please?" As she sat down, she explained, "I feel what these bodies feel as if they were my own. They're great for what I need done, but they can often be so cumbersome. Especially when they're so old they have trouble controlling their bowels."

Malice grimaced, but he made her some hot chocolate. He handed it to her, still studying her closely. Of course he was aware that she wasn't really herself. Still, could Boss hurt Malice through her somehow?

"Thank you," she said. "This is truly dreadful hot chocolate. Locked away in this woman's brain is the secret to making a delicious home-cooked meal and some hot cocoa. Would you like me to make you something? I mean you no harm and I wish to make a good impression."

"Yeah, sure," Malice said.

"Good, I hope you don't mind. Immortal told me you don't have much food here, so I brought some," she said.

Two young men came in with large brown grocery bags. They took everything out of the bags and helped her prepare the food. A third man came in with pots, pans, and cooking utensils.

They made lasagna with garlic bread for dinner, and she had brought a homemade apple pie. The three men took some of the meal and went back to the car. The old woman sat down at the table with Malice and they ate in silence. When she brought him a slice of apple pie, she smiled.

"The meal was excellent, was it not?" she said. "I hope by now you've had enough time to get over your shock. I trust that you are aware that I am Boss, and I'm possessing these people. You do not appear to be a simpleton." She paused a moment to grab herself a slice of pie.

"Perhaps now you will have a civil discussion with me?" she asked.

"Thank you for the meal. I haven't eaten this well in months," Malice said.

"I know this can be a bit of a shock. It was a mistake to introduce myself in the way that I did." She giggled. "I was just so excited to meet you. I knew it would be an awkward situation. That was why I brought so many people. It took me some time to decide, and even on the way over, I hadn't made up my mind. Obviously I settled on someone that resembled myself, as I stated. In hindsight the old woman, or even the attractive woman in the car, would have been better."

We underestimated him. Given our knowledge of his abilities, we estimated possession was unlikely, and if possible, certainly not to the degree he has achieved. You probably don't need the reminder, but we recommend

extreme caution. We will notify you if we detect anything.

"Yes, well, I apologize for punching you through the head. I have been hiding up here for a long time," Malice said to the woman. "You actually felt that?"

"Yes," the woman said. "I feel what they feel. Luckily the pain was over as quickly as it started. Normally nobody would be left to complain." She smiled warmly and took a bite of some pie.

This whole time, she and the other "guests" hadn't blinked once. It was a bit unnerving.

"Oh, I'm forgetting to blink again, aren't I?" she said. "Sometimes when I'm doing too much, I neglect simple things, like blinking, or keeping my mouth shut. In the early days I would sometimes stand there with my mouth open, drooling like a buffoon." She giggled and finished the last of her pie.

We cannot copy his power, like with the others.

Probably because he is not physically here. Our efforts at

blocking mental intrusion have begun, but there was no

way to test the effectiveness prior to now. Please try to

focus, and don't let your mind stray. We will help as much

as possible.

"So you spoke with Immortal?" Malice asked.

"Oh yes, we had a nice civil discussion, much as you

and I are now," she said. "After the unpleasantness of

abducting him, of course. That couldn't be avoided. He

would never have accepted an invitation, and I can't make

him. He is my prisoner, but he is quite comfortable. Even if

I wanted to torture him, it would make no difference. He

doesn't feel pain and he regenerates almost immediately."

"Did you take him to find me?" He asked.

"Oh no, I thought you were dead. Harmony and Noble

certainly made a compelling story of your death. You never

turned up, and despite extensive searches, no evidence of

your survival surfaced. I had Amy watched, of course, but you were smart enough to stay away. I'm embarrassed to admit it, but I am quite impressed."

"Why take Immortal then?" Malice asked.

"He probably never told you, did he?" The woman smiled. "Immortal is Mr. Gray's son. I hoped to use him as a bargaining tool with Mr. Gray."

Malice almost fell out of his chair. "What!" he yelled. "Why didn't he ever tell me? All this time I've been here and not a word of it."

"He told me it was nothing personal," she said. "Immortal wasn't sure what you were going to do. If you were a true threat to his father, he wanted to be there to stop you. They aren't particularly close, but they are still father and son. I'm sure you understand, having been a parent yourself."

Malice scowled, but kept himself in check and regained his composure.

"A sore point. I apologize. That was rather thoughtless of me," she said. "I assure you, Guardian acted on his own with that brilliant act of stupidity."

"Did you ever control the Paragons?" Malice asked. "The things they did, was it because of you?"

"Oh no," she said. "I made small suggestions to a few of them. Noble was the only one I had to alter. He was rather stubborn, probably a common affliction of the obscenely rich. He became rather unpleasant after that, so I never tried with the other Paragons. Unfortunately, a few of them grew rather unstable. You know what they say about too much power. I guess it applies to heroes as well."

"Okay, well let's get to the point. Why are you here?"

"I need your help," she said. "I find myself lacking in competent allies these days. Soon I will launch a counterattack against Mr. Gray and his political puppet. I need you to fight his new champion and the other monstrosity he created."

"Why would I help you?" Malice asked. "I am happy to see the Paragons crumble. It was your incompetence that cost my family their lives."

"It's true that the others became too infatuated with fame and fortune," she said. "As you have astutely pointed out in the past, we never killed the Fallen for a reason. Charisma convinced the others it would be best to keep them alive. We would keep them locked up for a time, let them out, and catch them again later. This way we were still important, and relevant."

The woman sighed and grasped Malice's hand firmly. "If they eliminated Lament and the others, we wouldn't be needed anymore. We wouldn't be heroes. I didn't care for all the attention. In fact, I have gone out of my way to avoid it. Charisma and the others were different, though. They truly believed they were above everyone else. Innocent lives began to mean nothing, and Guardian and Harmony in particular became quite sociopathic."

"I'm sorry," Malice said. "I'll be blunt: things don't add up to me. You make yourself seem free of blame. Everything I've heard is that you manipulated people and led the Paragons down the path of darkness."

The old woman cackled. "You still see everything in black and white do you? Oh, how wonderfully naive you are. I bet you think the country is improving, don't you? You think Mr. Gray is our lord and savior."

"Mr. Gray is a monster, and I trust him about as much as I trust you. Things have improved, though, as much as I hate to admit it. Would you go back to the greed and corruption you led us to?"

"I admit mistakes were made, but Mr. Gray is planning on global war. He now has firm control over the most powerful military in the world. He will use it, and he will create more creatures! We must stop him now!"

Malice shook his head. "I don't believe you. In fact, I think you're full of shit. I won't help you, so please leave.

If I have to, I'll kill all of your puppets. You'll find I'm much less compassionate since my family was murdered."

The old woman's warm demeanor disappeared. She pointed a crooked finger at him. "You will help me, one way or another."

The three men came in, and the old woman stepped aside. One of the men set a phone and an envelope down on the table.

"H-H-Hello?" a voice said through the speakerphone. "Malice, is that you?"

"No—you didn't?" Malice said.

"Yes, I did." The old woman sneered. "Immortal told me you probably wouldn't help, so I came prepared. I'm sure you recognize that voice."

"I'm so sorry!" the voice on the phone said. "We tried to lay low, but they still found us."

"Amy?" Malice said. "Is that you? Are you okay?"

"I'm sorry, I'm so sorry," she cried over the phone. "They have Stanton, too. I don't know what they're going to do. Please, just—"

The call disconnected. Malice quivered with anger.

"I wanted to do this the nice way," the woman said. "I didn't want to have to do it like this. I find it is easier if the person willingly does what I want, but one way or another, I always get my way."

The three men and the old woman walked to the door. The old woman stopped just before leaving the cabin. She turned to Malice and said, "Don't forget I have Immortal as well. I'll make the same threat to you that I made to Mr. Gray. I will lock him in a steel box and throw him into the deepest part of the ocean. If he lives, he will be very uncomfortable for a very long time. He will have it easy compared to Amy if you don't follow the instructions I left on the table."

"I'm guessing Mr. Gray didn't respond, or else you wouldn't be here," Malice said.

"You're smarter than you look," the old woman said, and she left the cabin.

Malice heard the car leave. He stood, staring at the envelope for a very long time.

We don't see this ending well. Whether you help Boss or not, Amy and this Stanton will probably die. What will you do?

"I don't know," Malice said. "I really don't know."

Chapter 44: Malice

The instructions were very straightforward. Malice was to meet Boss' associates somewhere, alone. Any signs of aggression were going to be taken as a sign of him failing to cooperate. If Malice didn't follow any instructions he received in person, he would also be failing to cooperate. Of course, either circumstance would mean the painful deaths of Amy and Stanton. It probably meant an eternity of suffering for Immortal as well, but Malice wasn't sure. None of it mattered, though, because he intended to go along with their instructions.

We will state again that this is not a logically sound decision. Your human emotions are dominating your decisions and clouding your judgment. Boss will have you in a location of his choosing, with preparations to counter you. We may be able to resist his control of your brain, but it likely won't be completely effective. Even if he can't manipulate you, he has incredible resources that could

succeed in killing us.

"Yes, I know," Malice said. "We're probably not going to be successful. It would make much more sense to leave to ensure our survival."

Malice looked down at the wedding ring on his hand. It was a constant, and often painful, reminder of the loss of his family. Vigilant had of course recommended removing it. Malice couldn't bear to part with it, and it was a surprising source of strength when his courage wavered.

"I couldn't do anything to help my wife and daughter," Malice said, choking back tears. "Maybe I can't do anything now either, but if I run from this, it will haunt me the rest of my life. I would rather risk death and failure than do nothing and always wonder what might have been."

Your emotions need not be a burden. We could remove them or at least lessen them to ease your pain and guilt. If you left now, we could aid you in this way. It ensures our survival and it will prevent further grief and sorrow.

"I'm afraid of what I may become without my emotions. Without them I may do something monstrous like Chaos. I understand your view of emotions being a useless hindrance. Give me time, and I think you will understand why I disagree."

We shall trust your judgment for now. While you are near Boss, we shall assist in keeping you in a calm, meditative state. It should help prevent Boss from reading your thoughts to some degree. We will continue to make adjustments and improvements to prepare. It would be wise to delay any action you may wish to take. The longer you are around him, the longer we have to learn of his power and resist it.

Malice remained silent. He continued to stare at his ring until his phone's alarm went off. He switched his phone off and left it behind. It wasn't a long walk to the meeting point, but he was anxious. The walk itself was probably only a few hours, but it felt like an eternity. It was tempting to use Justice's speed to rush over and be done with it. Rushing to what could be death or enslavement didn't sound appealing, though, so he walked at a normal pace.

When he finally arrived, he stood outside the factory he used to work at. The job was nothing special, but he missed it now. He had worked his way up from the bottom. Before he'd lost his family, he was managing production. It was simple, but it paid fairly well and it had normal hours. He wished more than anything that he could go back to that life.

A large black SUV pulled up beside Malice, and the back passenger door opened. With a sigh, Malice pushed away his feelings of nostalgia and climbed in.

Sitting in the backseat was an attractive young woman in a black business suit. She had more than a passing resemblance of his late wife. "Glad to see you have some sense," she said as the vehicle began to move.

Malice felt agitation building at the sight of her. He'd stomp Boss into a puddle when he got the chance. Suddenly he felt calm and at peace. Vigilant obviously sensed his anger and stepped in. Malice actually felt pretty relaxed now.

"My employer wasn't sure if I would anger you or calm you. Obviously he made the right choice. My name is Tonya, and I'll be walking you through the facility to meet him in person."

"Hello, Tonya. So your 'employer' isn't manipulating you right now?"

"Oh no, he wouldn't do that," she said. "It is a bit odd witnessing it, but he actually doesn't manipulate the thoughts of others very often. My employer informed me of his last visit with you and the use of his power. He mostly did it to show you the extent of his abilities and to ensure he communicated directly with you."

"How long have you been working for him?" Malice asked.

"Only a few months—not long after your encounter with Guardian. He has been researching you for some time. My employer even brought in some of your friends and former colleagues to try and understand you better. Immediately it became clear how much you loved your wife, so he found and hired me as his assistant just in case."

Malice remained silent, looking at the driver and the passenger. They were regular people, not the security guards he was expecting. The driver was a man in his late forties. He seemed indifferent to Malice's conversation. In the passenger seat was another young woman. She was staring forward and also appeared disinterested.

"Oh, you're curious about our other two occupants?" Tonya asked. She motioned toward the driver. "That's

Steve, he's normally a very pleasant man but he was good friends with Justice. He is awfully bitter about what you did to him."

Tonya looked at Malice, probably hoping for a grimace or some sign of emotion. Malice didn't really care; he just felt relaxed.

She pointed to the woman in the front passenger seat. "This is Samantha. She has been taking care of our new guests."

Samantha handed Malice some sort of tablet with a video feed of Amy, Immortal, and Stanton. They were separated, each in a decent-sized, fully furnished room. Amy seemed to be eating a meal, Stanton was reading a book, and Immortal was apparently trying—and failing—to get drunk. There were dozens of empty bottles of whiskey all over his room.

"As you can see, they are all quite comfortable," Tonya said. "Whether or not they remain that way is up to you.

Here are some videos of how some of our more unpleasant

guests have fared."

The video cut to a scene of a man Malice didn't

recognize chained to a wall. Samantha was peeling a small

chunk of skin off his arm while the man howled. He was

covered with dozens of similar wounds all over his body.

Another video appeared, of a woman this time. She was

screaming as Samantha prodded her with some sort of

electrical device.

Samantha smiled. "I have a lot more videos if you want

to see them. I've got a few fun ideas for your girlfriend in

particular. I'm kind of hoping you do something stupid so I

can hurt her."

Malice shrugged. "How many more videos do you

have? I'll watch a couple if you want."

Tonya looked bewildered. Malice figured that wasn't

the answer she was looking for. He knew he should care,

but he didn't. The videos didn't bother him at all. He was

just trying to be polite. Samantha looked him over and snatched the tablet out of his hands.

They drove for another half hour in silence. When they finally arrived, Malice saw a large mansion with an enormous flower garden. It was an old English-style building, but it looked like it had just been built.

"Welcome to Boss' estate," Tonya said. "Do you wish to have a look around or do you want to get straight to business?"

Malice shrugged again. "I don't care. Whatever you want, I guess."

"I am quite surprised. My employer did not feel that you would drug yourself. He figured you would be smart enough to know it wouldn't make any difference."

Malice just stared at her. He was going to answer, but then he decided he didn't feel like it. She frowned for a moment before leading him inside. As they walked in, there was a great marble stairway to the upper floor. They walked up, and Malice stayed silent, looking around. As they walked through the compound, he noticed paintings hanging on the walls. There were sculptures and other pieces of artwork in all of the hallways. Malice felt like he should be in awe, but he didn't feel anything.

Finally they approached a large mahogany door, carved with some sort of family emblem. It was a shield with a stag and a wolf. Malice didn't get to look at it too closely before Tonya opened the door.

"This is his study, and he has elected to meet you in person. I advised him against it but he felt it was necessary to gain your trust. He really does feel that you can have a great working relationship together."

He nodded and walked into the study. Tonya sighed and closed the door behind him. Behind a large desk was an older man smoking a cigar.

"Welcome! Come on in. I hope your trip was pleasant enough." The man stood and came to shake Malice's hand.

Boss was not an imposing man. Slightly taller than Malice, an average build but with a little bit of a bulge around his belly. Nothing particularly remarkable about him—just like Malice. He did have a pleasant and genuine smile and the grisly voice of a man that had smoked for a long time.

"Now I know we may have started out a bit rough, so let's be honest and acknowledge that was your fault. I'm ready to start fresh, though. If we work together, we can accomplish some amazing things."

Boss took a puff of his cigar, looking Malice over for a moment. "You seem awfully quiet, young man. Is something on your mind?"

"No, not really," Malice said. He heard and understood everything Boss was saying. It just didn't spark any thoughts or emotions in him. Just the sense that it should make him feel something.

"All right, I won't delve into your head as long as you don't do anything rash. It's sort of rude, isn't it? In my opinion, it's probably the worst sort of invasion. Entering someone's thoughts—it's like peering into their soul. It's an awfully private thing, so I try not to do it unless I have to."

Malice nodded. "That's good."

"While I was researching you, I heard many good things. You're a man of character, and I like that about you." Boss paused for another puff of his cigar, then flicked it over an ashtray. "I also heard that you are a very reasonable man, but that you have one hell of a temper. Something that you've struggled with your whole life."

"Yes, it got me into some trouble as a kid," Malice said.

"So far you have restrained your emotions very well, I anticipated some anger from you. You've surprised me, and that's not something that happens very often."

Malice nodded with a grunt of acknowledgment. "I don't mean to be rude, but can we please get down to business? I'm not usually concerned about small talk and pleasantries."

"Yes, yes, of course," Boss said, motioning Malice toward a chair in front of the desk. "My assistant has some concerns that you may have drugged yourself. I wish you wouldn't have done that. It doesn't accomplish anything other than making our conversation more awkward."

"I didn't drug myself," Malice said. "I'm just at peace with this and ready to move forward."

Boss sat in silence, puffing his cigar and staring at Malice.

He's attempting to read your thoughts. Right now he is receiving a calm, serene feeling from you. Nothing concerning yet.

"Hmm . . . all right," Boss said.

His intrusion is becoming more forceful. He seems much more interested now. He's attempting to access your memory. We're going to try something.

It was like a floodgate opened and all of Malice's grief and suffering came rushing out. The loss of his family and his guilt, rage, frustration, and despair all came to the surface at once. It was crippling; he wanted to curl up in a ball and fade away. Malice fought with every ounce of his being to stay seated and appear calm.

Boss winced, then began coughing profusely. The cigar fell out of his hands and he began shaking for a moment. Then it all stopped. He went back to feeling calm and serene again. The pain and despair vanished in a moment, the floodgate closed again.

We wanted to see if we could overwhelm and confuse him. It seems to have worked. He broke his probing after a few moments.

"Well, you're just a mess, aren't you?" Boss chuckled halfheartedly. "Sorry for the intrusion, but you're quite confusing and I couldn't resist a peek. Now I regret it. I don't know how you appear so calm on the outside when you're broken inside."

Malice shrugged. "I get by because I have to."

"Fine, well, let's get down to business," Boss said. "I need to show you something."

Boss hit a button on his desk and the wall behind him slid down. There was a large glass window, and Malice could see into a large room containing dozens of screens. Major cities, multiple views from space, some sort of weather radar station, and a man. The man was chained up and looked very haggard and disheveled. His face and neck were covered in a thick beard, and his hair reached down to his shoulders. He looked dirty, like he hadn't seen a bathtub in months or years. The poor man seemed to be asleep with his head tilted down.

"You probably don't recognize him, do you?" Boss asked. "And why would you. He's been gone a long time and he looks nothing like he did before. Say hello to Cataclysm."

Malice felt that he should be shocked or intrigued at least, but he just stared in silence.

"Honestly, you must be dead inside to not react to that," Boss said. "This is the reason Mr. Gray and I had a falling out. At the time, he felt that using Cataclysm as a weapon was a monstrous thing to do. Though I wonder if he would still feel the same after that DC stunt of his."

Boss stood up and walked over to the window. "When I need him I just point to an area and tell him what type of weather or natural disaster I want. He has proven very effective. Hurricanes, tornadoes, destructive lightning, and even severe droughts are at my disposal."

"Why do you need this?" Malice asked. "You can alter people's thoughts at will. What possible use could you have for this?"

"It's true, if I had the time and energy, I could bend anyone that matters to my will," Boss said. "After being in so many people's heads, it begins to feel revolting after a while. Every sort of evil that humans are capable of, horrors you couldn't even imagine, begin to seep into you. I can mostly navigate around those thoughts now, but doing it on a massive scale would be too taxing."

Boss pointed to Cataclysm. "He is the solution. Leaders and dictators around the world know that if they get out of hand, an anonymous individual will cause untold devastation to their country. A few examples had to be made, but word got around. Nobody knows who, of course, but they don't need to. Brute force is what people really bow to and understand more than any amount of reasoning. Perhaps our evolution isn't quite as complete as we would like to think?"

Malice shook his head. "There are still countless small wars, people suffering under cruel dictators. Apparently it isn't working as well as you would like."

"Apparently you don't understand the human mind very well." Boss shook his head and sat back in his chair. "If you push people too much, if you oppress them enough, they will fight back eventually. It's self-preservation, human nature at its finest. If I don't allow for some of those egotistical monsters to purge a village or two every once in a while, they'll begin to lash out in other more unpredictable ways. It could become a real nuisance. So I allow them to exert their power on occasion so they don't get too bent out of shape."

"You're beginning to make Mr. Gray look like a saint," Malice said. "You have the power to bring peace and stability to the world, or at least make it better. Instead you allow atrocities and suffering. Why?"

Boss began to laugh. "You really are naive aren't you? Peace is a fantasy, something for drum-circle hippies to jerk off to. It's not human nature to remain peaceful. There will always be clashing religions or ideologies. Always a scarce resource or borders to fight over. It just takes one charismatic lunatic to throw the world into war. There will never be peace. What I have established is the closest thing to peace the world can achieve. There have been no major wars since I began using Cataclysm, no genocides. This is as good as it gets."

"Maybe if you show people a life of peace, true peace, for long enough, it will become habit," Malice said. "Let Amy and the others go. Let's work together to bring peace to the world—it *is* possible. It's certainly worth trying, isn't it?"

"No," Boss said. "You're living in a fantasy world. My way is the only way. You won't be involved in dominating nations if it makes you feel any better. Your only job is to—"

Malice rushed over in an instant and slammed Boss's head into the wall, knocking him unconscious.

We don't have much time. There's no knowing what sort of security measures he has in place. Get to the computer at his desk.

Malice ran to the desk and inserted a device that Vigilant had designed from some basic equipment at Immortal's cabin. The computer immediately began bringing up files, and within seconds, Vigilant had what he was looking for.

This is fortunate. Apparently Amy and the others are being kept in this very facility. They are two floors below the ground floor. I will unlock everything and guide us there.

Without hesitation, Malice sped off through the complex.

A few minutes after Malice ran out of the room, Boss woke with horrible pain in his head. It took him a few more minutes to stand up and gain his bearings. When he looked through the glass, the room was empty.

"Oh shit!" Normally Boss would have reached out with his mind to his assistants, but his head hurt too much to do that. He pulled out his phone and called Tonya.

Boss said, "I underestimated Malice. He's gone and so is Cataclysm. Shut everything down and extract our guests if they're still here. We need to leave immediately."

Without even waiting for a response, he hung up and gathered his things. He wasn't about to wait to see if Cataclysm or Malice was still there. His head hurt too much to use his power effectively. Nobody in that building could protect him; it was time to cut his losses and regroup. He was angry with himself for being so soft and underestimating Malice's cunning. Every bit of information he had gathered made Malice seem like someone that was clueless and in over his head. Malice's background did not prepare him for this life. Apparently, he had adjusted quite nicely.

Muttering, Boss said, "That's fine, but next time the gloves are coming off. His misery will be my goal in life."

Chapter 45: Closure

Malice was successful in getting Amy, Immortal, and Stanton out of the building quickly and to somewhere safe, thanks to Justice's speed. Vigilant had found an abandoned bottling plant that went out of business a decade ago. Once they were all there, Immortal pulled out a bottle of champagne from his baggy jacket.

"I kept this on me at all times in case we managed to get out of there in one piece," Immortal said. "To be honest, I wasn't sure it was going to happen. Glad I decided to be an optimist for once. I didn't smuggle any glasses, though, so we'll have to drink it like a back-alley hobo."

Immortal took a drink from the bottle and passed it to Amy.

"You're as offensive and crude as ever!" Amy said. "Glad you're okay." She smiled and took a drink of the champagne and passed it to Stanton, who quickly gave it to Malice.

"It's a special occasion, but I still don't drink," Stanton said. "Plus I think our savior here ought to have the lion's share."

"With Immortal here, I get to share in his frustration of pointless drinking." Malice laughed and took a long drink.

"I made a mistake," Malice said. "I was in such a hurry to get you all out that I didn't kill Boss. Once he recovers, we'll have a real problem. In addition to that, overriding the security set Cataclysm loose."

"You should have left us in there," Immortal said somberly. "That guy is crazier than all of us super-powered freaks combined. Boss should have put him out of his misery."

"That's not what he likes to do," Malice said. "He likes to use people. Cataclysm was his instrument of global control. That's why there haven't been any large-scale wars in years."

Amy sighed. "So how many psychopaths are running around now?"

"There's Mr. Gray, Cataclysm, the Paragons . . ." Malice said. "I'm hoping Chaos was buried, but there's no telling what that thing can live through."

"Charisma was killed by something," Immortal said. "I think my father, or Mr. Gray as you know him, probably created it. I'm betting he's got more tricks up his sleeve."

"Torment has been rather quiet," Amy said. "She was seen fighting that creature and then she was rescued by Angel. Since then the news has been suspiciously quiet about it."

Stanton looked at Malice and said, "Are you still planning on killing them? What are you going to do?"

"This isn't a simple issue. Most of them aren't good people, but they're not all evil either," Malice said. "Drift isn't perfect, but he seems to help people. Torment didn't seem like she was out to hurt everyone either. The Paragons have some members that help, and others that don't."

"Well, we have one thing going for us," Immortal said. "Most of them want to kill each other in addition to us."

"We might have to use that," Malice said. "Right now I think the best thing is to leave. This place won't be safe forever."

"I say we go west." Amy smiled. "I've always wanted to go there, and it's far away from here."

Immortal snatched the champagne from Malice and took a drink. "I second that," he said. "There are a few places I know. I think we can be safe there for a while."

Stanton nodded and looked over to Malice. "Seems reasonable. What do you want to do?"

"Let's go," Malice said. "I'm anxious to leave. We can talk more on the way."

Made in the USA
San Bernardino, CA
01 June 2017